Boy Meets Earl

~

Catherine Stein

Copyright © 2024 Catherine Stein, LLC.

All rights reserved. No part of this book may be reproduced in any form without the written permission of the publisher, except as permitted by U.S. copyright law.

This is a work of fiction. Names, characters, places, and incidents are products of the author's imagination or are used fictitiously. Any resemblance to actual events or persons, living or dead, is entirely coincidental.

ISBN: 978-1-949862-51-5

Book cover and interior design by E. McAuley:
www.emcauley.com

Boy Meets Earl

Sebastian Wright will stop at nothing to retrieve his mother's heirloom pearls. Even if that means riding through a snowstorm to the house of a reclusive earl and disguising himself as a Bavarian lord. But Oliver, Earl of Fenwick, isn't the arrogant thief Seb expected. Seb likes Oliver's friends, his attitudes, and maybe even the earl himself. As the snow and the lies continue to pile up, Seb will have to untangle his web of desires and schemes to find his heart's truth.

Boy Meets Earl is an homage to Shakespearean comedy. As such, it contains implausible situations, anachronistic turns of phrase, ribald puns, over-the-top supporting characters, and plenty of blundering. **Content warning for a main character with social anxiety.**

Dramatis Personae

~

Sebastian Wright - the reckless one, twin brother to Helena

Helena Wright - the sensible one, twin sister to Sebastian

Oliver, Earl of Fenwick - a most(ly) eligible bachelor

Amabel, Duchess of Mirweald - a peeress with one suitor (too many)

Baron Georg Neufeld - conveniently absent

Sir Albert Fellowes - someone's cousin, a devotee of the arts

Casper Hawthorne - a master at crossing swords

Lord Tunsbury - a pretentious poet

Mr. Whitcomb - an aspiring actor

Mrs. Whitcomb - a lady of good manners and better aim

The Sapphic Ladies' Club

    Georgia/George Beauclair - a lady and a gentleman

    Maryanne - maybe Maryellen

    Maryellen - maybe Maryanne

Lord Rothmere - an old flame in need of extinguishing

Chapter 1

~ day one ~

SEBASTIAN WRIGHT WAS NEVER WRONG. Granted, his decisions didn't always have the expected results, but Seb considered a surprising turn of events an opportunity, not a failure. Consequently, when he arrived at Fenwick House—well after dark, in a raging snowstorm, without an invitation—he did it with a smile on his face and unshakeable confidence.

"You would be dead without me." Helena, his twin sister and partner in crime, hopped from her horse and led the animal from the cold carpet of white into the dimly-lit stables.

"Undoubtedly." It was good to see again. His cheeks still stung from the ice and snow that had pelted him during their ride, but at least now when he wiped the cold and damp from his eyes, they stayed dry. "But I'm not without you, am I?"

Sebastian swung down from the saddle and followed Helena, guiding his horse around the snoring groom who was probably supposed to be keeping watch. He tossed back his hood and shook the snow from his cloak. The stables weren't precisely warm, but neither were they damp and frigid. On any other night, Seb might have happily curled up here for a rest. Tonight, he had loftier goals.

The groom slept on as Sebastian and Helena tended silently to their horses. After a few minutes, the man let out a snort worthy of a legendary giant, startling himself awake.

"We have company," Seb observed.

Helena made no reply.

The groom rubbed his eyes and blinked several times, then scrambled to his feet. His nervous gaze homed in on Seb, and he executed an obsequious bow.

"Begging your lordship's pardon." The sentence came out as a single, long word. "Have I the honor of greeting Baron Georg Neufeld?"

Baron Neufeld was, as far as Seb knew, still miles away, sitting in front of a cozy fire at the Twisted Tree inn. Given the moonstruck way he'd looked at one of the young ladies in residence, Seb suspected the baron would be happy to remain snowbound for at least a few days.

"Good evening," Seb replied, adopting Neufeld's slight Germanic accent.

Helena, who had her back to the groom, scowled and mouthed a foul word.

"Welcome, welcome, my lord," the groom went on. "I will notify the household at once that you have arrived, and send footmen to convey your belongings to your chamber."

Seb waved a hand. "Never mind that. My carriage and my trunks were detained at the inn due to the weather, but I simply could not deprive the party of my company a moment longer. I have all my basic necessities in my saddlebags, and my valet will see to those."

"Of course, my lord. Shall I finish attending to your mount?"

"Nein, nein. I am almost finished with her." In truth, he didn't trust anyone else to see to the horses. After carrying him through the snow, they deserved better than a stranger.

The groom bowed again. "I'll notify his lordship of your arrival." He scurried away.

"Your valet?" Helena grumbled once the man was out of earshot.

"It's perfect." Sebastian couldn't suppress a happy bounce. "I'll play the baron, you play my servant, we cover the entire house. We'll have Mama's pearls back in no time."

Helena flung up her hands. "You don't speak German!"

"Mein Gott!" Seb cried. "Scheisse! Zum Teufel!"

"Profanity doesn't count."

"You're no fun."

"I'm plenty fun. Which is why I get to play the baron sometimes too." She patted her horse goodnight, then hefted their saddle bags onto her shoulders. "And you're hauling these back down when we leave."

"It's only fair." Seb grinned at his sister, studying the face so like his own. One of the best parts of their escapades was making the world believe they were one person.

"Good. I'll expect a full report tonight. Don't do anything foolish."

Seb chuckled at her departing back. Sometimes one needed to do foolish things. Fortunately, he excelled at that.

⁓

"Baron Georg Neufeld of Bavaria," the footman intoned, in a voice so pompous Seb couldn't help but strut a little in response.

All eyes focused on him. Which, to be frank, was a pleasant distraction from the unsightly Baroque styling of the so-called Painted Salon. Seb would rather meet the gaze of one hundred humans than look at any one of the creepy baby angels peeking out from behind the plethora of trompe l'oeil columns covering the walls. He smiled at the assembled guests and gave them an aristocratic nod of greeting.

"My apologies for my tardiness and my travel attire. The weather was inhospitable." Outside, the snow was still falling—if hurtling toward earth as though flung by furious angels could be considered "falling"—but, here in the house, the glowing lamps and crackling fire made the storm seem almost unreal.

A woman approached him. She was quite tall, with a regal bearing and a dress so laden with elaborate embroidery it was a wonder the fabric didn't collapse under the weight. Pink gemstones encircled her throat and decorated her upswept auburn curls. She may have been intimidating were it not for the unfashionable spectacles over her hazel eyes.

"Baron," she greeted him in a silky voice. "It is a pleasure to finally meet you in the flesh. Though I admit to some surprise that you would make such an effort to join us. Your most recent letter expressed a disinclination for a more intimate association."

Sebastian's brain whirred, sifting and sorting the information.

Dress and demeanor equals high rank. Duchess?
They have a correspondence but are not close.
Disinclination. Not lovers, not courting.

Seb bowed to the woman. "Cannot a man simply wish to join his friends in celebration, Your Grace? Nothing more need come of it than good cheer and good drink."

She laughed. "You do make an excellent point, Baron. Come, let me introduce you to our host."

Seb felt a telltale loosening in his shoulders. He had jumped the first obstacle, and the rest of the ride would be smoother. He accompanied the duchess across the room, mulling over the best tactics for charming a thief out of his ill-gotten gains.

Seb nearly tripped over his feet when the duchess stopped in front of the most gorgeous man he'd ever seen.

"No hiding like a hermit, Fenwick," she scolded. "Greet your guests properly."

"Neufeld." The earl nodded stiffly. "A pleasure. Her Grace has told me much about you."

"The pleasure is mine, my lord."

And it truly was. The Earl of Fenwick was lithe and elegantly muscled—probably a fencer. He wasn't exceptionally tall, but like most men, he had several inches on Seb. It was his face, however, that was most arresting. Wide blue eyes and full lips dominated the round shape, while wisps of blond hair fell across his brow. Soft, smoothly-shaven cheeks gave way to a strong, slightly pointed chin. His complexion was the pale white often called porcelain, overlaid with a profusion of freckles. What kind of earl had freckles?

He was, in a word, adorable.

"Call me Fenwick. I hope we will be friends." A hint of pink colored the earl's cheeks.

Oh, God, was he blushing? Freckles and blushing. Seb was a dead man. Already, he'd forgotten everything he'd meant to say.

"Wonderful!" the duchess exclaimed. "You two get to know one another. I'm for bed. Goodnight, gentlemen." A swish of fabric and she was gone, like a regal phantom.

Fenwick cleared his throat. "I hope your travels were not too arduous. There is considerable snow." He spoke in the austere manner Seb expected from a man of his station, but there was something nervous about him. His stance was too tense, perhaps, or his expression too bland.

Seb tried a joke to put Fenwick—and himself—at ease. "Ah, the weather. We are having a proper English conversation now!"

Fenwick's blush deepened. "I'm... not skilled at conversation. That's Amabel's strength." He scanned the room. "Alas, she has deserted me."

Not a social man, Seb noted. *Uses the duchess's given name.*

"I can talk for us," he said aloud. "It is very snowy outside. Very wet. Very cold. I was foolish to ride here tonight. My dear friend Maximillian von Wieseldorf would—What is the expression? Tan my hide?—if he knew. 'Georg,' he always says. 'Georg, you will find yourself dead in a ditch one day, and I cannot abide the thought of it. You know I look terrible in black, and I cannot possibly attend your funeral looking anything but my best.'"

Lord Fenwick's eyes grew wider, then his brow furrowed. "You're jesting."

Sebastian put a hand over his heart. "Not in the slightest."

Fenwick nodded, and some of the tension left his body. "Amabel said your letters had a cynical bent."

Well, that's a relief. Seb grinned. Sarcasm was always his friend. "She was not wrong."

A thoughtful expression washed over the earl's face, and he bit his lower lip. White hot flames of desire licked Sebastian from head to toe. God, how he wanted it to be his teeth capturing that lip, his hands cupping those freckled cheeks, his body making that blush spread clear down to Fenwick's toes.

"You're not here to propose to her."

Seb had to concentrate to understand the words. "To the duchess? Good God, no!" He only belatedly realized this was probably not the best thing to blurt in public. Worse yet, he'd forgotten to speak with an accent.

To his surprise, Fenwick only smiled. And bloody hell, what a smile. If it could have been weaponized, the war with Napoleon would have ended in seconds rather than years. In any other circumstance, Seb would have taken that smile as an invitation to sneak off for an extremely good time. Tonight, he could only stare.

"Excellent!" Fenwick continued to smile. "In that case, perhaps we truly can be friends."

Seb remained frozen.

The other man scanned the room again. "The party looks to be scattering, and your journey must have been exhausting. Perhaps we will speak again in the morning?" The blush returned to his cheeks.

Seb's jaw finally began to work again. "Yes. Of course. Goodnight, my l… Fenwick."

"Goodnight, Neufeld. Thank you for coming." The earl nodded hastily and scurried off as if he'd said something mortifying.

Seb leaned against one of the painted columns and took a steadying breath. This had to be how Fenwick carried out his crimes. He lured people in with a pretense of shyness, dazzled them with a morsel of seduction, and then picked their pockets clean. Seb was going to have to be on guard at all times. Because Fenwick wasn't an average thief. He was danger personified.

And Seb was never wrong.

Chapter 2

~ day two ~

Oliver prodded his toast, unable to compel himself to pick it up and eat it. How was he going to make it through twelve more days of this house party? He couldn't flee, that was for certain. Already the snow outside lay in deep drifts, and it was still coming down in buckets. Almost like fate was mocking him.

The party had started so well. Most of the guests were friends—more of them Amabel's friends than his, but they all knew him and his habits. He'd managed to greet the few new faces as a host should, and overall passed a satisfactory day.

And then Neufeld had arrived. Oliver had been exhausted after so much socializing, perfectly content to melt into the wall until he could retire to bed. Now he would have to spend the rest of the party knowing he'd embarrassed himself in front of Amabel's mysterious suitor.

The duchess eased into the seat beside him. "You don't look like a man brightened by a night of energetic bedsport."

Oliver poked his finger straight through the toast. "I… what?"

"I handed you the perfect opportunity for a night of debauchery." Amabel scooped a dainty morsel of jam and spread it on her own toast. "How on earth did you manage to bungle it?"

Oliver darted a glance around the room, but the few others

breakfasting at this hour sat at the opposite end of the long table, engaged in conversation.

"I can't believe you think I would hop into bed with the baron," he hissed. "He's here to propose to *you*."

Maybe. Neufeld had claimed otherwise and sounded sincere, but Oliver was hopeless at determining when people were lying.

"Oh, pish." Amabel dunked her jam-coated toast into her tea, a habit that never failed to make Oliver's nose wrinkle in distaste. "Neufeld has no interest in me. He stated as much in his correspondence. His family believes we would be a good match, and he initially wrote to me to determine whether we would suit. He has since concluded—with my encouragement—that we do not."

"And if he's a lying blackguard?" Oliver sighed. "I don't want him to be. I liked him. But you know I have a poor history with charming men."

Amabel patted his arm. "All charming men are liars, darling. It's simply a matter of whether their lies are meant to spread happiness or rob people of it."

Oliver had no chance to demand she explain further, because a dozen more guests chose that moment to stream into the dining room, Neufeld among them. Oliver hardly had time to take a single bite of his toast before the baron plopped down into the seat directly across from him.

"Guten Morgen!" Neufeld reached for the teapot. "I am excited to drink your strong English tea."

"It has been some years since you were in England for school, correct?" Amabel inquired.

"Ja." The baron poured a cup of tea and added a precise amount of milk with the deftness of any Englishman. "But I have not lost my taste for a proper cuppa."

Oliver took another bite of toast as an excuse not to say anything. He still wasn't hungry. He studied the man across the table. Neufeld was in his mid-twenties, at a guess, but could easily pass for younger, especially when freshly shaven. His features were delicate, his face elfin, a fact that was only magnified when he smiled. His eyes were golden-brown, and his skin a dark cream that suggested a Mediterranean ancestor. He wore his black hair cut short, but the ends curled up in various directions, creating an air of dishevelment that made Oliver blush. Again.

"You have a lovely home." Neufeld indicated the space around them with an expansive sweep of his arm. "Might I request a tour?"

Oliver swallowed hard. Was that genuine interest in seeing the house, one of those nonsensical things people said but didn't really mean, or a flirtatious implication that he wanted a more private tour?

"Of course," he replied neutrally.

"Good morning, good morning!" Sir Albert and his distressingly jolly demeanor joined the group, giving Oliver some reprieve from Neufeld's unsettling presence. "Heard we had a new guest arrive after I went off to work on my script last night."

"Yes." Oliver coughed. "Sir Albert Fellowes, Baron Neufeld."

"Splendid, splendid!" Sir Albert turned his terrifying smile on Neufeld. "Are you a devotee of the theater, sir? I am composing a short play to be enacted on the final night of our gathering and I do hope you'll participate. You would be perfect, in fact. The play is a love story, you see. A heart-rending tragedy that will make the ladies weep—but not too much—and leave us all touched by the bittersweet joy of our mortal existence."

Neufeld nodded thoughtfully behind a bite of poached egg. "How interesting."

Sir Albert took this as encouragement. "We will be performing the play in traditional fashion, with all the roles played by the gentlemen, while the ladies will be our audience.

I've assigned most of the roles, but I've been sadly lacking for someone who might play the fair young maiden. You, good sir, are exactly what I need. With that pretty face and a well-fitted gown you could pass for a lady in public, I'd wager."

Oliver squeezed his eyes shut. His friends wouldn't be offended by such a statement, but Neufeld was an outsider, and the average man walking down the street would probably be horrified.

"Maybe I have done."

Oliver's eyes snapped open at Neufeld's laughing reply. The baron was grinning at Sir Albert.

"It sounds like fun," Neufeld continued. "I'd be honored to play your fair maiden, especially if she gets to have a dramatic death at the end."

Oliver rocked back in his chair. Huh. Maybe Neufeld fit in here after all. Maybe Amabel was right that he'd missed an opportunity last night. Damn.

Sir Albert bounced up and down in his chair. "And you, my dear Lord Fenwick, will be playing the heroic prince, as befits your rank both as a peer and our host."

Oliver dropped the remains of his toast. "I…" He choked on the words. He couldn't possibly go on stage in front of everyone. He would freeze and then melt into a puddle of mortification.

"I'm still writing that scene, but trust me when I say it will be my magnum opus. When the two of you declare your undying love, embracing passionately, only to be interrupted by the wicked villain—"

Oliver's stomach lurched and he scrambled from his seat. "Please excuse me. I forgot… something."

He dashed into the empty hall, where he leaned against the cool marble of an Aphrodite statue, gulping in lungfuls of air. Bloody hell. If the mere thought of passionately embracing the too-handsome, too-charming stranger in front of an audience made him ill, he didn't stand a prayer of joining Sir Albert's ridiculous production, even in a minor role. Oliver wasn't certain if he'd manage the rest of the party.

Apparently his seclusion "for his health" had been too long and he'd forgotten all his coping mechanisms.

"She does have nice tits," Neufeld observed, "but I can't imagine they make the best pillow."

Oliver jerked upright and pulled his hand from the goddess' stone bosom. "I… Excuse me."

The baron flashed his fae-like smile. "Was that comment directed at her or at me?"

"Er…"

"Another jest." Neufeld waved a hand. "Shall we take the tour? You and me? You seem to prefer not to have an audience."

He didn't sound in the least put off by Oliver's social ineptitude. Oliver's heart fluttered. A pair of possibilities loomed ahead. One, Neufeld would really become a friend. Or two, there would be a repeat of The Incident.

"Yes, let's," Oliver replied.

Why not?

Maybe this was the step he needed to get out of his isolation. Make a new friend, maybe take a new lover. One-on-one interactions were so much easier than any sized group, and Neufeld had just handed him a golden opportunity. And if it all went wrong… Well, in twelve days the baron would be gone for good.

Chapter 3

Fenwick's shyness wasn't an act, Seb concluded, an hour and a half into the house tour. They had gone through several rooms, exchanging minimal conversation, before the earl had relaxed, but once they'd reached the portrait gallery, he'd started talking in earnest. Seb now knew which previous Earls of Fenwick had been arseholes of the highest order, which two—the first earl and Fenwick's grandfather—had been decent men, and how the fifth earl had jumped out a window to avoid being caught with the king's mistress and claimed thereafter his limp was from a mission in service of the crown.

Fenwick was delightful when he grew excited. His enthusiastic chattering enraptured Seb, so much so that he nearly forgot his purpose. Scanning rooms for potential caches of stolen goods while listening to the earl's rambles had taken all Seb's concentration. Exhaustion was setting in, and he hadn't seen a single conspicuously locked door or unlit corridor. If Fenwick had a forbidden room, it wasn't off any of the public spaces.

Guess you'll have to seduce him and sneak into his bedchamber. What a pity.

"I have one more room to show you." Fenwick jogged toward the stairs, eyes shining, cheeks pink with pleasure. "My favorite."

Sebastian followed in silence, as he had for most of the tour.

"Most people grow bored before we reach the end of the tour." Fenwick paused at the top of the staircase for Seb to catch up. "I almost never make it to the Big Library. But you seemed to like the Big Library, and you've been listening, so I thought you'd like this room too." His smile faded. "You have been listening, haven't you? I'm not taking advantage of your diplomatic politeness, am I?"

Seb grinned. "I haven't any diplomatic politeness. Please, continue."

"Excellent!" Fenwick frowned again, as if not sure he'd given the proper response, then brightened. "Right this way."

He pushed open a door to reveal a small chamber lined with bookshelves. A Venetian window at the far end of the room let in ample light. Several well-used chairs and footstools lay scattered around the room, indentations in the carpet suggesting they were moved often.

"This is the Little Library." The pride in Fenwick's voice caused a corresponding tightening in Seb's chest. "This is where I actually read and often take tea. This room was vital to me after—" He faltered. "While I was regaining my health."

"I love it," Seb replied sincerely. The room was cozy and elegant. The perfect space for relaxing alone or conversing with a few chosen companions, but much too small for a gathering of any size. "Is that shelf truly full of nothing but Minerva Press novels?"

Fenwick coughed. "Y-yes. I am an enthusiast of the Gothic genre." A panicked uncertainty appeared in his eyes again.

"It's an impressive collection." Seb looked straight at the earl, willing him to hear what he wouldn't say aloud. *You're not going to scare me off with unusual hobbies. Not with talking too fast, not with preferring solitude. Can't you see how damned endearing you are?*

"Thank you."

Can't you remember he's a thief? Seb's nagging conscience whispered.

Seb looked away from the earl and his freckles. "Do you have a secret passage in here?" Maybe Fenwick used his reading for inspiration. Maybe he stole from those who had wronged him. Seb couldn't imagine his beloved mother showing Fenwick anything but kindness, but the earl was quick to become nervous and defensive. In a situation with high social pressure, he might mistake an innocuous exchange for an insult.

"I don't, but it's a fine idea." Fenwick spun to face the door. He held up his hands as if measuring with an invisible tool. "I could have the door replaced with a bookshelf that swings open. And if the outside were painted to match the wall, it would blend in. It wouldn't be entirely secret, but it does sound delightful. A proper secret passage would need to lead somewhere dark and mysterious, don't you agree? Down into the cellars, perhaps. Or a tunnel out to a garden folly? Are follies still in fashion? It's a shame my grandfather didn't build any when he was in residence. Why haven't I been having fun with the house these past few years?"

He whirled back around so quickly he nearly collided with Seb. They both froze, near enough to touch. Almost near enough to kiss.

Fenwick didn't flounder or back away. His eyes darkened and his gaze dropped to Seb's lips. Seb lifted his chin and shifted his weight to the balls of his feet. Leaning. Inviting.

"Neufeld," Fenwick murmured.

Sebastian reeled and staggered backward. What the hell had he been thinking? No kissing. No seduction. He was here to find the pearls and get out. Not to toy with a man's affections. Fenwick had no idea who Seb really was. This mission didn't need any further complications.

"Well." Fenwick stuffed his hands in his pockets. "That's the end of the tour."

Seb's instinct was to bat his eyelashes and reply that he

hadn't seen the bedroom yet. He smothered the desire with a brusque, "Danke."

Fenwick nodded and walked from the room in silence. The spell had been broken.

Seb had to remind himself this was a good thing.

⁓

"Your turn to be the baron." Sebastian flung himself onto his bed. "I've learned nothing except that Fenwick is a strange man to be a thief."

Helena made a *give it here* gesture. "Jacket, waistcoat, and cravat, please."

"Ugh." Seb sat up and began to disrobe. "Did you pack any dresses? Sir Albert is a theater aficionado and wants me to act the swooning damsel in his play."

"The red dress is hanging in the wardrobe. You'll need to find some rags to pad the bodice."

"Easy peasy." He tossed the jacket and cravat at his sister. "Have you learned anything of interest so far? Something that might point to the necklace or provide tips for playing the baron?"

Helena brushed non-existent dirt from the jacket. "Oliver Henry Augustus Fenwick, ninth Earl of Fenwick. Twenty-nine years old, orphaned young and raised by his grandfather the eighth earl. Inherited the title three years ago. The neighboring property belongs to Amabel Esther Sophia Young, Duchess of Mirweald. It's a very old duchy, and she is duchess in her own right. Thirty-one years old, inherited at seventeen. She has been in residence here for many months, ostensibly due to renovations at her own estate. The two are fast friends and rumors of an affair have swirled for years."

Seb snorted. "And people believe that? Fenwick might have some interest in women, or at least in people with an androgynous appearance, but I don't think the duchess has any interest in men whatsoever." He tossed Helena the waistcoat.

"How'd you learn all that, anyhow? Have you become cozy with the staff already?"

"I asked a few discreet questions. But the specific details came from the conspicuously displayed copy of Debrett's in the library."

"The Big Library," Seb corrected automatically. He hadn't noticed any particular books when he'd been there, because he'd been too busy admiring Fenwick's smile. He flopped down on the bed. "Damnation. I almost kissed him."

"Fenwick?" Helena's voice rose higher in surprise.

"He's sweet. He has adorable freckles and is very passionate when he's not afraid of the whole world watching. I don't know why he would steal anything, let alone an innocent woman's jewels."

"He was seen by the doorman tucking an unusual gray and pink pearl necklace into his pocket as he left the charity dinner. Multiple people have confirmed that he left the event conspicuously early and alone. It was the first time he'd been in public in over a year. People would notice him."

Seb rubbed his temple. "I know, I know. It makes sense that he would only venture out for a charity event. It makes sense that he would leave early. It doesn't make sense that he would steal from Mother, or that he would do it with such lack of stealth."

"Thankfully, we have Baron Neufeld to find the answers for us." Helena walked to the window and drew back the curtain. "Also, it's still snowing, so we have at least a few days before we can leave. I acquired a maid's uniform to help us search rooms. It's in the wardrobe. Feel free to use it. With all the guests and their own personal staff here, there are plenty of unfamiliar faces about."

"Maybe I'll sneak into the duchess's rooms and read her correspondence with Neufeld." Seb tried to sound cheery, but he didn't feel much enthusiasm for the work.

Once Helena departed, dressed as the baron, Seb's

enthusiasm waned further. He didn't want to be jealous of his twin, but he couldn't help wondering if Fenwick would flirt with this new version of Neufeld.

He shoved himself roughly to his feet. "This is not a failure, it's an opportunity." He strode confidently to the wardrobe. He would become a maid or a valet and learn something new.

When Sebastian swung the doors wide, his gaze snagged on the red gown Helena had mentioned. A smile pulled at his mouth. Chances were, they wouldn't be here long enough to participate in Sir Albert's final performance. But Seb could still put on a show, one that would give him time alone with Fenwick and an excuse to search the house from top to bottom.

Given what had almost happened in the Little Library, it was probably a reckless idea.

Seb's smile broadened. "Needs must!"

Chapter 4

~ day three ~

THE CLASH OF SWORDS REVERBERATED off the high ceiling of the former salon Oliver had repurposed as his exercise room. Casper Hawthorne, Oliver's dear friend and fencing instructor, usually kept up a witty banter when they sparred. This morning, however, he had been quiet, contemplative.

Oliver lunged again, only for Casper to parry as calmly as if he were shooing a fly. Damnation! What did it take to hit the man?

Casper made an attack of his own, which Oliver swiftly countered. Oliver regrouped, then lunged again.

"You're aggressive today." Casper riposted, and the point of his blade caught Oliver square in the chest. "And unusually careless."

With a frustrated grunt, Oliver backed away and lowered his sword. "It was one mistake."

Casper shook his head. "That was far from your only mistake this morning. It was simply your worst." He waved the tip of his sword in a little circle. "Tell me what's bothering you."

"It's nothing." Oliver rolled his shoulders and settled into his en garde position. "Let's go again."

"Oliver."

Oliver winced. He knew that exasperated tone. He only ever heard it from Casper or Amabel, and it inevitably meant he was being an ass.

"I'm a professional," Casper continued. "I can tell when

one of my students is distracted. And I know you better than anyone. You'll make no improvements this way. You have two choices. One, I leave and you take out your aggression on a dummy. Two, you tell me what's got your back up and we fix it."

Oliver's shoulders slumped. "Everything. This bloody party. Amabel and I should have eloped. Taken Baron von Fuckable out of the equation."

"Oh, ho!" Casper cackled with delight. "I should have known it was him. He's entirely your sort."

"I think I offended him." Oliver stomped over to the fencing dummy and thrust viciously into its straw heart. "Devil take it! I thought I had a chance with him. This is the first time I've taken much interest in anyone since…"

"Since Rothmere caused your public humiliation," Casper snarled.

"No, you may not duel him. I'll not have you so much as nicked on account of that scoundrel."

"Please." Casper waved his sword. "I could defeat that man with my eyes closed."

"No."

"Very well. I'll leave him alive. For now. But only if you tell me about Neufeld. How did you offend him?"

Oliver yanked his sword out of the dummy. "I almost kissed him."

"Almost? No wonder he's offended! I would be too. You ought to have pushed him up against the wall and kissed him until he was begging for your mouth elsewhere."

"*He* pulled away." Oliver hung his sword in the rack on the wall. "Then he hardly even looked my way for the rest of the day. I swear he was flirting with Amabel, after he'd insisted he had no interest in a match." He threw up his hands. "I don't know. Maybe it's him. Maybe he's playing games with all of us."

Casper tapped a finger to his lips. "Hmm. Perhaps I should

seduce him? Get him away from the rest of you. I'm sure I can keep him interested for at least a few days."

"Please don't. I'd be in a worse mood if you succeeded where I failed. If you need to do me a favor, perhaps give Sir Albert a lesson and stab him? Not enough to do real damage, of course. But maybe a gash on his writing arm?"

"Oliver Fenwick, are you trying to ruin a man's theatrical dreams?"

"Yes."

Casper laughed.

"I can't get it through to him that I don't want to be in the play. He talks and talks and I can hardly get a word in."

"But, darling, the play will be wonderful fun! I am the villain! Shall we practice your death scene? Pretend to embrace your lover and I will run you through from behind."

"Absolutely not." Oliver stripped off his glove and padded jacket. "I'm not participating. I refuse to embarrass—"

"Knock, knock!" a voice called through the open door.

Oliver whirled to find Neufeld leaning against the doorjamb, arms and legs crossed. An impish smile played on his lips.

"Do you have a moment, Fenwick? I had an idea I wanted to run by you."

A grin lit up Casper's face. He put a hand on Oliver's back and propelled him toward the door. "He has many moments to spare. Take him away and do what you like with him!"

Oliver stopped himself from making a rude gesture. It would only encourage Casper.

"Please excuse my friend," he said to Neufeld. "Meddling in the affairs of others is his favorite pastime."

"Of course, darling," Casper drawled. "Affairs are so much more fun when one is participating."

Oliver kept his focus on the baron. "We can talk in my study. It's just down the hall."

Once out the door, the two men fell easily into step. It was as if the awkwardness of the previous evening hadn't existed.

"That's Hawthorne, yes?" Neufeld asked. "The fencing instructor? He seems an entertaining sort of chap."

"Casper is a dear friend and an excellent teacher. He is my opposite in that he loves parties and attention. He's also extremely protective and will whip out his sword at the slightest provocation."

Neufeld waved a hand casually. "What's a little light stabbing between friends?"

Heat crawled up Oliver's neck. "The study. Here." He lunged for the door. "Come in."

They settled into chairs on opposite sides of Oliver's desk, far enough apart to prevent any accidental touching, thank God. He needed to keep his head. The connection he'd felt between them yesterday was nothing more than his imagination.

"How can I help you?" he asked, trying to mimic his grandfather's formal mannerisms.

"I thought I might help *you*," Neufeld replied. "I understand you need to remove yourself from the party at times to avoid becoming overwhelmed. And I believe I am right in thinking that Sir Albert's theatrical is of particular concern?"

Oliver drummed his fingers on his desk. This was when people always gave him unhelpful advice.

Be a man. Have a few drinks beforehand. Visit a hypnotist. Drink this questionable cure-all potion. Imagine everyone else in their underclothes.

That last was especially terrible. The discomfort of others would only make him more uncomfortable.

"I'm not looking for help." Yes, he sounded surly. No, he didn't care if Neufeld was offended.

"It's not help so much as an excuse to spend time alone."

Oliver's fingers stilled. "Go on."

"I'm something of an amateur actor. My mother has many artistic friends, and through those connections I've learned a great deal. About acting, naturally, but also about the things that happen behind the scenes. Stage sets, lighting, costumes, props. People are easily fooled by what they see. Dress a king in rags and no one will recognize him."

Oliver only nodded.

"So." Neufeld leaned over the desk, his eyes shining. "I want to propose to Sir Albert that you and I take on the role of costume and prop management. Me because of my experience, you because you know the house and its contents. We can search together or you can simply read Gothic novels while I gather materials. We can also promise that we'll practice our lines together. Keep Sir Albert happy when you don't show up to rehearsals. We can practice in truth, if you want. It might make the role comfortable enough to perform for others. And if it doesn't, he will be so pleased with the effort we've put into the backstage work, he'll forgive you for withdrawing. I'm sure he can recite your lines himself if he needs a replacement. What say you?"

Oliver gaped, the words replaying in his head. "You are proposing I abandon my guests whenever I desire, under the pretense of gathering materials for an amateur farce?"

"Correct."

"And you'll prowl around my house while I'm tucked away in the Little Library?"

"Also correct. Unless you'd like to accompany me. I might require assistance finding things. I'll read the script and make a list of the necessary items."

"That is—" Oliver caught himself reaching toward Neufeld and forced his hand to still. "It's the most helpful solution to my social difficulties anyone has ever proposed. Thank you."

The baron's eyebrows rose and he rocked back in surprise. "Oh. You're welcome."

Neufeld didn't blush, but his smile was more bashful than Oliver could have imagined. Perhaps he wasn't as breezily confident as he usually appeared.

"I promised Amabel I would participate in her parlor games this morning." Oliver cringed. "I will no doubt need to recuperate when we have finished. Shall we begin our costume hunt directly after luncheon?"

Neufeld's easy smile fell back into place. "I'll be ready."

Chapter 5

"And then the farmer says to Max, 'Son, that's a ram.'"

The party dissolved into uproarious laughter. Which was impressive, considering that was one of the worst jokes Seb had ever told. Given the amount of alcohol circulating during this luncheon, he'd opted for juvenile humor. And it had worked.

Mostly.

At the far end of the dining table, the duchess smiled in a way that showed her teeth. An "I will murder you and enjoy it" smile. Fenwick, only two seats down from Sebastian, looked embarrassed, though Seb couldn't decide if it was because of the joke, the obviously intoxicated group, or too much time spent in company.

A woman attired in trousers—Seb thought her name was Georgia or George, but wasn't sure when she used which—nudged the man next to her. "Tunsbury, tell the story about the time you mistook Maryellen's mother for an actress!"

"They looked alike in the dark!" Lord Tunsbury protested.

Seb pushed his chair back from the table and rose to his feet. His own mother was an actress—a fact he'd nearly blabbed to Fenwick when explaining his plan—and he wasn't in the mood to hear drunken toffs treating the stage like a buffet of interchangeable delicacies.

"Speaking of acting, we have important work to do, eh, Fenwick?"

The earl flinched. "Oh. Yes." He stood. "Please excuse us, everyone."

"Won'rful!" Sir Albert slurred. He looked down at his wine glass, frowning when he found it empty.

Casper Hawthorne winked at Seb and Fenwick as they walked past. Fenwick blushed, as usual. The others might assume they were heading off for a tryst instead of a costume hunt, but that was fine with Seb. Everyone here seemed to accept unconventional people and relationships—something Seb had taken for granted growing up in the world of theater. He'd had quite the shock when his mother's marriage to a respected barrister had thrown him into a world where he wasn't supposed to flirt with men or swap clothing with his sister.

"Is everyone in this house queer?" he asked Fenwick once they were alone.

"I do not pry into the personal lives of my guests," the earl replied primly.

"You can say yes, Fenwick. You know I'm one of you. What of the servants? Are they similarly inclined or simply paid to be discreet?"

"What are you getting at, Neufeld?"

Seb stopped walking and crossed his arms. "You know what I mean. Is this a 'flirt but don't get caught in the wrong bedroom' situation, or—"

Fenwick held up a hand. "I grew up in this house with Grandfather, Grandmother, and Grandmama all living happily together. Does that answer your question?"

"It does. Thank you." Seb started walking again, although Fenwick was supposed to be leading the way. Constant motion soothed some of the churning in his stomach. This pull from two different directions was exhausting. What if he searched the entire house and didn't find the pearls? What if he *did* find them? He liked this place and the people in it. He wanted to walk out of here as Fenwick's friend, not his enemy.

Seb considered various scenarios in which Fenwick might

have come into possession of the pearls in a wholly innocent fashion. None were plausible.

Unless...

They looked alike in the dark, Tunsbury had said. An actress was beneath his notice, and so was a barrister's wife. A polite nod and he'd give her no further consideration. Could that be what had happened to Seb's mother? Had she been mistaken for someone else?

She wore her pearls often. The necklace was her sole remaining gift from Seb and Helena's father, and a treasured possession. It looked like the wedding gift it had been. As valuable as the baubles worn casually by rich men's wives and mistresses.

At a crowded event with poor lighting and many people wearing similar colors, mistakes could be made. Fenwick seemed unlikely to be so careless, but he might not have been acting alone. Perhaps he had friends, like Tunsbury, who snagged jewels from rich toffs to... What? Feed the poor?

"Are you and your friends radical activists?" Seb asked, as if it were a perfectly ordinary topic of conversation. "Not Gunpowder Plot types, but perhaps distributing obscene materials or establishing secret clubs? Speaking out in support of other queer people. Fighting for the freedom to love whom you will." *Stealing to fund your campaign.*

Fenwick opened his mouth, then closed it again. He glanced around, brow furrowed in uncertainty. "Do you have some ulterior motive for being here, Neufeld?"

Shit!

Seb plastered a neutral expression on his face. If he'd been caught out already, Helena was going to kill him.

"You said you weren't here to propose to Amabel. Why travel through the snow to a dull house party? Are you..." His frown deepened. "Are you here to recruit people for your— what did you call it—radical activists? I don't like groups, but Casper might—"

The knot in Seb's gut unraveled, and he stopped Fenwick with a wave of his hand. "I thought perhaps something was already in place. The duchess struck me as a crusader."

Fenwick's expression smoothed out. "Ah! Very much so. She has a publication. I write for it occasionally. She champions many progressive causes. I have copies if you'd like to read it."

"I would, thank you. But I suppose we ought to get on with our task."

What Sebastian ought to do was keep his damned mouth shut. He was utter rubbish at interrogation. Perhaps with someone else he could have flirted his way to answers. But with Fenwick, Seb always said the wrong thing. Half the time the earl misunderstood. The other half, Seb hardly understood himself. He'd taken a simple role of "suave nobleman who charms everyone to distraction" and turned it into "quirky flirt discombobulated by a shy eccentric."

In other words, the real Sebastian Wright. And that would not do.

He trudged after Fenwick, up staircase after staircase, until he couldn't stand the silence anymore.

"Sorry if I sounded like I was prying earlier," Seb said. "I must have come off like a snitch. You're an interesting person with interesting friends and I get excitable when I meet people like myself." *When I find a place I might belong.*

Damn, so much truth wrapped in so many lies.

"I understand completely," Fenwick replied. "Good companions aren't always easy to come by. It's taken me my whole life to accumulate this many people I can tolerate, and to be entirely truthful, most of them are Amabel's friends who hardly notice when I slink away."

I'd notice.

Seb couldn't imagine this house without Fenwick in it. The ballroom might go on as it was, but the small, quiet spaces would become empty and neglected. A house tour would be a recitation of facts rather than a passionate oration on history and Gothic novels.

Yes, Seb would enjoy the company of the other guests. But he'd miss the rosy flush on Fenwick's pale skin. He'd miss the freckle high on his cheekbone that was slightly larger than the ones around it. He'd miss the thrill of ferreting out each new detail of this complex, private man.

Fenwick stopped before an unremarkable doorway. "The attics are through here." He wore a slight smile. "This will be good fun, I hope. I played here often when I was a boy."

Another detail Seb filed away. "Then it's time you did so again. No one's too old to play. I'd have a dozen different rooms devoted to nothing but fun if I had a house like this."

Fenwick stopped with his hand on the doorknob and the door halfway open. "I thought you lived in a castle? What's different about it?"

Seb wanted to smack himself. *You fucking fuckwit! You are not Sebastian Wright. You are Baron Georg Neufeld. You live in a Bavarian castle, you are meant to marry a duchess, and you live a life of idle luxury!*

"It's very... fussy." Seb made a vague gesture. "You know Europeans. So much gold and frills..." He tried not to think about the Painted Salon with its baby angels and excessive decoration.

Fenwick laughed. "Good God, man, did you take no notice of the ballroom on our tour? The gilding alone could probably feed all my tenants for a year. If I didn't have obligations to host people—" He grimaced. "—I'd strip it all down and fund an orphanage."

"The ballroom has all the mirrors? I admit I didn't take much notice. I was distracted by your charming tale of the architect who designed the vaulted ceiling."

Much better. That was not only the absolute truth, but it was precisely what Baron Neufeld would say. Best of all, it brought an adorable blush to Fenwick's cheeks. Seb really oughtn't be so delighted by that.

"I do tend to ramble at times."

"A good thing in my opinion," Seb assured him. "I like a person who shows enthusiasm for topics that interest them."

Fenwick smiled bashfully and led the way into the attic. Unused furniture rested in the shadows, draped in white cloth like oddly-shaped wraiths. Trunks of varied sizes and ages filled the spaces between. The sunlight filtering through the crown glass window cast bullseyes of light over every surface. A bookcase of old toys listed to one side, causing its contents to pile up at the end of each shelf. Sebastian could picture a younger version of Fenwick in here, reading by the window, hiding beneath the tarps, or climbing up to the sloping ceiling on a solitary adventure.

"Clothing will be here." Fenwick indicated a stack of trunks. "Some of it might be too moth eaten or too small for most of the men. But it will be a start."

"We'll need jewels, too." Seb reached for the latch of the topmost trunk and sprung it open. "We can't have our prince and his court in anything less than their finest."

"Uh…"

Seb's fingers clenched in the fabric inside the trunk. He hated this. Every time he probed for clues about the pearls, a wave of guilt washed over him. He wanted to tell Fenwick the truth. Confess who he was and why he was really here. Enlist the earl's help in locating the pearls instead of constantly lying.

"Most of the jewels belong to Grandmother and Grandmama," Fenwick said. "They probably have some things put away at the dower house. But I expect they took their favorites with them while they winter in Italy. I don't know where costume pieces might be kept if not up here, but I can ask. If we don't find what we need, perhaps the other guests might enjoy making beads and pendants out of papier mâché."

"Good idea. It'll give everyone something to do besides

drinking." Seb lifted the fabric from the trunk and shook it out. "Petticoats. Always useful." He pulled out a few more underskirts, dropping them into an untidy pile as he uncovered what lay beneath. "Wait, what's this, then?"

Fenwick leaned in. "Are those powdered wigs? Dear Lord, I thought Grandmama had disposed of those decades ago."

"That one is pink." Seb pointed at the offending hairpiece. "And that one has a bird's nest in it. At least, I hope it's a bird's nest and not the home of a rodent."

Fenwick reached for the wig. As he lifted it, a cloud of powder puffed into the air, followed an instant later by an irate squeaking.

Seb shrieked. He sprang away from the trunk, caught his foot on a petticoat, and crashed to the floor in an ungainly heap of feminine undergarments.

"S-sorry." Fenwick's face pinched as he struggled not to laugh. He held up the wig. "No rodents." He choked back a snicker.

Seb threw one of the petticoats at him. "You fucking bastard."

Fenwick's control broke. He doubled over, his whole body shaking with mirth. "The look on your face..." His laugher grew louder. "And then the flailing and the p-petticoats..."

"I hate rats," Seb shot back, trying and failing to keep his own amusement out of his voice. "It wasn't—" A laugh broke free. "Fine! It was funny."

Fenwick chortled. He dropped to his knees beside Seb, tears dripping down his rosy cheeks. "Oh, God." He could hardly get the words out. "You going down and the skirts flying up—" He started wheezing.

Seb punched him in the arm. "Insensitive blackguard, insulting perfectly respectable underclothes."

He lost his composure and joined Fenwick's uncontrollable hilarity. Seb laughed until his sides hurt and his chest heaved. He laughed until he lay flat on his back, atop a crumpled petticoat, with Fenwick sprawled beside him and the bird's nest wig at their feet.

"I'll—" Seb gulped air and tried again. "I'll find out what you're afraid of and get you back."

Fenwick put a hand to his forehead. "Please do. I haven't laughed that hard in… forever." He blew out a long breath. "Thank you. I needed that."

"My pleasure." The words came out low and throaty, laced with innuendo Seb hadn't intended, but that he wouldn't take back given a chance.

Fenwick rolled to face Sebastian. "Shall we continue our costume hunt, or…" He let the sentence roll off his tongue, his generous lips remaining parted in invitation. His eyes bore into Seb, the irises a deep blue around pupils blown wide with lust.

Seb's body warmed all over.

Seduce him. Get into his bedroom and search for the pearls.

He mentally swatted at the nagging voice. Maybe it was the easiest way. Maybe he could do what he'd come here to do and be gone by midnight. But then he'd hate himself forever and nothing was worth that.

"Fenwick, I—"

"Oliver," the earl interrupted. "Please call me Oliver."

"Oliver." The name tasted like honey and brandy: smooth, sweet liquid fire down Seb's throat. He longed to rasp it against Fenwick's skin, to murmur it while he kissed every freckle, to moan it in ecstasy and hear his own name moaned in return.

Sebastian. He could hear it in Fenwick's—Oliver's—voice, in the unburdened, passionate tone he used when excited. *My God, Sebastian.*

"I would love to kiss you." Seb pushed himself away from the other man. "But I can't. Not now." He sat up and rubbed a hand across his face. "Maybe we can talk later?"

A small furrow of confusion creased Oliver's brow just above his nose. "Yes. Of course." His smile reformed, shy, but with a hint of temptation. "Somewhere more suitable for intimate conversation."

Seb swallowed hard and nodded.

Taking great pains not to allow even the tiniest brush of fingers, Seb assisted Oliver in examining the trunk of wigs and the next trunk below. An hour later, they had a pair of costumes worthy of the court of Louis XVI, including shoes, stockings, and a pair of outlandishly embroidered waistcoats. Seb thought he might pinch the one covered with little foxes and have it altered to a suitably modern style.

He gathered all the items into his arms and backed away when Oliver extended a hand to help.

"I'll take these to Sir Albert." Seb continued backing toward the door.

Oliver nodded. "But I will see you again this evening?" He flashed his shy-sexy smile again.

Seb fought the urge to fling everything aside, push Oliver against the dilapidated bookshelf, and kiss him until they both forgot who and where they were.

"Sure." He turned and fled, not to find Sir Albert, but to his own bedroom, where he dropped the garments in a heap and collapsed on the bed.

"Sebastian." Helena emerged from the dressing room, attired in the maid's uniform. "What have you done now?"

"I'm going to tell Oliver the truth," he vowed, then buried his head beneath a pillow. He didn't need to hear Helena cursing him to the iciest depths of hell.

Chapter 6

◦ day four ◦

Oliver sipped his port and smiled blandly, pretending he cared in the slightest about the impromptu poetry recitation happening around him. To his left, Casper sprawled sideways in a chair, smoking a cigar and misquoting Byron. Across from them, Sir Albert and Mr. Whitcomb stood before the hearth, rehearsing for the theatrical.

Oliver glanced at the empty place on the couch beside him. If the world were a kinder place, Neufeld would be sitting there. Oliver would sling an arm around his shoulders, lean in, and whisper, "Which waistcoat shall we give Whitcomb? The foxes or the periwinkles?" Then Neufeld would giggle and slide closer, the press of his thigh a promise for when they were alone.

Except that Neufeld was "indisposed," and had been since supper last evening. He'd appeared several times throughout the day, clad in a garish yellow dressing gown, to have a cup of tea and exchange brief words with people who were not Oliver. Every inquiry into the baron's whereabouts had been answered with, "His lordship is resting in his room."

Despite only seeing the man for a handful of seconds all day, Oliver had no doubt something was amiss. He couldn't say whether it was Neufeld's walk or the tilt of his head or an indefinable aura around him. But something was different.

Most likely he was suffering a bad headache or an unruly

stomach. It was only coincidence that this had happened after the near-kiss in the attic.

Oliver was damned tired of repeating this to himself. It hadn't helped that Casper had spent most of the day giving lessons and Amabel had been mysteriously absent, leaving Oliver with no one to confide in.

He rose and walked to the sideboard for a refill, then thought better of it. He set his empty glass beside the decanter and turned to address his companions.

"I'm off to bed, boys."

"By yourself?" Whitcomb tsked. "Terribly lonely."

Casper blew out a stream of smoke. "With Neufeld, assuming he's feeling up for it."

Several men snickered.

"I beg your pardon," huffed Lord Tunsbury. "You are disrupting my recitation of *Ode to a Blancmange*!"

"Do go on." Casper waved for Tunsbury to continue. "It can't be worse than *I Eat Thee, O! Sweet Strawberry Trifle*."

Oliver fled.

He took the stairs two at a time, not slowing his pace until he reached the soothing quiet of the family wing. Shaking some of the tension from his limbs, Oliver ambled down the dark hall. He'd never fall asleep at this hour, but perhaps he could read a book. He might even lie in bed with his eyes closed, enjoying the time away from people and noise.

"I could ring for a bath," he mused. That did sound nice. Hot water, fragrant soap, an erotic novel. He'd used the combination to settle his mind on a number of occasions.

Oliver pushed open the door to his bedchamber. His hand was halfway to the bellpull when he registered the single candle illuminating the room. And the man holding it.

"Neufeld?"

The baron stood at the foot of the bed, attired only in loose trousers and an untucked shirt. He held the candle too low for Oliver to read the expression on his face.

"My apologies," he mumbled.

"What are you doing here?" Oliver winced at his own foolish question. What did any half-naked man do in a bedroom?

"Invading your privacy?" Neufeld made it a question.

"I… suppose you are, at that." Oliver let the door swing closed behind him. "Which is not to say that an invasion must be unwelcome." Heat crawled up his neck. He needed to restrain the part of him that ascribed a double meaning to every word he exchanged with Neufeld.

The baron huffed a mirthless laugh. "You're far too trusting for your own good, Fenwick."

Oliver's jaw clenched. Neufeld wasn't wrong in his assessment. He'd been foolish enough to trust Rothmere, that pestiferous spawn of a moist turnip.

"What if I was a thief?" Neufeld pressed.

"If you were a thief, I would expect you to pinch the silver. There's nothing in my rooms worth stealing. And why would you come here, wait three days, and then steal something? That makes no logical sense."

People often do things that make no logical sense, Oliver reminded himself. He always forgot that. The same way he forgot that people would lie politely and expect him to understand that they meant the opposite of what they said.

The candle wobbled in Neufeld's hand, causing the flame to dance. "What if I thought you were hiding something of great importance and took it upon myself to search the premises until I found it?"

Oliver rubbed his temple. This conversation was making his head spin. Either he'd had far too much port, or far too little.

"You'd be mistaken," he replied. "I would be a terrible spy, and I haven't many close friends. Who would trust me with anything of great importance?"

"I would."

Oliver rocked back on his heels. "You would?"

"I'd wager ten pounds that if I entrusted something to you, you'd guard it with your life."

"Ten pounds." Oliver blinked. "Is that meant to be a large sum, or are you making sport of me?"

"Sorry. I ought to have said one thousand. Your cravat probably cost more than ten pounds."

"I have no idea what my cravat cost," Oliver admitted. He began to untie the blasted thing, in sudden need of more air. "Would you be a good chap and light the lamps? I'm getting spots in my eyes from staring at that bloody candle."

"Right."

As Neufeld went from lamp to lamp, Oliver removed his jacket and waistcoat. With the room nicely illuminated, he took a seat on the edge of the bed and began to unlace his boots.

Neufeld blew out the candle. "I suppose I'll be getting back to my own room."

Oliver fumbled the boot and it thunked heavily on the floor. He frowned up at the other man. "Look, if you don't want to fuck, you can say so. You don't have to be coy about it. I'd rather you tell me straight up instead of haring off each time I try to kiss you."

"It's not that." Neufeld began to pick bits of wax off the candle.

Oliver tossed his other boot aside. "Are you a virgin?"

"God, no!"

"First time with a man?"

"Not that either."

"Then what's got you tight as an overwound pocket watch? You're making me seem like the normal one."

Neufeld's eyes widened, the gold flecks among the brown sparkling in the lamplight. "I have no interest in normal people. You do us both an insult to imply any such thing."

"That sounds like something Casper would say."

"He's an intelligent man. I told you I liked your friends."

Oliver shrugged his braces off and let them dangle. "Shall I continue to disrobe, or would you rather come here and kiss me first?" Might as well do this the straightforward way. He'd had more than enough of vagueness and miscommunication. Flirtation took far too much energy, and the house party had already sapped most of his.

Neufeld turned away. "I shouldn't."

"For God's sake, why not?"

The baron's shoulders rose and fell as he expelled a deep breath. "Because I'm not who you think I am."

There. He'd said it. Seb sucked in another shaking breath. He'd told the truth. Fenwick would probably relegate him to the stables until the snow melted enough to make the roads passable. His mother's pearls would remain forever lost. Helena would refuse to work with him ever again.

But at least he hadn't succumbed to the temptation to sleep with Oliver under false pretenses. Damn, he was going to miss those freckles.

"Could you clarify that statement?"

The question startled Seb enough that he turned around. "I beg your pardon?"

"Is there some meaning to your statement that I don't understand?" Fenwick asked. "Because I think you are a charming young man who is interested in me the way I am interested in you. What part of that is wrong?"

"None of it. I spoke plainly. I'm not who you think. I'm not Baron Georg Neufeld of Bavaria."

"Oh." Oliver stared off into the distance. He ran a finger across his lower lip, seeming to ponder the matter.

Seb tried to look anywhere except at that lip, tried to force his mind to think of anything besides how it might feel under his own finger.

"My name is Sebastian Wright. The man at the stables mistook me for Baron Neufeld. I ought to have corrected the error at once, but I was cold and tired and your household was welcoming."

"I see." Oliver's gaze remained focused on nothing, and his finger continued its slow slide. Back and forth. Back and forth.

Seb swallowed hard. "I am entirely at fault for perpetuating the deception. Please convey my apologies to the rest of the party. I'll take no more of your time, and I promise to depart as soon as it becomes safe to travel." He swiveled toward the door.

"A moment, Neu— Mr. Wright."

Seb paused with his hand on the knob, but didn't look back. "Yes?"

"If you are not the baron, why did you come to this house in the first place?" Fenwick's voice was the epitome of aristocratic politeness. Seb would have preferred a fist to the face.

"A matter of business. One I will no longer be pursuing. Again, my apologies."

Sebastian pushed the door open and hurried away, the unlit candle still in hand. He didn't stop moving until he was in his room, in bed, with the sheets pulled up over his head. He was right. He knew he was right. He'd done the decent thing, and he was a better man for it. It was the irrefutable truth, no matter what anyone else might say to him.

If only it didn't feel like one more misstep down an endless road of wrongs.

Chapter 7

◆ day five ◆

Oliver poured himself a fourth cup of tea. He added neither milk nor sugar, despite the questioning glances of the others gathered at the table for breakfast. No one tried to engage him in conversation, thank heavens. Anything to come out of his mouth would surely be as muddled as his thoughts.

All night he'd tossed and turned, trying to wrangle his emotions into a semblance of order. Was he angry? Yes. Hurt? Yes. Confused? Undoubtedly.

But there were more layers than that, ones he hadn't quite identified, or perhaps hadn't wanted to examine, tangled as they were with lingering lust for a man who didn't exist.

Oliver waved away the offer of another pot of tea. He had to get up. His guests wanted entertaining, and he couldn't slink away until he fulfilled his duty to them.

"Neufeld! Here you are at last," Whitcomb called out. "Thought you might miss breakfast entirely."

Oliver turned slowly. The faux-baron strode casually into the room, dressed in his usual attire of black trousers and jacket. His waistcoat today was pale blue, and his wine-colored cravat had been loosely knotted. That, along with the slight curl of his dark hair, gave him an aura of insouciance that lured Oliver like a moth to flame. The magic of a conjurer, still working even after he had learned the trick.

A more capable man might have pulled the imposter politely aside, then banished him from the house with a few pointed words. Oliver sat in paralyzed silence as the opportunity passed him by.

"Late night?" Casper smirked at Wright. "Please, have a seat and tell us what could possibly have kept you up."

Wright cocked a hip and returned Casper's smirk. "I have better ways to occupy my lips than with idle gossip."

"Oh, ho!" Tunsbury lifted his teacup in salute. "His tongue is as sharp as your sword, Hawthorne. Perhaps he should give you lessons."

Wright slid smoothly into the seat beside Tunsbury. "I don't believe the swordmaster has much care for the cunning arts of a linguist."

The party broke out in laughter and Tunsbury slapped Wright on the back.

Oliver stared. The theatrical playing out in front of him was as bad as the one Sir Albert was planning. It was as if the character of Baron Neufeld, aka Sebastian Wright, had been written by a pair of feuding scribes. Oliver hadn't known what to expect after last night's awkward conversation, but it certainly wasn't this.

This version of Wright laughed and flirted as if yesterday hadn't happened. Oliver might have thought it a dream except for the note of falseness in Wright's voice. The difference was subtle, and Oliver doubted he would have noticed if he hadn't been so attuned to the other man these past few days.

Wright made another joke and the table once again erupted in laughter. He was definitely acting a part. It almost sounded as if he were mimicking his own voice. Why, Oliver couldn't fathom.

He pushed his chair back and excused himself, mumbling nonsense about stepping outside to evaluate the snow. He wanted no part in whatever game "Baron Neufeld" was playing. No amount of outrageous behavior would tempt Oliver to expose the scheme in front of the rest of the party. He knew the consequences of a public argument all too well.

The snow was indeed snowy. Cold and wet, even. It was also inconveniently deep. No more was falling, but the air was cold and the sky overcast. It took no more than two ticks of his watch to convince Oliver no one would be going anywhere soon. Which meant he couldn't order Wright to leave even if he wanted to. Perhaps the best strategy was to continue on with the charade until the roads were passable.

Trapped between his need to play host and his desire not to speak to another living soul, Oliver set himself the task of organizing the papier mâché prop making. He helped his footmen arrange tables in the Painted Salon, then spent the remainder of the morning circling the room to ensure that everyone had sufficient access to paper, scissors, paste, and brushes.

With outdoor pursuits still severely limited by the weather, the party threw itself into the endeavor with the exuberance of schoolchildren. Ladies and gentlemen alike rolled beads and sculpted oversized pendants. Whitcomb attempted to craft a sword from a damp stick he'd plucked from a snowdrift—with predictable results. Casper began to fashion a crown he intended to steal from Oliver at the climax of the play. Oliver pointedly ignored him.

Most of the guests drifted in and out, but Wright was conspicuously absent.

"Where *has* Neufeld taken himself?" Amabel asked, when the crafting began to wind down.

Oliver—who was rearranging finished pieces that had been perfectly fine where they were—paused and looked up. The duchess caught his eye, and he had a sudden fear that she could read every thought in his head.

"Gone to the stables to spend time with the horses," Sir Albert reported. "But he did promise to be back in time for rehearsal. I want to focus on the love declaration scene today, as it is key to engaging the hearts of the ladies. I trust you've been learning your lines, Fenwick?"

Oliver jumped so hard he upended a plate of beads. The sticky balls went flying, and he scrambled to pluck them off the carpet before they ruined it. By the time he finished, the room was deserted.

⁓

Luncheon was a casual affair, during which Oliver had an excellent conversation with Amabel about his idea for an article on the queer undertones in a recent popular novel. By the time they finished, he had plans for a whole series of articles on the same theme. Someone would probably cry obscenity when he denounced publishers for their refusal to print happy endings for anyone they deemed "immoral."

But since the entire pamphlet was anonymous, Oliver would write whatever he damn well pleased. He had money, he had a pen, and he had things to say. Maybe he couldn't make speeches, but he could do this. A smile formed as he recalled the conversation about radical activism. Neufeld would approve.

Oliver shook off the memory. *Wright, not Neufeld. He's probably a thief. He's probably absconded with something valuable and that's why you haven't seen him since breakfast.*

"Ah, Fenwick, my boy! Here you are, right on time!" Sir Albert's voice echoed through the empty room.

Oliver winced. "Oh, no," he grumbled.

Amabel patted his hand. "Spare the man a few minutes. His play is possibly the only thing keeping the party from drinking your cellars dry."

"Right in here, Neufeld," Sir Albert continued. "Place the box on the table. There's a good lad."

Oliver squeezed his eyes shut. Of all the rotten luck. If only he'd been a fraction less enthusiastic about his articles for Amabel's magazine. He could even now be hiding in the library with a book.

"Please excuse me, gentlemen," Amabel said smoothly.

The slide of her chair and the swish of her skirts announced that she was rising, leaving Oliver with no choice but to do the same. He steeled himself before turning to face the men.

"Sir Albert." Oliver hesitated too long before adding, "Neufeld."

The name felt sour on his tongue. It didn't belong here. It didn't belong to the bleary-eyed young man before him. Wright must have been woken from a nap. He looked pale, weary, and in need of a brisk cup of tea. Or a whole pot.

"You changed your cravat," Oliver blurted, his gaze landing on the patch of bare skin above the haphazardly knotted white neckcloth.

"Er…" Wright tugged at the cravat, exposing the bob of his Adam's apple when he swallowed.

"Have fun, boys!" The door thunked closed behind Amabel.

Sir Albert clapped his hands. "Let's get to it. You two are the heart of this story. There's the comedy, of course. And the terror of the villain and the pathos of the tragic ending. But for those things to be believed, the audience must care for you and your love." He pulled some papers out of the box on the table. "I've lines for you to read, in case you haven't memorized them yet."

Oliver hadn't so much as glanced at the script, nor did he have any intention of doing so. "I must beg your pardon, Sir Albert, but I cannot possibly perform for an audience. It is simply not in my nature."

Sir Albert pressed a paper into Oliver's hands nonetheless. "Stage fright, eh? No matter, no matter. It's all down to practice, you see. Let me tell you about my younger days, when I was so shy of the spotlight I cast up my accounts on the leading lady's dress. Now…"

Oliver caught Wright's gaze in a desperate attempt to tune out what was no doubt a distressing story.

Wright shrugged and stepped closer, reaching for his own

copy of the script. He lifted the paper to hide his mouth, then whispered, "Sorry."

Sir Albert began pulling props out of the box as he rambled: a parasol, a red silk scarf, a lopsided bouquet of faux flowers.

"He ambushed me on my way to find food," Wright explained. "I didn't know he meant to find you until we entered the room."

"There's an urn of coffee and some fruit and cheese remaining on the sideboard," Oliver whispered back.

"Thank God. I haven't eaten all day and I'm famished." He started across the room.

Oliver nearly pointed out that Wright had been at breakfast, but at that moment Sir Albert waved a pair of props in Oliver's face.

"This scene begins with you bestowing a gift on your lady love," the older man declared. "We must find the appropriate thing. Jewels?"

He jiggled a rope of pink and gray pearls that seemed vaguely familiar, though Oliver couldn't place them or guess where in the house Sir Albert might have found them.

"No, too extravagant." Sir Albert tossed the necklace back into the box. "Flowers?" He waved the sad bouquet. "Too common." The flowers followed the pearls into the bottom of the box.

Oliver lifted the paper with his lines. "Perhaps someone else—"

"Of course!"

Oliver jumped back in alarm.

"Poetry!" Sir Albert did a little dance. "The prince is a man of words. Naturally, he will woo Lady Alice with a poem." He tossed the remaining props into the box, with the exception of the parasol. "Oh, Lady Alice—that's you, Neufeld—come join us. We are ready to begin."

Wright turned around, a cup of coffee in one hand and a wedge of cheese in the other.

Help, Oliver mouthed.

Wright downed the entire cup of coffee, then ambled over, gnawing on the cheese. He allowed Sir Albert to position him facing Oliver, the closed parasol propped on one shoulder.

"Excellent. Now let us read through the scene once before we begin to make adjustments." Sir Albert motioned for Oliver to begin, then backed away to view them from an observer's perspective.

Oliver stared blankly at the paper in his hands.

"Read it badly," Wright murmured. "If we're rubbish at it, he won't make us do it in the play."

The weight of Oliver's anxiety eased. It was a fine idea. Wright was a skilled enough actor to play the role of Baron Neufeld. Across from him, Oliver would resemble a bumbling oaf. No one would want him to read a part ever again.

He did have to wonder why Wright was helping him. In thanks for not exposing him to the others, perhaps. Or maybe he was a decent man after all, albeit one who made questionable choices at times.

Sir Albert cleared his throat.

Oliver looked down at his lines. "My dear Lady Alice," he recited, as if reading the morning's correspondence.

"Your Highness," Wright answered, the words garbled due to the cheese he hadn't yet finished.

"I beg your forgiveness for my intrusion, but I must speak, though I fear my words come too late." Oliver didn't stumble over a single word, and couldn't help smiling at the unexpected burst of pride this elicited.

"I will deny you nothing, sir." Wright idly twirled the parasol. "Surely you must know this. My loyalty to you knows no bounds."

"Emotion, emotion!" Sir Albert called out. "You two are madly in love."

"Darling Alice," Oliver recited. "Always will I treasure

your goodness and fealty, though they are but fleeting shadows when I cannot have your heart."

"Muh harth?" Wright asked around the last mouthful of cheese.

Oliver almost laughed. He wasn't merely acting a farce; his life was one.

"Your heart, my love. I know it is not mine to claim, but I yearn for it. My own has been yours since the moment I lay eyes upon you." Oliver squinted at the paper. "Oughtn't it say 'laid'?"

Sir Albert hurried over, his expression pained. "Begin again. *Be* the character. Look into your lover's eyes. Lean closer. You are desperate for one another. Dying of longing to touch. Have passion!" He held out his arms in entreaty, either as an example or because Oliver truly was rubbish at this.

"Lie, lay," Oliver murmured. "You don't 'lie eyes' on someone."

"I think I need a different voice," Wright suggested. "Should it be higher?" He touched the tip of the parasol to the floor and leaned coquettishly over it. "I will deny you nothing, sir!" he squeaked, each word higher than the last.

Oliver burst out laughing. This acting business wasn't so terrible after all—in a closed room with a pair of very silly companions.

"No, that's all wrong." Wright straightened up, gripped the handle of the parasol with both hands, and looked up through his lashes. "I will deny you *nothing*, sir," he purred, low and seductive.

Oliver's blood went hot.

"Surely, you must know this." Wright took a step forward, one hand outstretched. "My loyalty to you knows *no bounds*." He crooked one finger in a come-hither gesture, a sly smile stealing across his lips.

The words were ridiculous, and not truly meant for Oliver, but he could only gape, tongue-tied.

"No, no, no." Sir Albert rushed over again. "That was

excellent passion, Neufeld, but you are an innocent maiden, not a courtesan. You must be demure. A blushing virgin."

Wright blinked as if confused. "A what?"

Sir Albert ignored him and turned to Oliver. "You are perfect. Keep that lovesick look on your face and recite your lines as if he is your entire world. Let's try the end. You'll be moving closer together. Neufeld, you are holding the parasol like a shield because you are shy, but you move it aside as Fenwick reaches for you. When he leans in to kiss you, use the parasol to hide your faces from the audience, to spare their delicate sensibilities."

Oliver rubbed his temple. "Why? No one in this house would be even mildly startled to see two men exchange a kiss, especially in the context of a stage play. I don't see a need to hide anything." Theoretically. If he were the type to perform in public.

"No, no, it's all for show," Sir Albert explained. "We must pretend that the ladies have delicate sensibilities, whether they do or not. And by hiding your kiss, you force them to use their imaginations. If they are delicate, they blush. If they are worldly, their imaginings go beyond a mere kiss. Do you understand?"

He didn't, honestly. If he were watching such a thing, he'd see the parasol and assume they were using it so they didn't have to kiss at all.

"Try it," Sir Albert instructed. "Neufeld, begin with, 'You are as dear to me…'"

Wright popped the parasol open and took up a defensive stance behind it. He then declared, in rather ardent tones, "You are as dear to me as all the earth, the moon, the stars, and all the universe."

Oliver laughed again, then coughed and read his own line. "Alice, my heart! My love!" He frowned at the accompanying stage directions. "Apparently I am now to 'clasp you to my bosom.'"

"Yes, embrace," Sir Albert urged. "Closer, closer. Lift the parasol."

Wright did, but the movement was in no way amorous. "Are you well?" he whispered. "I've been trying to make you laugh, but I may also have embarrassed you? I'm so sorry if I did."

Oliver's chest tightened. Wright's antics were all to make Oliver comfortable. Not for his own gain, not for his own entertainment. He seemed to genuinely care.

"I'm..." Oliver didn't know what he was, other than inarticulate. "Thank you."

"Again, again," their frustrated director said. "You've nearly got it, if you can only remain serious. Think romance, love, desperation. You are *pining* for one another."

Wright repeated the line about earth and moon and so forth, but Oliver didn't hear it. He was mesmerized by the imploring look in Wright's dark eyes. *I'm trying*, the look said. *Please forgive me.*

Oliver took a step forward, extending a hand. He didn't understand Wright's lies and strange behavior, but he understood remorse. God knows he'd fucked things up an uncountable number of times. Bad people weren't sorry for their mistakes.

And maybe this was yet another example of Oliver misreading a person. Maybe he'd come to regret it. But at the moment, all he wanted was for Wright to take his hand.

"My lady," Oliver intoned, not remembering his lines, but prepared to improvise. "Take my hand, as you have taken my heart." *I am your friend, if you wish it.*

Wright curled his fingers around Oliver's and tugged him close, shielding them once again behind the parasol. His smile was radiant, and Oliver's knees went suddenly weak at the sight.

"Friends?" Wright murmured.

"Friends," Oliver agreed. And then he bent his head for a kiss.

This time, Wright didn't pull away.

Chapter 8

Fenwick's kiss was gentle, but earnest, the mark of an agreement sealed. Relief washed through Sebastian. He wouldn't be cast out or exposed. He'd been forgiven. Best of all, he hadn't lost the first chance he'd had in ages for a real friendship.

The moment his tension ebbed, the feelings he'd been studiously ignoring asserted themselves like a blow to the head. He staggered into Oliver, clutching at his coat to drag him closer. Oliver was all long limbs and lean muscle, rock solid against Seb's softer, more delicate form. A hint of fragrance clung to his skin, clean and floral, and Seb couldn't help but wonder what fancy soap he used.

Which conjured up an image of Oliver in the bath, water sluicing down his naked body, rinsing everything away until all that remained was freckled skin and that enticing scent.

Seb groaned, and Oliver took it as an invitation to deepen the kiss. His lips were luscious, his mouth tasting of strong tea and cranberries. He never demanded, only offered, and with the same pure eagerness he exuded when sharing his interests.

Seb flung himself into the kiss. He had to make this good. Whatever happened tomorrow or the next day, he wouldn't let Oliver regret this. He slid his tongue in and out, teasing and tempting, dragging it over Oliver's plump bottom lip, then nipping gently with his teeth. Oliver let out a gasp of pleasure.

A pair of sharp claps startled them out of their amorous haze.

"Boys," Sir Albert chided. "While I appreciate the enthusiasm, your osculatory arts are beyond the scope of this production."

Oliver jumped back, red-faced. "M-my apologies."

Seb picked up the parasol he'd abandoned sometime during the proceedings, and folded it closed. "Excellent rehearsal. We won't take up any more of your time, Sir Albert. Come along, Fenwick. I know you have work to do. Alone, in your library."

Oliver's eyes widened. "Oh. Yes. Please excuse me." He rushed for the door.

Seb followed, and as soon as they'd left Sir Albert behind, he said softly, "I'm sorry for embarrassing you again."

"It's fine," Oliver replied, in as bland a tone as a child reciting from a schoolbook.

"It's really not. I shouldn't have done that with someone else in the room."

Oliver's head tilted, and he studied Seb like a curiosity. "I forgot myself as well. But thank you for considering my... sensibilities."

"You're welcome. I do earnestly desire your friendship, and friends should have a care for one another's needs." He nudged Oliver with his elbow. "You've had a busy few days. Go read for a few hours. You can tell me all about the book at dinner."

Oliver's smile nearly knocked Seb off his feet. "I'd like that." He hurried down the hall and disappeared around a corner, but not before casting one last adoring look over his shoulder.

―

The bedroom door flew open, nearly smacking Seb in the face. He yelped, then froze at the sight of Helena, dressed in a suit nearly identical to his own.

For an instant, she looked as startled as he was. Then she

grabbed hold of his arm, dragged him into the room, and shut the door.

"What the bloody hell, Sebastian?" she hissed. "Have you lost your damned mind? We can't both be out wandering the halls as the same man."

Seb crossed his arms. "Well, excuse me," he retorted. "I was asleep when you left, without so much as a note. How was I supposed to know you'd decided to be Neufeld today?"

Helena adopted the same pose. "You might have noticed that one of our two suits was missing?"

"You're overestimating my mental capacity upon first waking."

She growled and turned away. A few seconds later, she turned back, her face impassive. "Fine. Nothing terrible happened, so we'll put this behind us. You'll need to take off those clothes. Be a valet or a maid, whatever you like."

Seb shook his head. "I need to be Neufeld at dinner. I promised Oliver."

Helena raised an eyebrow. "Oliver? Are you and Fenwick on such intimate terms now? Don't tell me you intend to reveal your identity to him."

"I did that last night." Seb met his sister's gaze defiantly. "I should have told you right away, and for that I'm sorry. I wasn't thinking straight."

"You don't say?" She tried to scowl at him, but her fond-but-exasperated smile broke through.

"I mucked it all up, and I was convinced we'd be thrown out at first light. I panicked, and spent the night frantically searching for the pearls while feeling sorry for myself. By the time I went to bed, you were asleep."

"And then I went down to breakfast with no notion Fenwick knew anything of our scheme." She rubbed her temple. "Devil's teats, this is officially the worst communication we've ever had. Bollocks! I'm sorry I've been so distracted these past few days."

"You? I thought I was the distracted one."

Helena shrugged. "Let's not place blame. We need to decide what to do about Fenwick. You didn't tell him *why* you're here, did you?"

"God, no! I'm not going to accuse him of a crime I don't think he's guilty of. But we talked more today. You don't have to worry that he'll throw us out into the snow."

Helena huffed.

Seb held up a hand. "I mean it. We're friends. He's a good man and we rub along nicely." *And the way he kisses is intoxicating.*

Helena clapped a hand over her eyes. "Oh, my God, you're in love with him."

"Don't be daft," Seb replied, a little too quickly. Oliver was adorable and sweet, and Seb was absolutely going to kiss him again. It was friendship mixed with lust, nothing more.

"You are. You're head over heels in love, and you're going to let him get away with stealing from Mother because of it."

"Helena." Seb sighed and looked up at the ceiling. "He didn't do it. He wouldn't. I'd bet my life on it. If he were going to steal—which I doubt—he'd be picking the pockets of Tories and spreading the wealth like bloody Robin of Loxley." He met his sister's gaze again. "Maybe we *should* tell him everything."

"Don't you dare. You can be his friend. You can be his bedmate. But do not ruin this. I didn't come all this way, ride through shitty weather, and endure meddlesome duchesses, only to fail. You go have your fun; keep Fenwick busy. I'll find the pearls, and then we can leave."

"What if I don't want to leave?" What if he wasn't here for pearls after all? What if he was here for something far more valuable? Something Mother would prize more than all the jewels in the world.

Helena placed a gentle hand on Seb's shoulder. "You'll get over him, Sebastian. You always do. A month from now, another pretty face will come along and you'll move on." She gave him a pat. "Let's sit down and make a list of all the places we haven't yet searched."

Seb flopped on the bed. "The billiard room, because it's always occupied. The kitchens. Fenwick's personal study. The butler's pantry."

Helena responded in kind, but most of it flowed right past Seb. His mind was too clogged with her previous statement. *Another pretty face will come along.*

When Seb closed his eyes and tried to imagine leaving Oliver behind, the list of *Things Seb Would Miss* went on for miles. Oliver's laugh. His Gothic novels. His awkward charm. His passionate ramblings. His queer friends.

His pretty face wasn't even in the top ten.

Chapter 9

~ day six ~

THE NEXT MORNING DAWNED clear and bright, conferring a childlike energy on the entire household. The snow lay in deep drifts, and the trees swayed in the winter wind, but the unbroken sunshine promised to ease the sting of the cold for all who dared to venture out.

Seb added his voice to those clamoring for the outdoors, and soon enough the entire party tromped out to the garden, bedecked in hats, mufflers, coats, and capes of all sizes and colors. Oliver even invited the servants to join in, swelling their numbers to nearly three dozen adventurers.

The duchess led the procession with her customary regal elegance, until she deemed the party appropriately far from the house and held up a hand to halt everyone.

"Tally-ho!" she cried, then flopped onto her back in the snow, waving her arms and legs to make the imprint of an angel.

The crowd cheered. In an instant, the garden became a hive of activity. Amorous couples chased one another, falling into snow drifts wrapped in each other's arms. Snow forts and snow creatures rose into the air, decorated with twigs and leaves and icicles snapped from bowed branches.

Seb ran through the snow, enjoying the freedom of the outdoors and the burn of exercise in his limbs. When he grew tired, he settled beside Oliver, who hummed happily as he erected a structure of neatly-packed snow bricks.

"Will this be a pyramid?" Seb added a brick to the stack.

"A stepped pyramid," Oliver confirmed. "All rectangular bricks and right angles. If we're successful, then we can consider adding specialized blocks to create a sloped facade."

"You're so fucking cute."

Oliver's cheeks, already pink from the cold, turned scarlet.

Across the garden, Casper attacked a listing snowman with a stick, while a group of pupils mimicked his movement. Among them, Seb spied a figure in a familiar knitted blue cap. He couldn't remember which twin the hat had originally been gifted to, but they'd been fighting over it for a decade now, swapping it back and forth between them.

Along with *his* hat, Helena wore a scarf wrapped around her nose and mouth to conceal her features. A mere nod to good sense. Seb grinned. He loved when her own reckless streak got the better of her. Today was brilliant. Later he would kiss Oliver again, but right now, he would laugh and play.

He rolled a handful of snow in his palms, forming a neat ball. When Helena turned her back to attack the snow dummy, Seb tossed the snowball in a long, graceful arc. It hit her right between the shoulder blades.

She retaliated immediately, naturally, lobbing a snowball of her own while urging those around her to do the same. One of the balls smacked into the pyramid, starting a small avalanche down one side.

"We're under attack!" Oliver cried. "Take cover!" He hauled Seb behind the partial structure. "Start rolling balls. We'll need a stock of ammunition."

Seb peeked around the pyramid, ducking when a snowball came flying at his head. Most of the revelers had joined the snowball fight, and factions were beginning to emerge. Helena knelt behind a toppled snowman with a group of housemaids. The duchess crouched behind a leafless bush, calling out orders to a team of hangers on.

"Death to men!" shouted Georgia Beauclair. (A full suit

meant George, a skirt meant Georgia, and anything else was ambiguous, Seb had learned.) "Victory for the Sapphic Ladies' Cl—" Her words dissolved into a shriek when a woman dumped snow down her jacket. "Maryanne, how could you? Traitor!"

Another barrage of snowballs slammed into the pyramid and Seb scooted closer to Oliver. "We may need to shore up our defenses. I appear to have started a war."

Oliver chucked a ball straight into the bush, where it exploded among the branches, showering the duchess. "Someone always does."

A wool-swathed body plunked down next to Seb. "Guess I'm throwing my lot in with you two," said the muffled voice of Lord Tunsbury. "Better than being Her Grace's minion. We'll all lose to the Whitcombs, naturally."

Seb piled more snow atop the pyramid, no longer caring about the aesthetics. "Why?"

Tunsbury slapped Seb on the back hard enough that he almost fell over. "Forgot you're new here. Mrs. Whitcomb has a colorful past. Born a boy in the East End, ran with gangs for years. She's still got the arm strength to prove it. She always destroys us at these winter games."

Oliver poked his friend. "Stop chatting and make snowballs."

Tunsbury did neither of those things, but their small group acquitted themselves well nonetheless. Even half-built, Oliver's pyramid presented a sturdy target, and it took the efforts of several other groups to destroy it.

When arms began to ache and the snow fortifications had been reduced to piles of rubble, the cold, wet combatants helped each other to their feet, brushed snow from hats and cloaks, and offered hearty congratulations. Everyone retreated into the house to change into warm clothing and fill their bellies with hot drinks.

Tunsbury slung a damp arm around Seb's shoulders as they made their way up the stairs to the guest quarters. "You're one of us now, Neufeld. You've witnessed multiple peers of the realm behaving like wild children, and now we can't let you leave, for the sake of our reputations."

"Never fear, my lord. I'll tell no one of your appalling lack of snowball fight skills."

"That's the spirit!" He slapped Seb on the back with a bit less force than the previous time, then skipped off toward his own room.

Seb's stomach flip-flopped. Tunsbury could be a pompous ass, but he seemed to genuinely care about his friends. Now he'd extended that friendship—that trust—to Seb. Who didn't deserve it.

"Shite," he muttered.

Longing thrummed inside him, an uncreasing pulse of *want, want, want*. He wanted room to be himself. He wanted queer friends. He wanted love and companionship and people around him who liked to play in the snow and read Gothic novels. He wanted Sebastian Wright to be welcomed the way the fake Baron Neufeld had been.

Oliver had been tolerant of the deception, but Seb couldn't guess how long that would last. Until the snow cleared? Until the real Baron Neufeld arrived? Until they'd gone to bed a few times and weren't so lust-stricken?

Seb shoved open the door to his room and began stripping off his sodden clothing. Until now, he'd been having a perfect day.

Bugger.

∽

Oliver couldn't have dreamed up a more perfect day. The fresh air had been rejuvenating, and the snowball fight the best in years. For a while he'd been a boy again, free from the concerns and expectations of adulthood.

Now, after a hot bath and several cups of whisky-laced tea, he relaxed on a sofa in the Green Salon, book in hand.

Sebastian Wright sat beside him, engrossed in a book of his own. They hadn't touched since the snowball fight, but the air between them remained heavy with promise. Every few pages, Oliver adjusted his position, inching closer and hoping Wright would do the same.

The room was relatively quiet, given the number of people present. At the opposite end from where he sat, a group played a game of Forfeits. This particular variant appeared to involve some kissing, frequent slaps on the arse, and constant giggling. Casper, of course, was the ringleader.

Closer to Oliver, Amabel and Mrs. Whitcomb sat side-by-side, chatting while they embroidered. They were genteel ladies from tip to toe, without a hint of the snow-hurling hoydens from earlier. They did, however, occasionally glare at Tunsbury, who hunched over a nearby desk, scribbling poetry. The man had a bad habit of reciting rhymes aloud when searching for a word.

Tunsbury put his head in his hands. "I need a word that rhymes with 'siren.' As in, 'I hear your call and come, my siren.'"

"Alas for you, you're no Lord Byron," Wright quipped, not looking up from his book.

"Sod off," Tunsbury replied good-naturedly. "I'm going to use that, just to show you up." He began to scribble.

The smile creeping across his friend's face did something to Oliver's insides. Amabel and Mrs. Whitcomb were grinning too. They all liked Wright. It really shouldn't have mattered. Oliver didn't need his friends to like the people he slept with. He didn't like all their lovers. He'd actively despised some of Casper's lovers, and it hadn't impacted their friendship in any way.

But this thing with Wright—Oliver craved approval in a way he never had. He wanted all his friends to pat him on the back and say, "Good for you." He wanted them to expect Wright's presence next time they all congregated here.

Oliver squirmed in his seat and forced his eyes to look at his book. He was being silly. He was antsy because he hoped to take Wright to bed tonight. And after Rothmere, he needed outside reassurance that this wasn't a foolish decision. Nothing more than that.

He relaxed against the back of the couch, satisfied with this entirely logical deduction. As the story sucked him in, he lost track of the rest of the room. The laughter and voices blurred together into a comfortable background hum.

Wright moved closer, until their shoulders touched. He didn't speak or try to pull Oliver out of his reading. Chapter after chapter they sat there, together in their separate pursuits. When Oliver finally looked up from the book, the sun had set and his invaluable staff had quietly turned up the lamps.

Warmth spread through his chest, filling a wound in his heart that had been gaping for a year. He'd missed this space between socializing and isolation, where he could simply be. He'd missed having people surrounding him who had no further expectations beyond his presence. In all the days his guests had been here, not one of them had chided him for disappearing for hours at a time or remaining silent while they talked.

Had he really spent all this time fretting about misstepping? Even in front of his friends? Thank God Wright had arrived to shake him up a bit, or he might have continued on heedless.

Oliver must have shifted, because Wright lowered his book.

"This is the third time the hero—supposedly a trained soldier—has been kidnapped. I don't think he actually wants to rescue the heroine. I think he's fucking the 'cruelly handsome' villain."

Amabel looked up from her embroidery. "Is that the book with the underwater dungeon? I loved that one. There's a delightfully erotic hair-brushing scene between the heroine and her maid."

"Excellent." Wright slammed the book shut. "And they all lived happily ever after." His voice held a hint of wistfulness, and his smile didn't quite reach his eyes.

A desire for happy queer stories? A dozen new ideas for his article formed in Oliver's head. Ways stories could hurt or help. Ways fiction could show truth more starkly than fact.

Because that's what Wright was, wasn't he? A fiction. A veneer of Baron Neufeld atop his genuine self. Maybe his lie allowed him to be what he ordinarily couldn't.

Oliver nudged him. "Would you like to go upstairs?" he asked quietly.

"God, yes." Wright hopped up and extended a hand.

Oliver let the other man help him to his feet, but didn't let go. Fingers intertwined, they left the room together.

Chapter 10

They were kissing before the bedroom door fully closed. Where their previous kiss had been spontaneous and experimental, this one was deliberate. Wright didn't hesitate to press Oliver back against the door, trapping him between hard oak and soft lips. Oliver grasped Wright's waist and brought their bodies flush, taking some of the weight from the shorter man when he went up on tiptoe to improve the angle.

Finally, finally.

The thought pulsed in rhythm with Oliver's heartbeat, steadily faster, as the kiss grew to a needy, lip-bruising frenzy.

Wright sank back down, dragging his mouth over Oliver's jaw to his neck. "I'm too short," he murmured. His lips pressed against a throbbing vein, sending a shudder of longing straight to Oliver's groin.

Oliver's head lolled against the door. "You're the perfect height," he gasped. "Don't stop."

God, he'd been wanting this. He'd been raging with desire since the moment Wright had walked into this house and flashed his impish smile, those warm, dark eyes shining.

Wright tugged Oliver's cravat loose and dropped it on the floor. He kissed down the column of Oliver's throat, hands sliding beneath his coat to work the buttons of his waistcoat and shirt.

"Sebastian." The name slipped from Oliver's lip like a prayer, then he stiffened in alarm. "May I call you that?"

Wright's lips met the junction of Oliver's neck and shoulder, sparking an involuntary shudder. "You may and you should," he murmured. He sucked at the delicate skin. If he continued in this manner, it would leave a mark, something Oliver usually tried to avoid.

He let out a whimper and grasped Sebastian tighter. Today he didn't care. No, that wasn't quite right. Today he *wanted* it. He wanted to look in the mirror tomorrow and remember exactly this moment.

"Fuck, Sebastian."

Wright ground his erection against Oliver's thigh. "Want you."

"Want you too," Oliver panted. "Can't stop thinking of you." He slid his hands down over Sebastian's beautifully rounded arse. "Wanted you the moment I saw you. That damned smile."

"For me it was your freckles," Sebastian responded, prying Oliver's shirt open and kissing below his clavicle. "So many fucking freckles." Another kiss. "On your face, your neck, right here." Kiss. "Are they everywhere?"

"You like my freckles?"

"I want to kiss every one on your body."

Oliver's cock throbbed. Heat seared his skin. He was going to be one of those cases of spontaneous combustion, and be forever known as That Earl Killed By Freckle Kissing.

Sebastian pawed at Oliver's clothes, trying to free his shirt from his trousers for more access. "Every damn one," he growled, the low tones causing Oliver's cock to twitch again.

"That would take a long time," he replied, because his brain was unhelpfully literal and his mouth became uncontrollable in times of heightened emotion.

A flash of anguish sliced through him.

"How can a man be expected to maintain a cockstand while listening to your inane drivel?"

Rothmere. Fucking Rothmere ruining fucking everything.

Oliver almost pushed Sebastian away. Maybe he couldn't do this. Maybe he'd isolated himself for too long to engage in normal human interaction. Or maybe he never had and never would understand what "normal" even meant.

Sebastian leaned back to look up at him. "Are you all right? You've tensed up. Did I do something you didn't like? Please tell me so I won't do it again."

Oliver closed his eyes, as if that would hide his embarrassment. "It wasn't you. I say foolish things sometimes."

"I didn't hear anything foolish." Wright laughed. "Also, you are talking to a man who's pretending to be a Bavarian lord. I think I win the foolish contest. Now take off your shirt so I can search for more freckles."

"Take yours off too." Oliver scrambled to undress, trying to shove away the unpleasant memories. He didn't need to panic. He didn't need to second-guess his every action. Wright wasn't Rothmere.

Oliver tossed his jacket and waistcoat aside, then pulled his shirt over his head. When he wriggled free, he was greeted by the sight of Sebastian with his trousers half-unbuttoned.

Wright tugged his shirttails free, then discarded the garment, leaving him bare from the waist up, the trousers hanging low on his hips, the bulge of his cock straining against the remaining buttons. Oliver couldn't remember ever wanting anything this much in his life.

"Bed?" The question ended on a breathless rasp as Sebastian flattened his palm on Oliver's chest.

Sebastian slid his fingers through the pale curls of hair, tracing a path down to Oliver's waistband. "Or I could take care of you right here." He undid a single button. "Kiss a few more freckles."

"I don't know if I have any down there," Oliver admitted. "Never thought to check."

It was another absurdly matter-of-fact statement for the

circumstances, but the ensuing spike of anxiety was squashed flat in an instant by Sebastian's provocative smile.

"I'd best see for myself then." He went down on his knees.

Oliver hissed out a curse. God, it had been so long since he'd felt anything but his own hand. Wright's fingers were slim and nimble. In moments he had Oliver's trousers shoved down far enough to begin a torturously slow perusal of his cock and balls.

"There's one." Sebastian pressed his lips to a spot on Oliver's thigh. His fingers traveled up the length of Oliver's erection, then down again. "And here's another."

"Sebastian."

"Mm?" His hands continued their alarmingly light strokes as he kissed another patch of freckled skin.

Oliver's legs began to tremble. "You're going to kill me."

"Only a little." Sebastian swiped his thumb across the head of Oliver's cock, spreading the drop of moisture he found. He licked his thumb clean, humming in pleasure.

Oliver's knees almost buckled. He tangled his fingers in Sebastian's hair. "Please. God, please."

"Happy to oblige, gorgeous." Wright grinned wickedly, then took Oliver's cock into his mouth.

All coherent thoughts fled Oliver's brain. His pulse beat wildly in his chest, and his breathing became ragged. If he was even breathing at all. He wasn't sure. The world had gone hazy except for the bob of Sebastian's head and the heat of his mouth.

Oliver babbled—words that might have been *yes* or *please* or *good*. He couldn't stop talking any more than he could stop from arching up into Sebastian's mouth, or clenching his fingers in locks of wavy, dark hair.

Sebastian wound him up like clockwork, lips and tongue stroking up and down his shaft, teasing the head, licking and sucking until Oliver could hardly remain upright. He could feel the orgasm hovering, ready to tear him to pieces. He spouted more nonsense words as his body trembled.

"Fuck, please, yes, oh, God, Seb—" His words faded into a prolonged moan when his release hit. White hot pulses of pleasure swamped his senses, and he spent hard and fast into Wright's eager mouth.

"Bloody... hell..." Oliver gasped, slumping against the door, legs wobbling like a molded jelly.

Sebastian eased off him and rose to his feet. His lips—gleaming and red from his ministrations—curved into a broad smile. "Utterly wrecked is a good look on you."

A warm glow of happiness settled in Oliver's chest. "You may wreck me at any time." He pressed a hand to his brow, finding it damp with perspiration. He felt limp as a washrag and twice as wrung out. "Give me a moment. Then I'd like to return the favor."

Sebastian kissed him, slow and gentle. "I'm all yours," he murmured.

⁓

A thoroughly-pleasured Oliver possessed the kind of beauty poets would rhapsodize over. Or the kind they ought to rhapsodize over, in Seb's opinion. He would read more poetry if it was all about the aroused flush of his lover's skin, the glazed look of bliss in his eyes, and his half-hard cock, glistening with the remnants of spend and Seb's saliva.

Seb reached for his trouser falls to free his own aching erection. He hadn't been that excited to suck somebody in… well, maybe ever. Oliver's squirming and frantic babbling had left him so hard he figured he could bring himself off with no more than a few brisk strokes.

"Lie down on the bed," Oliver instructed, sounding more in control of himself than he had moments ago. He swayed a little as he bent to remove his shoes and stockings and pull his trousers fully off. "If my limbs never work again, I will blame you."

"Apologies for my wholehearted lack of remorse." Seb gave Oliver a smile of smug satisfaction.

"You are entirely too proud of yourself. I think it's time I repaid you in kind."

"Yes, please." Seb shucked the remainder of his clothing and clambered onto the bed. He flung his arms wide. "You may have your wicked way with me."

Oliver lay down beside him. "What do you like?"

"Anything. Everything. Hell, I'll probably fall apart the moment you touch me."

"That hardly seems fair." Using a single fingernail, Oliver grazed a meandering path up Seb's thigh.

Seb sucked in a sharp breath.

Oliver's finger traced its way back down to a ticklish spot behind Seb's knee. Seb jerked reflexively, knocking Oliver's arm aside and nearly kicking him.

"Shite! Sorry."

Oliver laughed. "So sensitive. Do I need to hold you down for my own safety?"

"No, but you can be on top if you like."

Oliver moved over him, straddling his hips and pressing him down into the cushion of the bedding. "I would absolutely like." Oliver's breath ghosted across Seb's lips, and then their mouths crashed together, an exuberant clash of tongues and teeth that made Seb curl his hands into fists and thrust up against Oliver's muscled torso.

"Patience," Oliver murmured. He bent his head to nuzzle Seb's neck. "I'm still recovering from your efforts. You deserve my best in return."

"Doesn't have to be fifty-fifty." Seb wriggled, trying to increase the friction against his cock. Oliver skimmed his hands over Seb's hips and along his ribs, every feather-light touch a flame against his skin, threatening to set him alight. "Can make up for it... next time."

Oliver flinched, and a bit of fog cleared from Seb's mind. Dammit. Would there even be a next time? He shouldn't assume, shouldn't make this anything more than two friendly blokes taking the edge off. He always fell too hard, too fast and came up bruised because of it.

Oliver moved lower and swiped his tongue across one of Seb's nipples. "You should have my best every time," he said, before using his teeth on the tight little nub.

Seb groaned. He wanted to say yes, to beg for many more times, as slow or as fast as Oliver liked. Anything, so long as this wasn't the end. Words wouldn't form. He didn't have Oliver's ability to spew words during sex, and inevitably he would reach the point where he couldn't form words at all.

Oliver applied the same treatment to Seb's other nipple, causing another needy moan. "I love how sensitive you are."

Seb had no further recourse but to respond with his body. He bucked and writhed as Oliver continued to map his torso with fingers, tongue, and teeth, animalistic noises standing in for words even his mind could no longer form. Oliver cupped Seb's balls in his palm, and Seb would have arched right off the bed were he not pinned down.

"Do you need me, love?" Oliver asked, voice husky and soothing. He wrapped his other hand around Seb's cock, and Seb thrust up in reply. "Yes, I see that you do." He stroked slowly at first, then matched his pace to the rhythm of Seb's hips. "That's it, darling. Take what you need."

You. I need you. Oh, fuck. Oh, God. Oh...

Pulses of perfect agony shot through Seb's body. He went rigid, the force of all his muscles centered on one final drive into Oliver's fist. Sticky fluid spattered his belly. He let out one last breathless cry, then went slack.

When he opened his eyes, Oliver was gazing down at him, blue eyes soft with affection, his smile a little crooked.

"Hey, beautiful. You're an absolute pleasure to watch."

"Yeah?" Seb asked hoarsely.

"Without a doubt." Oliver planted a gentle kiss on Seb's cheek. "I'll grab a cloth so we can clean off. Will you stay the night?"

Seb didn't think he could move right now, even if he wanted to. The door seemed miles away, his own room a foreign land. A man of better sense would overcome such an obstacle. He'd force his body up and away, knowing he had to stop the fall before he hit the rocky ground below.

But Seb wasn't that man. He'd flung himself off this cliff without looking down. Probably he'd be dashed to pieces at the end, but right now there was nothing but the open sky and the peaceful cushion of the air around him.

He gave Oliver a bleary-eyed grin. "I'll stay."

Chapter 11

~ day nine ~

SEB TWIRLED, the fabric of the dress fanning out around his ankles, its shimmering red fabric a perfect complement to the walls of the Green Salon.

"What do you think?"

His audience of one applauded. "You look adorable," Oliver replied, favoring Seb with his now-familiar intimate smile.

This was the first time Oliver had seen the gown, even though they'd spent hours working on costumes over the past few days. Sir Albert wanted to begin dress rehearsals tomorrow, which meant tonight was Seb's final chance to show off in private.

"Where did you find it?" Oliver asked. "It looks like it was made for you. The cut suits your short hair and flat chest."

Seb twirled once more before responding, enjoying the swirl of fabric around him. "It was made for my sister, in fact, but we often share clothes. I habitually carry an assortment of different garments when I travel, for however I wish to present myself. If I wanted to be perceived as a woman, I'd wear a wig and pad the bodice out a bit."

Oliver, lovely man that he was, accepted this unconventional behavior with a nod of approval. God, how Seb longed for a life like this. To simply be *normal*, in whatever way that manifested for him. Home meant fretting about his mother and stepfather. They deserved every happiness, and he didn't want them bombarded with nasty people saying, "I heard your son is a molly." And as much as Seb liked his theater friends, he wasn't an actor. He'd wear himself to dust if he lived their hectic lifestyle.

"You'll make a beautiful Lady Alice, or whatever her name is," Oliver said. "But I like you best as yourself."

Seb danced over to the nearest chaise lounge. "Say that again."

"Pardon?"

"The 'I like you best' bit."

Oliver's brow furrowed, but then he shrugged and said, "I like you best as yourself."

"Yes, that. Ugh, so romantic." Seb flung himself onto the couch in a melodramatic swoon. "My delicate constitution can't handle it."

Laughing, Oliver crossed the room and knelt beside him. "Do you require me to carry you to bed and tend to your needs?"

Seb nearly replied in the affirmative. Three days now, this had been their life—playing and teasing and making love. They'd cuddled in front of the others and snuck away to "rehearse their lines." They'd existed in a bubble of bliss, wildly in love and free from any outside constraints.

But bubbles were fragile things.

Seb looked automatically out the window. Night had already fallen, but he knew what awaited him in the darkness. Two days of rain had obliterated the snow. Today had dawned fair and warm, drying out the muck left behind. The roads were passable, or would be soon.

Anxiety had wormed its way in like a parasite, multiplying all day, until it was eating him from the inside. The bubble could burst at any moment. He was no longer snowbound, and change was inevitable. The party would end. He would need to vanish forever or explain his deception to everyone. He would have to ask Oliver about the pearls—in a way that didn't sound accusatory—or else leave alone and defeated.

"Sebastian?" Oliver brushed a finger along his jaw. "Where did you go?"

Seb blinked. "Sorry. A lot on my mind, I suppose. We should finish laying out the costumes for tomorrow. We can turn in after."

Oliver gave him a swift kiss. "A good plan."

They reconvened across the room, where the costumes and accessories lay strewn about. Some were neatly folded, but many lay in heaps, abandoned by the actors after their final fittings. Seb and Oliver each grabbed a garment, shook it out, and spread it neatly on the floor.

"These hose go with that doublet." Seb tossed the pair at Oliver.

"And you need this waistcoat."

They traded and sorted, matching up costumes and searching for mislaid pieces. When they finished with the clothing, they began adding wigs and other accessories.

"I'm impressed with your papier mâché jewelry." Seb dangled a necklace from his fingers. "Now that they're painted, they look fabulous, and the bright colors are going to catch the eye of the viewers. We've only to decide who should wear which piece."

"You give me too much credit. I only supervised."

"You organized the entire project and you did a damn fine job of it."

Oliver blushed. "I suppose."

Hell and damnation, this darling man! Seb's entire body ached with longing and a horrid uncertainty. What was to come of them tomorrow, or the next day? He wanted to memorize the precise color of Oliver's cheeks and the exact placement of his freckles. He needed to imprint the warmth of his skin on his fingers, and inhale his scent so deep into his lungs it would abide forever.

The fragile pendant Seb was holding crunched in his hand. He jumped, tearing his gaze from Oliver to the mangled craft.

"Blast. I've ruined this one. I'm glad we have extras." He tossed the piece aside and began matching the remaining accessories to costumes, taking care never to let his gaze linger on Oliver for too long.

You're already in too deep. Don't make it worse. This is surely a passing fancy for him anyhow.

"What about your costume, Prince Fenwick?" Seb asked, trying to keep the mood light. "Riding boots, evening jacket, and a crown? Maybe we could find a sash of some sort for an accent."

Oliver's shoulders slumped. "I don't know if I even want to do this. I know all the lines, and I can recite them when it's only the two of us. But I haven't even attempted acting across from anyone else, let alone in front of a group. I should tell Sir Albert to take my place. Otherwise I'm liable to get nauseous and run away." He put his head in his hands.

"Hey." Seb scooted closer and put an arm around him. "I honestly think you can do it, but you don't have to if you don't want to. I'll have your back if you decide to tell Sir A to go shove it. I'll be right there with you, whatever you do."

Oliver straightened up and turned toward Seb. He leaned in until their foreheads were touching. "You are a treasure."

Seb's heart stuttered. "I—"

A drugging press of lips saved him from rashly confessing his feelings.

"Thank you," Oliver said, when he drew back. "Your understanding means a great deal to me. I ought never to have isolated myself for so long. It's made everything harder."

"Why did you do it?"

"Oh, I forgot you don't know." Oliver chuckled, running a hand through his hair. "It feels like we've known one another forever, rather than a few days."

"It feels that way to me too."

Christ, Oliver's smile was tearing Seb to pieces. He looked

delectable, disheveled and still a bit flushed. Heading to bed was sounding better every second.

"I should explain." Oliver stared out at a distant point as he spoke. "Do you know Lord Rothmere?"

"No." Seb knew no aristocrats except the ones at this party. Another reason to keep his head on straight. Another reason he would probably ignore.

"Consider yourself lucky. He has charming manners, but he uses them to manipulate. As I'm sure you've noticed, I'm not skilled at reading people. I'm particularly bad at recognizing lies."

Seb nodded.

"Rothmere and I were lovers for a time. I was foolishly infatuated. Thought he made the sun rise and set, despite warnings from my friends. I ignored the cutting remarks he made, assuming them to be my fault. I'm strange. I know that. But I tried to be what he wanted. Be like everyone else. It's what I've always been told to do."

"Fuck that," Seb growled. "You be you. You're brilliant just as you are."

Oliver covered Seb's hand with his own and gave it a squeeze. "Thank you, darling. In any event, Rothmere tired of me after a time. Sent me a letter telling me he didn't want to see me anymore. It was terribly vague and full of obfuscated references to our relationship, and I'm shite at all that, so I didn't entirely understand what he was saying.

"In hindsight, I shouldn't have confronted him at a ball, nor should I have brought the letter with me, but I was hurt and confused and not thinking straight. He'd told me he loved me when we'd last parted. Surely I was misreading the letter and he would explain it all."

Seb could see where this was heading. "Oh, Oliver. I'm so sorry."

"He snatched the letter from me and read it aloud." Oliver sighed heavily. "Or parts of it, I suppose. He left out anything that might suggest it was his letter. And, of course, he emphasized the meaning behind each insinuation. Made everything I'd been uncertain of sound obvious. God's teeth, it was mortifying. The entire crowd knew that not only had I been spurned by a lover, but that I couldn't even decipher my own rejection letter. Rothmere tossed the letter in the fire at the end, to ensure no one would see his name or his handwriting. I was an object of public ridicule, at his hands, while he was the clever fellow who had made everyone laugh. So I left Society. Hid out here and saw no one, save Amabel from time to time."

Seb let his head fall onto Oliver's shoulder. "Can you introduce me to Rothmere someday? I'd like to slug him. Or maybe Casper can teach me to fence and then I can run him through in a duel for your honor."

"You're sweet."

"We'd have to move to the Continent if I killed him, but I hear it's a nice place for chaps like us."

"Sebastian." Oliver drew out Seb's name in fond exasperation. "I will not have you dueling on my behalf. Let me finish the story. I was alone for a year. Some weeks back, I tried to go out in public for the first time. I had a few drinks to help me relax, and at first it seemed to be working. I'd hardly eaten that day due to my restless stomach. By the time I began to grow anxious, I was soused enough to drink even more. Eventually the anxiety blossomed into full-fledged panic. I don't remember much, only the terror and the certainty that I would be sick in front of everyone and become a laughingstock once again. Somehow I managed to get to my carriage and flee for home. I honestly don't know if I can ever show my face in Society again. A private party like this one might be all I can handle."

Well, shite.

Seb's mind whirled. Rage at Rothmere and anguish for Oliver twisted and tumbled with a sudden spike of fear. If Oliver had been so deep in his cups he couldn't remember that night, perhaps he was responsible for the disappearance of the pearls after all. Though even an inebriated Oliver didn't seem a likely thief.

Seb rubbed the bridge of his nose. He needed to think. He needed to talk to Helena. She was the sensible one. She'd have some idea of how to tactfully bring up the matter with Oliver.

Or she would if he ever spoke to her again. He'd hardly seen her over the past few days, and when he had she'd seemed preoccupied. It was possible she was angry at him because he'd been spending all day and all night with Oliver. But Seb would never apologize for that. Time was running short, and he didn't want to waste it.

"Let's get you some accessories and call it a night," he declared. Thinking could come later, when he was tucked snuggly into bed at Oliver's side. "Something red to match my dress would be best."

Oliver glanced around. "Where's Sir Albert's box of props? The one he got the parasol from? I think there was a red scarf in it."

"Oh!" Seb jogged across the room. "I shoved it in the corner because I thought it was all rubbish. Let me look."

He located the box and knelt down beside it. It really did look like rubbish, full of worn fabrics and silk flowers missing half their petals. He pawed through the scraps, until a flash of red caught his eye. *Aha!*

Seb tugged on the fabric, but it had snagged on something. He knocked a few more crumbling bouquets aside. The scarf lay at the bottom of the box, tangled up with a looping rope of pink and gray pearls.

Seb almost fell over. He blinked several times, certain he must be seeing things. Heart hammering, he reached out, slow and deliberate, as if the necklace was a snake that would lash out at any sudden movement.

The pearls were cool and smooth beneath his fingertips,

and entirely real. Seb's breath hitched. He unwound the strands from the scarf, hands trembling.

"Fuck," he breathed.

"Sebastian?" The soft thud of Oliver's footsteps on the carpet rolled through the room like distant, ominous thunder. "Did you find what you needed? Shall we go to bed now?"

Panic clawed at Seb's chest. He would have to explain. He would have to demand that Oliver explain. With the roads clear, he would have no reason to stay. Mission accomplished. Curtain closed. Show over.

He stuffed the necklace down his bodice and whirled to face Oliver. "Fine," he blurted. "It's fine." He scrambled to his feet. "I should go. I… have a headache."

Seb lifted his skirts and ran from the room, his memory already burning with the look of confusion—and hurt—on Oliver's face.

Chapter 12

~ day ten ~

Oliver arrived unusually late to breakfast. He'd been surprised how empty his bed had felt, after only a few nights of Sebastian's presence. He hoped his lover had slept more soundly than he had. Their parting last night had been so abrupt and odd.

As always, Oliver's first instinct had been to question himself. *What did I do wrong? How did I upset him?*

But after a night's worth of thinking and rethinking, he'd concluded—intellectually, if not emotionally—that he'd done nothing to be ashamed of. Sebastian had needed to be alone for reasons of his own, and that was that. Maybe he truly had a headache. Maybe it wasn't any of Oliver's business.

Oliver walked to the sideboard, where Sebastian stood eyeing the coffee urn as if engaged in a confrontation. His business or not, Oliver could hardly stop caring. God knew he wasn't particularly skilled at opening up, but he'd managed it last night with Seb's gentle coaxing. He wanted to offer the same in return. To be the person Sebastian could turn to with his problems and fears.

When he opened his mouth, however, what came out was, "This is why I prefer tea. I don't have to wrestle it into submission before drinking it."

Sebastian laughed. "Head in the clouds again, sorry." He reached to fill his cup.

Oliver placed a hand on the small of Seb's back. "I've

noticed that tendency. How are you feeling? Is the headache gone?"

"Fine. I'm fine." He didn't turn around, but he leaned into Oliver's touch.

"Good. Let me know if you need anything." Oliver dropped a kiss on his jaw. "Please."

Oliver stepped aside and gathered his usual breakfast, taking care that the egg didn't touch the toast. An attentive footman placed a pot of tea on the table as he sat. Oliver poured himself a cup, then spread a single pat of butter evenly over his toast.

Sebastian sat down beside him, plate piled haphazardly with food in a way that made Oliver smile. He would cringe if that were his own plate, but on Seb the chaos was charming. He was colorful and creative and a little bit wild. Enough to fascinate Oliver and encourage him to stretch his boundaries without overwhelming him.

He felt a flutter in his chest. One he'd felt several times over the past days without acknowledging it. But what was the point in dissembling? He was in love. In love with a man who might possibly—hopefully—like him exactly as he was.

"The post, my lord."

Oliver blinked and turned to find his butler holding a small tray with a pile of letters. All the correspondence that hadn't come through during the snow. Mostly invitations to parties he wouldn't be attending, he guessed.

"And one letter for Her Grace." The butler circled the table and placed the single letter before Amabel, then bowed and departed.

Oliver poked at his own pile. Nothing seemed urgent. Most of it he could ignore entirely. The rest could wait until after the house party ended.

When Sebastian is gone. Hell and damnation.

"A letter from Neufeld?" Casper, who sat next to Amabel,

chuckled. "A bit late to inform you that he's coming to the party."

Oliver's head snapped up. Beside him, Sebastian shifted, though he kept his attention on his food. They hadn't discussed telling the others the truth. Oliver had hoped not to bring up the subject until the guests had gone. When he could explain in writing—with Sebastian's approval, since it wasn't Oliver's story to tell.

"It seems the baron intends to marry." Amabel smoothed the letter out on the table, where anyone sitting close to her could read it.

"Marry whom?" Tunsbury asked. "Fenwick? Because I know a vicar who might assist with that."

Oliver couldn't tell whether he was joking or not. Either way, the comment only added to the nervous quaking in his stomach.

Casper craned his neck to read the letter. "That's dated yesterday." His usual melodious tenor dropped nearly to a baritone. "'On the morrow we will at last be departing the inn...'" His gaze locked on Sebastian, his whole body radiating fury.

"I suppose this is my cue to explain," Seb said halfheartedly. "Not my preference, but needs must."

"You think this is a joke?" Casper snarled. "Who the fuck are you?"

Oliver held up a hand. "Whoa. Casper, relax. It's a simple misunderstanding."

Casper's fingers curled around his butter knife. The blunt-tipped instrument could hardly make an effective weapon, but the intent was clear. Casper had witnessed the entirety of Oliver's humiliation, and knew the story of his past with Rothmere better than anyone. He'd threatened multiple times to call the bastard out. He wouldn't hesitate to fling himself at anyone else who hurt Oliver.

He brandished the knife like one of his fencing swords. "Explain yourself."

Sebastian leaned against the back of his chair and let his hands fall into his lap. "My name is Sebastian Wright. I'm not Baron Neufeld, and I don't know a thing about the man except that the boy in the stables assumed I was him when I arrived. I used that to get into the house, and I honestly can't say I regret the lie. It got me out of the snow and I met all of you." He held Casper's gaze for a moment, then looked around the table, nodding to Tunsbury, Sir Albert, the Whitcombs, and even Amabel. "I had no compelling reason to tell the truth to strangers, and by the time I discovered how well I fit in here, well… This moment was bound to happen. And I told Oliver days ago, if that makes any difference to the rest of you."

"It bloody well does not." Casper looked perilously near to leaping from his seat. Oliver braced to fend him off if he went for Sebastian's throat. "Who are you? A thief? A spy? A confidence trickster? A blackmailer?"

"God, no, stop!" Seb threw up his hands. "I'm… me. I'm no one special. I never meant to hurt anyone, I swear. I made a mistake and I'm sor—"

The door to the room banged open and a second Sebastian stormed in, eyes narrowed in anger. In his fist he clutched a rope of pink and gray pearls that sparked the hint of a memory in the back of Oliver's mind. In any other circumstance, he might have been able to grasp it. Now, though, he could only gape while his brain tried to make sense of the impossible.

"Goddamn you, Sebastian Wright, how long have you had these?" The second Sebastian shook the pearls. "How could you keep this from me?"

This Sebastian's voice was different, Oliver realized. A touch higher. Their stride was similar, but with a bit less sway in the hips. As they neared, he began to pick out subtle differences in their face: softer around the cheekbones, a pointier chin. No hint of stubble along their jawline in that one particular place Sebastian seemed to perpetually miss while shaving.

It was made for my sister, in fact, but we often share clothes.

Bloody bollocking hell. This explained those times when Sebastian—no, Baron Neufeld—had seemed different. Because he had been. Had the two swapped places other times when Oliver hadn't noticed?

A wave of nausea swept over him, and he clutched his stomach.

"I swear to Almighty God I haven't been drinking this morning," Whitcomb said. "Why the devil are there two of you, Neufeld? Or whoever you are."

His wife stilled him with a hand on his arm. "They're twins, honeybee. Honestly, men are so melodramatic."

"I'm not a man," Sebastian's sister snapped. "This nonsense is entirely my brother's doing." She stalked toward him. "How long have you had these, Sebastian? How long have you been lying to me?"

"I haven't," Seb implored. "Helena, I just—"

"How could you do this to me? We were partners. We were in this together. I came here for a *purpose*, not so you could play Fuck-the-Toff for a week!"

Sebastian's eyes darkened to almost black. "I am *not* playing. And what do you care, anyhow? You'd handle it and I only had to 'keep Fenwick busy,' wasn't that what you said?"

Oliver couldn't breathe. His limbs couldn't seem to move. He wanted to scream, wanted to flee, but panic was closing in on him with such crushing force that it took everything in him simply to sit and stare.

Around him, the room erupted. Casper lunged at Sebastian, but Amabel seized hold of his jacket, keeping him just out of reach. Tunsbury had turned a sickly green. He stumbled from his seat and hurried for the door. The Whitcombs clung to one another, as if for sanctuary. Amabel's sapphic friends kept out of the mess, whispering and shaking their heads.

Helena hadn't stopped screaming at her brother, but the words no longer penetrated Oliver's brain. He was going to be sick. Or maybe he'd simply pass out. Already the world had gone a bit hazy, the edges of his vision dark. He kept staring at the necklace clutched in Helena's fist, as if it held answers. He'd found those pearls once. In his pocket?

When he tried to focus on the memory, it only amplified the panic and nausea already threatening to overpower him.

"Oliver." Sebastian's voice, full of concern. "Oliver, I'm so sorry. This has nothing to do with us, I swear on my life. Please, tell me what I can do to make it better. Do you need to be alone? Do you need someone who's not me to take care of you?"

The words sounded right. Like everything he wanted to hear. A fever dream, perhaps? It must have been. Certainly he couldn't have heard all that through the deafening noise.

God, there was so much noise, so much movement. Too much all at once, stabbing into his skull. His brain wanted to shut down and make it all go away, but the sights and sounds kept coming, bombarding him.

"Stop," he groaned, closing his eyes and covering his ears with his hands. "Stop. Please, stop."

Sounds continued to intrude. Crashes of overturned chairs. Clinks of plates and teacups knocking together. He heard his name again, followed by a rustle of movement at his side.

Then suddenly, all at once, silence fell.

Oliver had to count to ten before he trusted himself to open his eyes and uncover his ears. The room had mostly emptied. Casper paced in a corner, silently fuming. Amabel still sat across the table from Oliver, her bearing regal despite the sorrow lining her features.

"I handled that badly," she said quietly. "I ought to have brought all of this up with you long ago."

Oliver blinked at her. "You knew?"

"Not all of it. I knew they were masquerading as Neufeld, among other disguises. I didn't know the why of it."

"And you said nothing." Oliver stared down at his uneaten breakfast. The plate had been bumped hard enough that the egg now rested half atop the toast, and a puddle of tea had begun to seep beneath both. Strangely, the sight didn't make him sick. In fact, he couldn't really feel his stomach roiling anymore. Couldn't feel much of anything.

"I had no idea you'd actually fallen in love with him." Amabel reached out a hand, but Oliver flinched away.

"Excuse me." He pushed his chair away from the table and rose to his feet. No weakness, no trembling. Only more nothing, like he'd been hollowed out or drained of all sensation. He turned away without another word and walked from the room.

Sir Albert leaned heavily against the wall in the corridor, looking haggard. "Lord Fenwick—" he began.

Oliver shook his head and kept walking.

Behind him, a piteous lament rose to the heavens. "What does this mean for my theatrical?"

Chapter 13

~ day eleven ~

A DISTANT CLOCK TOLLED a hollow one. Seb crept down the dark corridor, ears pricked for any sounds of human activity. He'd spent most of the day in the Big Library, hiding behind an armchair and funneling his heartache into lurid prose. When he'd run out of paper, he'd stared at the wall, contemplating his life choices. Hours later, his only conclusion was that he did not want to talk to anyone. Which was why he was now slinking through the house in the dead of night, hoping everyone else was asleep or otherwise occupied.

He put a hand to his stomach. Oh, God, what if Oliver was "occupied"? What if Casper or Tunsbury or someone was busy comforting him, making him forget Seb had ever existed?

"Don't be daft," he hissed aloud. *It's not like it's any of your damn business anyway. You made this bloody mess, you get to lie in it.*

And there was the crux of it. He'd been wrong. So very wrong there was no recovering. No opportunity. None of the avenues open to him would give him what he wanted. He couldn't turn back time, so the only recourse was to move on.

Slivers of light crept from beneath the doors to a few of the guest rooms Seb passed, but thankfully nothing disturbed the silence. He slipped into his own bedchamber, easing the door open and closed so as not to wake his sister.

The scratch of a match being struck sounded in the

darkness. A halo of light flared, illuminating Helena as she reached to light a lamp.

"Thank God." Lamp lit, she blew out the match on a heavy breath. "I was worried about you. I almost thought you'd left, except the horses are still in the stables. Where have you been?"

Seb held back the dozens of curses that leapt into his mind at the sight of her, still dressed and waiting up for him. He began to strip off his own clothes. He was going to bed and not talking about anything, and that was that.

"Seb, I'm so sorry." Helena crossed the room to him, but didn't touch him. "I should never have confronted you like that. My mind's been in such a muddle all week, and when I found the pearls in our bags, I snapped. I reacted impulsively and out of anger, and that was wrong of me." Her voice choked. "We were a team. Always together. And now I feel like I've driven a wedge between us, and… and…"

Seb blinked moisture from his eyes. He turned to Helena and pulled her into his arms. "Hey. I still love you, Hellion."

She sniffed a laugh. "You haven't called me that in years."

"Well, you had to go and turn all sensible on a chap. Nice to know you still have your wild moments."

Helena pressed her face into Seb's shoulder, her tears dampening the fabric of his shirt.

"If you soil my clothes, I'll make you swap with me," he warned.

She laughed again, with more cheer than before. "I was certain you'd hate me, and here you are being your usual ridiculous self."

"You know I can never stay angry for long. And this morning—yesterday morning, I suppose—was as much my fault as yours. I lied too often for too long and it came around to bite me in the arse."

Helena nudged him toward the bed. "Tell me how you found the pearls, and then you should get some sleep."

Seb shrugged and resumed undressing. "They were in a

box of props Sir Albert had scrounged for the theatrical. I don't know where he found them. The clasp looks to be broken. Maybe the pearls simply fell off. I told you Oliver didn't steal them. I'm not even sure he recognized them. Apparently he was a bit worse for drink that night."

"Hmm." Helena kicked off her shoes. "Still a number of holes in the story, but that's for another day. Would you like me to apologize to Fenwick?"

Seb flopped on the bed. "No. I should do it. I'll speak with him in the morning, and if he throws me out, I'll leave without another word. If he doesn't want to speak to me ever again, the choice is his." Sebastian rolled over and buried his face in his pillow. "Dammit all, he could have been the one!" The tears he'd been holding back all day began to flow.

Helena slipped into the bed beside him, wrapping her arms around him. "You're such a romantic." She stroked his hair soothingly. "You could have dozens of lovers with a crook of your finger, but you only want one, don't you?"

"I don't want—" Seb hiccupped "—to be loved for my body or m-my cocksucking skills. I want to be loved for being *me*."

Her embrace tightened. "I love you for you. And if your earl is as extraordinary as you seem to think he is, he will too. Mistakes and all. Give him time. If he doesn't see how wonderful you are, I'll call him out."

"Don't. Oliver takes lessons from Casper. He's good with a sword."

"Well, you would know."

Seb choked on a half-laugh, half-sob. "That too."

Helena resumed stroking his hair. "Sleep now, love. Tomorrow is a new opportunity."

Seb wasn't sure he believed that, but he let himself relax into her touch regardless. Maybe he'd fucked himself over. But there were two Wrights, and maybe it simply took both of them to fix a wrong.

Oliver went to bed angry. He woke angry, performed his ablutions angry, and breakfasted angry. He was beginning to think angry was his new basic state of existence.

His friends weren't helping his mood. Casper wouldn't stop whipping his sword out every thirty seconds. Amabel hovered like a mother hen. Tunsbury was avoiding Oliver for unknown reasons, and Oliver was avoiding Sir Albert for obvious reasons. The Whitcombs thought to comfort him with the tale of how they had hated each other for three years before realizing they'd never actually spoken—a story Oliver had heard at least fifty times before. And he didn't want to turn to Amabel's Sapphic Ladies' Club friends. Because while he knew Georgia/George Beauclair from a brief affair years ago, he'd forgotten which of the other ladies was Maryanne and which was Maryellen, and now it was much too late to ask without embarrassing himself.

"That marsh about a mile off, that's on your property, Duchess?" Casper leaned in the doorway to the study, where he and Amabel had cornered Oliver once again.

"It is." Amabel took a sip of her tea with all the hauteur of a woman who had just poisoned her fifth husband.

"Capital. We'll dump the body there and never have to worry someone might find it."

"Get out." Oliver pointed sharply at the door. "I'll have no more talk of murder or dueling. It's not funny and I'm bloody well sick of it! Come back when you can stop acting like a bullying older brother who hits anyone who looks at his siblings funny."

Casper straightened. "I beg your pardon!"

Amabel waved him off. "He's right, Hawthorne. There's no need for histrionics. The proper solution is to send Mr. Wright packing with a warning to stay away lest we take more drastic measures in the future. Speaking of which, why haven't you sent him away?"

Oliver glared at her. "I don't know, Amabel. Why didn't you tell me you'd noticed suspicious goings on?"

Her back, which was always ramrod straight, managed to stiffen further. "I was attempting to unravel the mystery and resolve the matter in a way that would cause the least disruption. I perhaps was hasty in allowing Hawthorne first glimpse at the letter from the real Baron Neufeld. But I could not have known Miss Wright would choose that moment to expose herself to the world." A touch of bitterness had crept into her voice, but Oliver wouldn't allow himself to feel sorry for her in any way. Not yet.

"Resolve the matter," he scoffed. "Take care of things behind my back like I'm a poor little child who can't make a decision for himself."

"I did not say that."

"Nor did I," Casper added. "It's only that after your exile—"

Oliver pounded his fist on the desk. "I'm incompetent? Weak? Afraid of everyone and everything?" He kicked his chair back and stood. "Maybe I am. Maybe I'm pathetic and helpless and need looking after. But did you ever once think to *ask*? No. You all simply barge in and start doing things for me. Yes, I needed help. I even wanted help. But not one of you ever bothered to ask what I wanted."

No one but Seb. From the props and costumes idea to a gentle, "Do you need time alone?" Sebastian had always offered help, never imposed it. And didn't that just make everything hurt all the more.

"I'm done here," Oliver declared. "Don't follow me. I've had more than enough of your meddling. I won't be your charity project any longer." He walked around Amabel, shoved past Casper, and stomped all the way to the Little Library, where he yanked the door closed behind him and locked it.

"Eep!"

Oliver jolted at the startled squeak. Sebastian stood beside the shelf of Gothic novels, hands full of papers. He was dressed in the same traveling outfit he'd worn the day they'd met. Oliver's heart skipped a beat.

"Don't leave," Oliver blurted.

"Don't leave the house? Or don't leave the room? Or…" Sebastian let the sentence trail off.

Don't leave me.

Oliver fought to keep the words from spilling out unchecked. He scrambled to come up with an ordinary sort of thing to say. "We need to discuss certain matters." Good. That was good. Sensible. "We can start with what you're doing here."

Seb shifted nervously. "Doing in the house at all, or doing here, now, in this room?"

"I'm not being clear," Oliver said, at the same moment Seb added, "Sorry, I'm being pedantic."

They shared an awkward laugh. Christ, was everything between them going to be awkward from now on? In that case, he was better off if Sebastian left as soon as possible.

His stubborn brain swiftly rejected that idea. "Please, sit down and let's talk. I need explanations about… everything, frankly."

"And I owe them to you," Seb agreed. "Let me put these papers away first." He tugged a book from the shelf. "I, uh, wrote an alternate ending to that novel I was reading."

Oliver took an involuntary step forward. "May I read it?"

"Of course. That's why I— Do you mean now?" Sebastian glanced apprehensively at the papers, then slowly extended his hand. "Be my guest." The moment Oliver took the papers, Seb threw himself into the nearest armchair, starting resolutely out the window. "If it's terrible, don't tell me."

Oliver lowered himself into a nearby chair, already focused on the words. Sebastian had captured the tone of the novel perfectly, overlaying it with his wry wit. With a few neat turns of phrase, the vague sexual tension between the hero and the villain from the original text morphed into sparkling chemistry.

Oliver flipped pages frenetically, relishing each stolen glance and near embrace.

All at once, the final page was in front of his face, and the two men were kissing and declaring their love amidst the rubble of their ruined castle.

"The whole world can crumble around us for all I care," the former villain said. *"I have you, and you are home enough for me."*

"Sebastian," Oliver gasped. "This is good. This is really good."

Seb jerked to look at him. "It is? The ending is rather abrupt. I ran out of paper."

Oliver clutched the papers to his chest. "I adore it. You should write books like this. Queer books."

"Oh. Well." Seb shrugged. "No one would publish them, and I can't afford to do it myself."

"Amabel would do it." The idea blossomed in Oliver's mind. "I'm writing about queer subtext for her next issue. It's to be the first of a series of articles. This could become a lead up to a book or many books." He began to bounce, unable to suppress his excitement. "They'd be serialized in the paper first and then printed and bound after completion. Some people would cry pornography, of course, but even if we were banned from open production, word would be out, and we could continue distribution through other channels. Work to get the books into the hands of people who want them and need them. We'll be the premier underground publisher of subversive literature. What do you think? Is that something you'd be interested in?"

Sebastian's jaw worked. "I… suppose?" he replied haltingly. "But I thought none of you wanted anything to do with me from now on?"

"Huh?"

Oliver had to shake himself out of his fantasy. When he came back to himself, he found Seb staring at him with an expression of such naked longing he nearly slipped into another sort of fantasy altogether. He rocked forward onto the edge of his chair.

"Tell me the truth." Oliver's words were barely a whisper. "Tell me everything. Then maybe…"

He didn't know how to finish that sentence. But hope simmered inside him.

"We came for the pearls," Seb began. "Helena and I. They belong to our mother, and they're precious to her. The necklace was her wedding gift from our father, the only fancy thing they ever had. He went off to war and never returned, and the pearls were all she had to remember him by. Aside from a pair of unruly infants, I suppose."

"I'm so sorry."

"Thank you. So you see why we wanted to recover the pearls. Mother lost them at a recent charity event. And when we made inquiries, we were informed that you had been seen leaving the premises abruptly with the pearls in your pocket."

The memory that had been poking at Oliver's mind burst into sudden focus. "That was when I was fleeing the crowd. I was drunk and ill, and probably staggering. But I remember now, feeling something in my pocket and pulling it out. It was those pearls. The pink and gray color pattern was so unique that it stuck in my mind."

Sebastian was now also perched on the edge of his chair, tilted toward Oliver. "You have no idea how they came into your possession?"

"None whatsoever. I was confused, but needed to leave, so I stuffed the pearls back in my pocket and kept going. I arrived home hours later—nothing could have compelled me to remain in town—exhausted and with a raging headache. I did realize eventually that the necklace must have belonged to someone at the party. I hung it somewhere, I believe, thinking to make inquiries the next day."

Seb winced. "Let me guess. It was an 'extremely logical'

place to put them, which you promptly forgot about until this very minute and still cannot entirely recall."

Oliver grimaced. "You sound as though you speak from experience."

"Oh, yes."

"Then I suppose you won't hate me for what happened?"

Sebastian caught his gaze and held it. "I would never. I came here under false pretenses, yes. But I realized almost immediately that you couldn't possibly be the thief we'd assumed. You're artless. You're kind. I should have confessed everything to you then, or at least when I told you who I really was. But I was afraid you'd throw me out, and I liked it here. I liked your books and your friends and the freedom to act like myself. I liked *you*. I didn't want to lose that." He laughed mirthlessly. "Guess I cocked that right up."

"Sebastian." Oliver reached out a hand, but Seb looked away.

"I never meant to hurt you. The last thing I ever want to do is hurt you. I'm so sorry."

"Sebastian." Oliver pushed up from his seat and went down on his knees at the other man's side. "I understand. I do. You didn't know me, of course you didn't trust me. Hell, I don't even trust myself half the time!"

Seb turned back to Oliver, and the corner of his mouth hitched up. "Don't underestimate yourself, Oliver Fenwick. You're a remarkable man. A far better man than I deserve."

Oliver's chest tightened. Hope was now a roiling boil, threatening to bubble over. It had the power to scald him, and the Oliver of twelve days ago would probably have run from it. Bugger that. He was bloody sick of old, scared Oliver.

"I think you're exactly what I deserve," he replied. Then he pulled Sebastian in for a kiss.

Chapter 14

This didn't feel like a goodbye fuck. They never did. Which was why Seb assumed this would be the end. One last hurrah. Go out with a bang. Another instance of "I like you, but…"

Oliver broke the kiss and rocked back on his heels. "You're drifting away again. If you don't want to—"

"I do. I'm sorry my brain is unruly."

Oliver laughed so hard he choked and had to cough a few times before his breathing steadied. "Believe me, Mr. Wright," he said, voice scratchy. "I fully understand the perils of an unruly brain. I wouldn't undo it, however, given the choice. If I were anything other than me, I wouldn't be where I am today. And that's none too shabby a place to be, all things considered. And I'm not simply talking about money and luxuries and the things I have by accident of birth. I mean the people who love me. They're blockheads, the lot of them, but they go to absurd lengths to defend me."

"Like Helena defends me," Seb agreed.

"Like you defend her," Oliver amended. "And your mother. And me."

Seb shifted so far forward he nearly fell off his chair. "Defend you? By sneaking into your house and lying to you and all your guests?"

"Don't be daft, you bloody fool. I mean by devising ways for me to be alone. By listening to my unfiltered ramblings. By insisting on giving me your real name before we became intimate. By giving a damn what I thought and felt from the moment you walked into this house, when you hadn't the slightest reason to!"

"Oh."

"I won't insist upon you staying if you're no longer comfortable here. I have no right to do so. But if you're not in any hurry to leave…"

Oliver left the sentence hanging. He plucked at a loose thread along the hem of his jacket, his eyes averted.

Seb teetered on the edge of the chair, his ears ringing with the harsh sound of his breath sawing in and out of his chest. Here again was that cliff he'd thrown himself from. He'd thought he'd crashed at the bottom, but now in the silence he could look around and see he'd only tumbled onto a ledge partway down. He could back away now and lick his wounds. Or he could let Oliver pull him over.

Oliver looked up. His eyes were the clearest, most inviting blue Seb had ever seen. There was nowhere to hide behind those eyes. If someone looked into them long enough, they would see everything written on Oliver's heart. They only had to let themself fall in.

And fall Seb did. He didn't need to be pulled after all. He was content to go down, down, until he could wrap himself around Oliver's soul. He'd fall through rock and dirt and hell itself. Casper could run him through a thousand times. The duchess could flay him open with her sharp words. But Sebastian wasn't going anywhere. Not unless Oliver told him to go.

Seb slid off the chair to kneel at the other man's side. He put one hand on Oliver's hip, the other on his chest. "I could show you what I think the villain and the hero were doing after those kidnapping scenes."

Oliver flung his arms around Seb and tumbled them both to the floor. They kissed wildly, tugging at buttons, each trying to be the first to get hands on bare skin.

Oliver won that contest. He had Seb's shirt fully untucked and unbuttoned before Seb could even get down to Oliver's waistcoat. Damned form-fitting aristocratic suits.

"Am I the hero or the villain?" Oliver asked, his lips against Seb's throat.

"Villain. Rich blond toff. Blast, I should have given him freckles in my new ending."

Oliver kissed down Seb's chest. "Save the freckles for your original erotic novel."

"Who says I'm writing one?" Seb meant the words to sound impudent, but Oliver's tongue was on his nipple, and the pulses of desire racing to his groin made everything come out breathless. "Not putting in that work… without a… contract."

Oliver laved the other nipple, humming in pleasure as he worked. Seb squirmed, pressing up against Oliver, needing more friction against his cock. Oliver continued without pause. He licked and sucked at Seb's skin, still making those humming sounds.

Fuck, Seb was going to explode from the erotic impact of Oliver's pleasure noises. He sounded delighted—maybe even sated—as if Seb were a banquet to be leisurely devoured. Seb moaned something that he meant to be a curse, but more likely was garbled nonsense.

"I think," Oliver murmured, low and throaty, "you are going to tell me every detail of your erotic novel, so I might perform each act precisely as you describe. If you are very good about it, I may even release you from my dungeon." He slid a hand between their bodies, finding Seb's cock and cupping him through the layers of cloth. "You want release, don't you, my sweet?"

Seb made another incoherent sound. When Oliver peered up at him, quirking one blond eyebrow, Seb choked out, "Y-yes."

"Mmm. Tell me more. Shall I inflict my depraved desires

upon you?" He slid lower still, dipping the tip of his tongue into Seb's navel.

"Please."

"Then tell me what you want." Oliver's voice was almost a growl, as if he really were the sexy villain from that silly novel. He moved back up Seb's body until he could whisper in his ear. "Tell me how to torture you until you scream."

Seb's eyelids fluttered closed. "I'm… in your dungeon," he panted. "Ch-chained to the floor."

Oliver let his full weight settle on Sebastian, crushing him into the carpet. He pinned Seb's wrists to the floor, as if he were manacled. When he let go, Seb remained frozen, restrained by the imaginary bonds.

"You like being trapped here, don't you?" the villain purred.

"I do," the hero breathed. "I let you kidnap me."

"I know." Oliver nipped gently at Seb's earlobe and then once again began leisurely mapping his torso. "They call you a paragon." He pinched Seb's nipple and Seb's fingers dug into the thick plush of the carpet. "A pure soul." A swipe of the tongue then another pinch, a little bit harder. Seb's back arched. His cock was aching, but he was pinned beneath Oliver and could only squirm helplessly. "But I know the truth."

"I'm wicked," Seb admitted.

Oliver sat partway up, but Seb didn't move. He kept his eyes closed, his body still.

"Worse than that." The villain's fingers grasped the waistband of his captive's trousers and began unfastening buttons. "You *enjoy* being wicked. You love it. You love me because I'm evil. Because you know I will satisfy every devious little secret desire of your heart."

"Fuck, you're good at this," Seb blurted, only partly in character. And then Oliver got his cock free and wrapped a hand around it and he lost the thread of the story entirely. "O-Oliver."

"Tell me what you want, darling boy."

"Your mouth," Seb wasn't sure the words were recognizable, but he was so insanely turned on, he would have attempted anything Oliver asked. Especially once Oliver began to pump him in long, easy strokes. "Please. God, please."

He almost died when Oliver's tongue swiped over him. He was already leaking, already harder than he could remember being in his life. Either his heart was going to burst or his balls were, and he didn't much care which.

Oliver took Seb deep, and god-bloody-dammit, he began making those noises again, like nothing could possibly taste better than Seb's cock. Like he didn't mind that Seb was bucking and thrusting and losing all control, and his mind was melting, and he was going to shatter, and he needed more, more, harder and faster and please oh please oh please—

Seb didn't register that he'd screamed until it was over and his muscles had gone limp and he was a wet, sticky puddle. When his eyes finally opened, Oliver was grinning down at him, lips red, a rope of spend smeared across his freckled cheek. Oliver wiped it up with one finger, which he licked clean.

"Roll over," he commanded.

Seb wasn't sure if the order came from the Gothic villain or the Earl of Fenwick, but he obeyed without hesitation. "Haven't got any oil. Sorry."

Oliver tugged Seb's trousers down almost to his knees, then climbed atop him, rubbing his erection against Seb's thighs and the cleft of his arse. "Keep your legs together."

Seb sighed as Oliver thrust between his thighs, sliding easily, slick with perspiration. He liked bossy Oliver. Loved bossy Oliver, who could demand what he wanted without fear or shame. Seb would give him this every day for the rest of his life if Oliver let him. He'd be the safe space, the soft, vulnerable one or the strong hand to hold, as needed.

"Yours," he murmured. "I'm all yours."

"Yes." Oliver's words became pants as the pace of his

thrusting quickened. "Be mine. Mine now, mine tomorrow, mine forever. Sebastian." He groaned in agonized desperation. "My Sebastian."

Seb felt Oliver stiffen and shudder, spilling pulses of hot come over his skin. Then his full weight came down on Seb again, a tight embrace and a warm blanket all in one.

"How are you so damn perfect?" Oliver asked.

"Natural talent," Seb answered breezily, and they both laughed. Seb wasn't accustomed to laughing after sex, but Oliver made it seem as ordinary as breathing. "Speaking of talent, you said you couldn't act, and then you play the seductive villain like you were born to it."

Oliver rolled over and dug a handkerchief out from somewhere in his rumpled clothing. "It doesn't take much talent to enjoy fucking you." He urged Seb onto his back and began to wipe him clean. "Very little playacting required." He went suddenly still. "Bloody hell, tomorrow is Sir Albert's theatrical." His gaze locked with Seb's. "You're not leaving, are you? Not before the play? I can't possibly do it without you."

Not before the play. But what would happen after? Sebastian worried his lower lip between his teeth, shaking his head.

"I wouldn't abandon you like that," he promised. "I'll be here as long as you want me."

"Thank you." Oliver kissed Seb's temple and resumed wiping up their mess.

Seb closed his eyes again, and allowed himself to savor Oliver's gentle care. Not a bad way to go, if this was the end.

"As long as you want me," he whispered.

Chapter 15

~ day twelve ~

OLIVER ADJUSTED HIS SASH, trying to secure the unwieldy papier mâché sword at his hip. His equally unwieldy crown listed to one side.

"Do I look ridiculous? I feel like I look ridiculous."

Sebastian placed a hand on his arm. "Sweetheart, Whitcomb has on a pink powdered wig. You have nothing to worry about. Can you get the top button of my dress? It's a bitch to do up myself."

"I'd be happy to."

In truth, Oliver was happy to do anything to distract himself. A distraction that involved touching Seb was all the more welcome. He let his fingers glide over smooth skin, lingering on a freckle between Seb's shoulder blades. If they were alone, he'd be kissing that freckle right now. Teasing Seb about how unfair it was that he had so few of them.

"Your attention please, gentlemen!"

Sir Albert clapped his hands twice, the sound painfully loud in the crowded nook abutting the Green Salon. If he was trying to replicate the chaos of a real theater backstage, he was doing a stellar job. Oliver was ready to run on stage simply for breathing room.

"The ladies are assembling," Sir Albert intoned, "and in a few short minutes I will be welcoming them to the show. Well done with the costumes. Don't forget jewels and hats and such.

Neufeld—er, whatever your name is—have you the long, blond wig for Lady Alice?"

Seb pointed, and Oliver's gaze fell to the mop of golden hair puddled on the floor. Maybe he could step on it, or tangle it up with something and render it unusable. Because he didn't care for the idea of reciting passionate lines to someone who didn't look like Sebastian.

It's pretend. You're not confessing your feelings. It's only acting.

The way it had only been acting when he'd played the villain to Seb's hero on the floor of the Little Library?

"Bloody hell, shite, and bugger," he hissed under his breath. He could not do this. He absolutely could not go out in front of even a single person and put on any kind of persona. Not when all he could think about was Seb's eyes, nearly black with desire, soft and trusting. Or the way he'd so eagerly sprawled beneath Oliver, offering himself up for the taking.

A hand clamped down on his shoulder. "Yes, think passion, Fenwick. That's a good lad."

Oliver gaped at Sir Albert, but the man was already turning away. "Hawthorne, I love that look of pure loathing on your face! Keep up the good work. I say, is that a real rapier? Can't have anyone getting hurt now."

Casper glowered at Sebastian. "Blood won't show on that red dress."

Seb folded his arms across his chest, squishing his fake breasts. "Oh, sod off, Hawthorne. If Oliver wants to talk to me or touch me or do anything at all with me, that's his choice, not yours. Hate me all you want, but shut your mouth and stop waving your prick around. All you're doing is making him uncomfortable. Sulk on your own time and come back when you can be a decent friend."

"I've known him for more than half his life," Casper retorted. "This is, what? Your twelfth night? You think you can seduce everyone with your naughty quips and your perfect femme-boy looks, but let me tell you—"

"Stop!" an agonized voice interrupted. "I can't stand it anymore! This is all my fault!"

Every eye darted to Tunsbury. He sat huddled in the corner of the room, a flask in his hand and his costume hanging limp and unbuttoned. Dark circles lined his eyes.

"What the devil—" Casper began, but Oliver cut him off with a sharp gesture.

"This is my house. I'll do the talking." He pushed past the others and held out a hand to Tunsbury. "John, are you well? You look a wreck."

Tunsbury blinked. "Fuck's sake, Fenwick, you sound like my mother." After a moment's hesitation, he took Oliver's hand and allowed himself to be dragged to his feet. "Forgot you even knew my Christian name."

Oliver checked that his friend was steady before letting go. He didn't seem drunk, thank God, but he was certainly underfed and overtired. "We met when we were five years old, you clod. Now tell me what this is all about."

Tunsbury scuffed the carpet with one shoe. "The necklace. The one your beau's sister was screaming about. It's my fault you had it."

"*You* stole—" Sebastian stopped himself. "Sorry. Go ahead Oliver."

Oliver's heart did something funny, and for a moment he forgot how to speak. Seb had more right than anyone to be furious over Tunsbury's admission. But he was holding back and placing his trust in Oliver. Again. And Oliver would sooner step out on stage in front of a thousand people than let him down.

"Did you steal the necklace, Tunsbury?"

"No. Not..." Tunsbury squirmed. "I found it on the floor, all right? The clasp was broken. It could have belonged to anyone. I'd run up some debts of honor—you know how it is—and suddenly there was a solution, lying right in front of me. I scooped it up and tucked it in my pocket. I began to doubt myself, felt this uncertainty, you know—"

"Guilt. It's called guilt, John."

"Yes, yes, I felt guilty. Are you satisfied? I saw you were leaving the party early, so I slipped the pearls into your pocket. I'd retrieve them later, I thought. Give myself some time to reflect on my plan. It seemed harmless. How was I to know a pair of charming twins would storm your house, take on a secret identity, make everyone fall in love, and break your heart?"

"Our next theatrical needs a secret identity," Sir Albert mumbled to himself. "I must make a note of that."

"You understand?" Tunsbury spread his hands helplessly. "None of this would have happened if it weren't for me. Don't hate each other. You all did what you thought needed doing. The blame falls solely on me. I'll take my leave of you. I'll be seeing some of you at dawn, no doubt."

Amabel appeared in the doorway. "Tunsbury, stop blubbering. The ladies are waiting for the play to begin and I believe you're in the first scene. Into the next room with you all. I need a moment alone with Fenwick. Mr. Wright, you may remain as well. Quickly, gentlemen, I haven't all day."

A roomful of bewildered men stared at the duchess. Surprisingly, it was Tunsbury who broke the silence.

He bowed deeply. "As you wish, Your Grace." He scampered away, buttoning his waistcoat as he went. Others began to follow.

Oliver caught Casper's arm. "Please don't call Tunsbury out over this."

Casper heaved a sigh. "I'm rather weary of being your champion at present. And you were correct. You can champion yourself and I shouldn't interfere unless you ask."

"Hey," Sebastian cut in. "Instead of murdering me, maybe

you could give me a fencing lesson and relentlessly mock my ineptitude?"

Uncertainty flickered across Casper's face, then smoothed away. "A truce, then. For as long as you make Oliver happy." He shook Seb's hand, then walked calmly out the door.

Oliver let out a breath of relief. One of his favorite people appeased. Now to face Amabel.

Amabel who was, he realized in shock and horror, attired in nothing more than a dressing gown. The hem swished around her bare feet and calves, and the top gaped enough to expose her stays.

"What are you wearing?" he blurted. "Or *not* wearing?"

Amabel waved another person into the room—Helena, similarly unattired.

The duchess looked directly at Oliver. "Get out of those clothes," she commanded.

"I beg your pardon!" He took a stumbling step backward.

Amabel unknotted the tie of her dressing gown and the garment slithered to the floor. Oliver clapped a hand over his eyes.

"Calm yourself, Fenwick. I'm not here to seduce you. You of all people know I have no interest in men." She said this last with the same air of disgust one might use when speaking of vermin. "But I have wronged you and I owe you a good turn. Now hand over your costume. I'm taking your place."

"Is that an order?" Seb retorted. "Because I didn't hear a 'please.'"

Oliver's hand dropped from his eyes as he shifted into a ready position, prepared to fling himself between Sebastian and Amabel. But the duchess wasn't glowering. In fact, the expression on her face was one Oliver had never seen before. Was that... contrition?

"You have my apologies, Oliver," Amabel said slowly. "I have been trying to control your life, and that has hurt you and hurt our friends. Now here I am, doing it again. Allow me to offer you a choice. Miss Wright and I are willing and able to take your places in the theatrical. We've read the script. If you don't want to perform for the ladies, we will. What is your decision?"

Oliver ripped the crown from his head and tossed it at her. "I accept your apology and your offer. Sebastian can speak for himself."

Seb was grinning at his sister. "Be my guest." He kicked the tangled blond wig in her direction.

What ensued was a mad scramble to swap costumes, culminating in a rumpled prince and Lady Alice racing away to make their entrance on time. Oliver and Sebastian found themselves suddenly alone, nearly naked, and giggling.

The voices of emoting actors drifted in from the Green Salon. Oliver shook with half-suppressed laughter. His cheeks were burning, partly from the absurdity of standing in nothing but his drawers, a mere room away from a houseful of guests, and partly from the sight of Sebastian in the same state.

Another bubble of giggles escaped him. "I feel like a mischievous schoolboy getting away with something," he whispered.

"Welcome to my world." Seb's smile was a little bit flirtatious, a little bit naughty, and entirely radiant. "I spend approximately ninety-five percent of my waking hours feeling that way."

Oliver closed the distance between them. "One of the many reasons I love you."

Sebastian's eyes went wide and his jaw dropped.

Panic clawed at Oliver's chest. "I… That is… You don't have to feel the same. I understand—"

Seb pressed a finger to Oliver's lips. "I love you too. I've loved you for… well, days, I suppose." He chuckled. "Is that peculiar? Have we both lost our minds?"

"It's likely."

"Well, I don't care. You're the sweetest, most adorable man I know. You're loving and accepting and much stronger than you think you are. I want to read all your books and write erotic novels for you and listen to you ramble on about the queer architect who designed your ceilings and how he hid tributes to his lover all over the house—"

"You really *were* listening!" Oliver pulled Sebastian into an embrace. "Of course you were listening. You always do. You always care. You're a wild, whimsical spirit, but your heart is so damn big and you impulsively bare it for all the world to trample on. You make me want to hold you and protect you forever."

Seb began to nuzzle Oliver's neck, where the love bite from a few days prior was fading. "I want to do the same for you."

Oliver pressed a kiss into his hair. "Will you stay, then?"

Seb looked up at him, dark eyes misty. "I need to return the pearls to my mother. But then I'll be back, if you'll have me."

"For as long as you desire." Oliver lowered his mouth to Seb's in a deep, thorough kiss. A promise of days and nights to come. A life stretching out before them.

Some time later, Seb broke the kiss, panting. "What if I desire forever?"

Oliver brushed a lock of wavy hair from Seb's eyes. "Then forever you shall have."

A beatific grin lit up Sebastian's whole face. "I knew I was right to ride here in a snowstorm!"

He leapt up into Oliver's arms, wrapping his legs around Oliver's waist. Oliver staggered for a few seconds, then backed Seb up against the wall, kissing him greedily. They rocked against one another, hearts pounding and chests heaving, fierce and desperate and joyful. Oliver would have been content to continue all day, were it not for a sudden burst of applause from the next room.

He backed away, lowering Seb gently to the floor.

"Maybe not here?" Seb licked his lips and glanced up at the ceiling.

Oliver nodded. "Come, let's to bed, my love." He took Sebastian's hand and kissed his knuckles before casting a final glance toward the exit to the Green Salon. "To all: good day. And may your night be passionate and gay."

Exeunt.

THE BARON
of
Twisted Tree Inn

~ *an epistolary romance* ~

Maria never expected to be the heroine of one of her "horrid novels." But when a snowstorm strands her at the Twisted Tree Inn, where she encounters the mysterious (and handsome) Baron Neufeld, her imagination begins to run wild. Is the gnarled old oak outside a portent of evil? Is the baron plotting her demise? As Maria details her adventure in letters to her sister, she begins to unravel fact from fiction. And with a romance blossoming between herself and the baron, Maria can't help but wonder if her own story has a chance to end happily ever after.

Day 1

Dear Lucy,

I am stranded. You will not receive this letter before I place it into your hands, but I must write to someone about my predicament. The snow has been coming down for hours now. Late this afternoon, we were forced to postpone our journey as the roads had become too hazardous. Everything was first covered in ice, and now the snow has begun to build up on top of that.

The inn is full of other stranded travelers, and I am thankful we arrived when we did. We were able to procure a room for myself as well as a room for my traveling companions, Mr. and Mrs. Henry Tilney. You will remember Mrs. Tilney from when she was Miss Catherine Morland. Lucy, you know not how relieved I am to have her here with me. Without a friend to talk with, I am not certain I will retain my sanity. There are whispers that we might be here a <u>full sennight</u> before the roads are navigable.

There is one thing here at the Twisted Tree (is that not a chilling name? It gives me gooseflesh to write it) that might provide an occupation for my mind during our isolation. It is also perhaps more disquieting than the inn and the claw-like branches of the gnarled oak that gives it its name. Sometimes, when I look out the window, I see wooden fingers reaching out, threatening to drag me into the cold night. I am certain it was the tree itself and not the wind that caused my cloak to snag on a low branch upon arrival. I ought to have known at once that we would not be leaving this unsettling place.

Oh! But let me not keep you in suspense any longer. There is a mysterious man among the guests. We have not been formally introduced, but it is impossible not to interact with everyone here to some extent. He calls himself Baron Georg Neufeld and he hails from Bavaria. He is handsome, of course, but not the way any of the men Mama would approve of might be. His hair is very dark, and overlong. He has made no attempt to tame it with oil or tie it back in a queue. He also has a dark shadow of facial hair, as if he has not shaved in some days. I find it distressingly alluring, though I know beards are not at all the fashion. His eyes are nearly as dark as his hair, and they stand out all the more due to his pale skin. They are very brooding eyes, and I cannot help but think he must be plotting. He is quiet and solitary. Polite, but terse. I spotted him throwing correspondence into the fire. Is he burning secret documents? Hiding evidence? I could not see what was written on the papers, but I am suspicious. To be sure, he is everything I would expect from a villain.

Catherine says I have read too many horrid novels and advises me not to assume such things truly happen, as this leads to terrible misunderstandings. She says she speaks from experience. But she agrees that the baron looks dastardly. I think he is watching me as I write this letter. I do hope he will not murder me in my sleep. I shall use my hair ribbons to tie something to the door tonight, so it will make noise and wake me when he enters.

I shall update you on the morrow, unless I am murdered.

Your loving sister,
Maria

Dearest Lu,

I am not murdered. The snow has not stopped and the drifts outside grow ever deeper. I have never seen anything like it. I fear I shall never be able to leave this inn. Already my skin itches with the need to go outside. You know how poorly I fare when I cannot move my body enough.

I have no doubt now that the baron is watching me. My ~~occasional~~ frequent unladylike tendencies have drawn his notice. I talk too loud or I laugh too much. I read fully half of a horrid novel last night, and I am certain I exclaimed far too vigorously while discussing it with Catherine. (I will give you the book when I see you. There is a hapless hero who has been kidnapped three times and a mysterious dungeon beneath a lake.) In any event, I was most excited to talk about it. I happened to look up in the midst of this discussion, and the baron was looking <u>directly at me</u>. When our eyes met, he did not look away! He smiled!

Oh, Lucy, he has such a nice smile. It makes dimples in his cheeks and makes his dark eyes seem so inviting. This is how he lures his victims! He will smile at me and I will become entranced, and then he will ravish me!

He is looking this way again. I had a momentary respite while he conversed with Mr. Tilney and some of the other gentlemen. But now Henry and Catherine have slipped away to gaze adoringly at one another and the baron is alone. I can feel his eyes on me. He is sitting at a desk, as if writing letters, and he occasionally rises to cast another paper into the fire. Either he makes many mistakes or he is hiding something. Perhaps tonight will be the night I am murdered.

Still alive,

Maria

Day 3

Lucy!

Oh, heavens! We have spoken! I have exchanged words with Baron Neufeld, and they were... not seductive? I am puzzled. I was finishing the horrid novel. (The ending was shocking! You will swoon!) I was seated by the fire, and the baron passed me. He inquired after my book. He has very little accent, and I understand that he studied many years in England as a young man. (I do not mean to imply that he is no longer a young man. He is an old young man. He is not old, I mean. Perhaps six-and-twenty?)

I informed him (with great pride, because I will not feel shame for the books I enjoy) that I was reading a most compelling Gothic novel.

"Ah," he said. "The one you were telling your friend about yesterday? It sounds very interesting."

The innkeeper called him away at that point, to inquire after his well-being. The innkeeper is terribly anxious to have foreign nobility in his establishment and wishes to give the baron every comfort.

But you see, Lucy? This is proof that the baron has been spying on me! He is studying my reading habits! He must know now that I suspect him of villainy because of what I have learned from my books.

I heard him request more writing paper for a letter he is

"attempting to compose." I think he is working on creating a secret code for his dastardly correspondence.

Catherine says I appear smitten with the baron. I cannot understand what she means. I have not been watching him except for my own safety.

Yours in bafflement,

Maria

Day 4

Dear Lucy,

Tonight is the night. I shall surely be murdered after what has transpired. I told you about my restlessness in a previous missive. Today it got the better of me at last. I put on my cloak and my overshoes and went out into the snow. Catherine declined to accompany me, and instead disappeared somewhere with her Mr. Tilney. Again. I would say she has taken ill, except she has been of a markedly cheerful disposition, especially for someone trapped in an inn for days.

The outdoors was so beautiful and peaceful, and I walked for a time, slowly tromping a path around the inn. I am not certain I have ever felt so refreshed as I did then. My arms and legs were in motion. I drew in cold, clean air with every breath. The wind did sting my cheeks, but I have never minded anything so little. I was outside, where I could be free and unfettered by rules and boundaries. This is how the heroines in novels feel when they are struck by the sublime majesty of nature. I know it. It is a moment outside of time and space, full of pure joy.

In this ebullient state of being, I scooped up a handful of snow, shaped it into a ball, and hurled it as far as I was able. It made such a cheery SPLAT when it landed in a snowdrift, that I could not help but throw another. But as I threw a third snowball, who should appear from around the corner, silent as the grave, but Baron Neufeld!

So startled was I by his unexpected appearance, that I

jumped high in the air and my throw went awry. The snowball hit the baron squarely in the chest.

I know I should have apologized, but I shrieked and ran. I am mortified.

Terrified. I meant to say terrified. Surely the baron will never look at me again until the moment he strikes me down.

Your soon-to-be-deceased sister,

Maria

Dear Lucy,

I begin to despair of ever leaving this place. I walked again today, over the path I trod yesterday and the nearby path that must have been of the baron's making. The weather remains cold and the carriages cannot traverse the roads. I wonder if all who come here are cursed to remain as long as the Twisted Tree stands. I did not see anyone on my walk today, and I did not throw any additional snowballs.

Conversing with the baron is no longer shocking. I was seated across from him at dinner, and he was everything amiable. He asked if I had enjoyed my walk and spoke of his own fondness for exercise and the outdoors. I was surprised to learn that we have much in common. And I do not mean only a love for walking and a hatred of turnips.

I stated (very foolishly, many would say) that I believe girls should have equal schooling with boys so more women might become leaders and help to make important decisions. We are half of the world, after all, and many women have been excellent rulers. I know because the stories of those women are my favorite things to read when I am not in the mood for a horrid novel. I may have said this all in a loud, forceful, unladylike voice.

Baron Neufeld neither scolded me nor laughed at this. He smiled and then he agreed! He spoke of a friend who is a duchess in her own right and said that more women should have such opportunities.

"I see no reason," he said, "why women should not study medicine, law, or any other profession. Women have brains as clever as men."

When another man replied that the female constitution is not sturdy enough for the rigors of such work, Baron Neufeld asked who was the only one among us hearty enough to venture outdoors today for the improvement of body and mind.

Everyone knew it was me. I am certain I turned most awfully red. But I held my head high, as I am proud of my penchant for exercise.

The obnoxious man did not speak again, and the baron smiled at me for the remainder of dinner. Catherine and Henry both say Neufeld is smitten with me and I with him. They are clearly wrong.

However, I am less certain of the baron's villainy. I think he might be nice. This requires further study.

Your hearty, clever-brained sister,
Maria

P.S.

Neufeld is reading my horrid novel! I saw him just now, as I was folding this letter and preparing to retire for the night. He is sitting in front of the fire, with his feet propped on the bricks of the hearth, reading intently! He didn't even notice when I paused to discover what book he held.

It is my book! I am certain because it has a small stain on the back cover from when I set it down atop a letter that had not finished drying. I must have left it here in the main room by mistake.

Unless he crept into my room and stole it!

But this is not even the most shocking thing. Lucy, he is wearing spectacles! They are perched just so on his nose, and his hair is falling into his face. Now and then he tucks a lock of hair behind his ear, but then it falls again. His beard has continued to grow during our days here. It looks soft.

I think I will not retire quite yet after all.

-M

Dearest sister,

I can hardly recall a lovelier day. The sun came out at last, and some of the snow has begun to melt. (Do not think this means I will soon escape. The drifts are still large, and the few places free from snow are nasty pools of mud. One man attempted to depart, and his carriage became stuck mere yards down the road. It is still there, and the man is staring despondently into his drink.)

But I digress. The beautiful day! I went out for my now-customary walk, laughing as I slid over icy patches and admiring the shimmering icicles. As I was finishing my first circuit of the inn, I saw Neufeld emerge. He inquired whether he might join me on my rambles, and I said yes.

This was perhaps too forward of both of us? No one else had ventured out yet, so the baron would have had every opportunity to ravish me. (He did not.)

We walked together for some time, talking about this and that. He is a most amiable conversationalist and has wide interests, from books to art to the theater. He told me of his homeland, and I said I would very much like to visit someday. We then spoke of all the many other places we should like to visit and what we might see and do there. Neufeld said that if we ever find ourselves together in a fancy city like Paris or Vienna, he will take me to the opera. Such a thing will never happen, of course, but it was a lovely fantasy. I told him that because of his hair and his beard the other theatergoers might mistake him for the villain and ask for his autograph.

He laughed, but then his expression became serious. He leaned down toward me, and said in a low, rumbly voice, "I am no villain, my dear, but I am lately plagued by wicked thoughts."

We stared at one another for some time, and I grew awfully warm, despite the chill of the wind. Is this the moment where I should have feared ravishment or murder? Because I did not. I felt entirely safe, despite his being rather large and piratical. In fact, I am certain that if a highwayman had happened upon us, the baron would have shielded me with his own body and fought off the scoundrel. Could it be that Neufeld is a dashing hero who has been disguised as a villain? Horrid novels do so often have disguises, and even though Catherine insists that they do not depict real life, I am certain there must be some truth behind the stories.

I do not remember which of us was first to look away. Perhaps we both did at the same time.

We returned to the inn, then, in silence. Whatever discomfort was between us soon dissipated, and we spent much of the remainder of the day reading side-by-side. In the evening, myself, the baron, and the Tilneys had an engaging dinner conversation about the horrid novel with the dungeon under the lake. Neufeld believes it would be ridiculously expensive to build and maintain and perhaps this is why the villain has lost all of his fortune. It was an excellent point, I agreed. I proposed that if Gothic novels were true, there would be crumbling ruins with eerie dungeons and secret passages every few miles down even the smallest road.

Henry quipped that perhaps this was true on the Continent, which made Neufeld exclaim in mock indignation in his native tongue. He then taught us a few phrases in German. I can now say "guten Morgen" (good morning), "auf wiedersehen" (until we meet again), and "Ich liebe dich" (I love you). This last was for Catherine and Henry, but perhaps I will need it someday.

If tomorrow is as pleasant as today was, I shall not mind terribly that we have been here a full week already.

Your contented sister,

Maria

Day 7

Dear Lucy,

Today was another most enjoyable day. The sky was gray again, and the air cold, so no more snow has melted. This did not deter me from my daily constitutional, nor prevent the baron from joining me. Today our walk was filled with observations of the most careful sort. We paused to comment on rocks and plants that looked different beneath the clouds. We followed tracks left by an animal (we decided it was a squirrel) to where they ended at the base of a tree. We made studies of the icicles and the snowdrifts. It was my slowest walk of the week, but very rewarding nonetheless.

Neufeld was in a jolly mood, joking and teasing, which sometimes made me smile and sometimes made me blush, especially if our hands happened to brush or our shoulders to bump while we made our observations. My body has an unusually strong reaction to his touch. Or perhaps I was shivering from the cold.

I was prepared to return to the warmth of the inn, when Neufeld asked me if I wished to throw a few snowballs first.

I blushed furiously and stammered something about how my attack on his person the other day had been entirely unintentional, but he seemed only amused. He proposed we have a contest. He selected a particular knot on the Twisted Tree to be our target, and said that we would each hurl ten snowballs at it. The one to hit the target the most times would be the winner.

He offered to allow me to stand closer, but I refused. He would have been better served if he had stood closer, as only five of his snowballs hit the target as compared to eight of mine. I did not tell him this, but he would have an easier time of it if he would take more care crafting his snowballs. I pack mine tighter and rounder than he does, and the difference in their flight is significant.

As my prize for winning the contest, he took me inside, sat me by the fire to warm up, and brought me a book and a hot drink. The remainder of the day is almost a blur. I know only that we spent it together by the hearth in a mix of chatter and companionable silence. I have become so at ease with Georg the baron, more than I ever had been with any man. I should like to be his friend permanently. Sometimes, when my mind wanders, I find myself wanting other, more scandalous, things too.

I am beginning to fear that Catherine and Henry are correct and I may be smitten.

Your hopeless sister,

María

Dear Lu,

The weather today is miserable. A cold rain has been pouring down since morning, turning everything to slushy muck. This means that the snow is melting and we will not be stuck here indefinitely. I am not as excited as I would have expected. I have grown accustomed to life here, I suppose. I'm sure having us all leave will be a great relief to the innkeeper, who has been working without pause and surely needs to restock his pantry. I find myself in no hurry, however, even though I am in a state of agitation.

I spent most of the day reading and talking with Neufeld. I have loaned him another horrid novel. This was all as pleasant as ever, but I cannot suppress my restlessness. I miss our walks. I miss the movement and I miss the time alone with him. Are you scandalized? Well, it is nothing but the truth. I relish my time alone, unchaperoned, with a handsome man.

I am so grumpy today that I had to start this letter before our evening meal, as I needed to get these feelings out. I must pause now to eat, but will finish later.

Lu! You will never believe what has happened! (Oh, it is nothing dire, please do not panic.) As the dishes were cleared away, all the gentlemen rose from their seats and began to move the tables! We ladies were entirely stunned, murmuring and gasping in our seats.

"His Lordship has arranged a surprise for us this evening!" the innkeeper announced.

The baron murmured that he needed no thanks and, when he said it, he was looking at me! Even now I am trying not to think about what this means.

All the tables were swiftly relocated to the corners of the room. Then the chairs were gathered and stacked atop the tables. I hoisted my own chair, thank you very much, but I had to do it while Georg was occupied carrying the chairs of a pair of elderly sisters. They blushed and giggled and flirted with him terribly and it was both sweet and funny.

While this was happening, a couple by the name of Mr. and Mrs. Whitby scurried off to their room, only to return with instruments. Mr. Whitby plays the flute, and Mrs. Whitby has both a small drum and a tambourine. They struck up a lively tune, and all the guests, the servants, and even the innkeeper himself began to dance.

I'm certain you can guess who I danced with the most. I promise I did not spend the entire evening in his arms, but we did take many turns together. There are more men here than women, so everything was a silly, muddled mess, no matter what we did, and we had ladies dancing with ladies, and men dancing with men, and ladies leading men, and we all clapped and laughed and had the most wonderful time! This is how a ball should be. Not stuffy and proper, but lighthearted and fun. Imagine how much easier it would be to find agreeable partners! You would only need to look around the dance floor, spot someone having fun, and extend your hand. You wouldn't have to dance in straight lines or perfect circles or anything complicated. And if you danced with the same gentleman, say… half a dozen times? No one would think anything of it. Or at the very least, they wouldn't assume you are about to marry him.

It was magical, Lucy, truly. I know I keep saying that I am having lovely days or lovely evenings, but this was the best of all. Everyone was smiling. Georg was shy with the other ladies, and I have never found him more adorable. With me he was all laughter and energy. I hadn't realized that his aloofness all those days ago was merely a touch of nerves when meeting strangers. He talks with Mr. Tilney and a few of the other gentlemen, but it was clear tonight that his dearest friend in the inn is me. Me!

Oh, Lucy, what shall I do? I am smitten. I cannot deny it. He is my brooding but kind heroic villain, and I wish he would carry me away to his crumbling castle and ravish me! We would pick wildflowers on our walks and rebuild the castle walls together. We could fill a library with horrid novels and read them aloud and act out all the scandalous parts.

No. No. I must stop.

This is a silly fantasy. The snow will be gone soon. The mud will dry up, and the roads will be clear. I'm sure the baron is meant to marry someone fancy, such as a princess or his friend the duchess. We are friends but cannot dream of romance. After we depart we are unlikely to ever see one another again, and this will become nothing more than a fond memory.

I apologize for the smudge. My hand is not trembling. I am merely tired. I will take myself off to bed and dream of pleasant things. Not ~~Georg Neufeld~~ a certain person.

Your absolutely not heartsick sister,

Maria

Day 9

Dearest Lucy,

I shall begin, as I have often done, with the weather. The day has been fair and warmer than any in several weeks. Most of the snow is gone, and the mud is drying out. The stablehands have freed the stuck carriage and brought it back to the carriage house to be cleaned and (re)prepared for departure. We all may be able to leave the Twisted Tree as soon as tomorrow. Certainly by the day after.

I must confess, this is almost worse than the terrible weather of yesterday. While I am not confined to the indoors, I do not feel the sense of freedom I ordinarily would. In all honesty, I would characterize my mood as morose, and my behavior as listless. Perhaps I am coming down with a cold. I do not think I am feverish, and I have no sniffles or cough.

I should be honest with you. I fear it may be something worse than a cold. It may be heartbreak.

Even the horrid novels have failed to improve my mood. They may even be exacerbating it. (Isn't "exacerbate" an excellent word? I love the way it feels and sounds, all sharp and formidable.) Something I have noticed in these Gothic stories is that it doesn't signify if the hero is a prince or otherwise unobtainable. Somehow the heroine will marry him in the end. She will be a secret princess or heiress.

I am not a secret anything.

Georg and I did not talk much today, and I know I am at fault. I was short with him, only answering in single words and gruff tones. I let my sour mood affect my speech, and did not realize what I was doing until it was too late.

When we walked, he mentioned a bird he'd spotted in the branches of the Twisted Tree.

"I'd rather not see it," I grumbled. "What is the purpose of admiring something when it will just fly away from you?"

"I thought you believed in happy endings," he retorted.

"Only in stories," I huffed.

He said nothing after that, simply walked away, leaving me by the tree, listening to the bird I could not bear to look at.

We sat apart at dinner. Oh, Lucy, why was I so horrible today? I didn't mean to hurt him! I only fear that our time together is ending, and this causes a terrible ache in my chest and a sickness in my stomach. I do want to be his friend, but how do I tell him so without revealing too much? I cannot tell him of my romantic fantasies when he must know how unsuited we are. Regardless, I am certain I have ruined any affection he held for me.

Your absolutely heartsick sister,

Maria

Day 10

*O*H, MY GOODNESS!

I must beg your pardon if this letter is illegible. I am writing it in the wee hours of the morning by the light of a single candle. But I simply must relate what has happened. If I do not, I might suddenly awaken and everything that has transpired will fade away like a dream. I <u>will not</u> allow that to happen! I will write all night if I must.

But I shall keep you in suspense no longer.

I retired to my room in the evening, where I penned the previous letter in this ever-growing packet. I was melancholy and frustrated, but I forced myself to go to bed and think nothing more of my baron and our star-crossed love.

Needless to say, I was unsuccessful. I lay awake, growing ever more restless, imagining all the ways I might possibly apologize to Georg and all the possible reactions he might have. Truly, I had become a novel heroine, crushed by an onslaught of emotion. Had I a less sturdy constitution, I would have swooned. Also, I would be pale and slender and terribly empty-headed. I am greatly relieved my story is not one such as that.

Some time after midnight, my tossings and turnings were interrupted by a soft tapping at my door. I bolted upright, thrilled, but certain I must have misheard. The tapping came again.

I told myself it must be Catherine, or a maid coming to check the fire. Still, I sprang from the bed and rushed to open the door.

I expect you already know who was standing there.

"I couldn't sleep," he said.

"Neither could I," I replied.

He took my hand, lifted it to his lips and kissed it. "My darling. I must humbly beg your pardon."

I was baffled by this and insisted that, no, it was I who must apologize. After a bit of confusion, we determined that we had both been gruff and disagreeable throughout the day and it was the fault of neither and both of us. This resulted in much giggling, and I ushered him into my room, lest we be spotted laughing together by a poor soul rising to use the necessary.

The moment the door closed behind us, the atmosphere changed. Truly, the air felt thick, and it buzzed with a peculiar energy. We were standing so close, neither moving. I could hardly breathe, and I swear that my heart beat loud enough to hear.

We didn't need to talk, we simply fell into each other's arms. I clasped him to my breast and he whispered my name. "Maria, Maria, Maria."

When I lifted my head to meet his gaze, he bent to meet me halfway. Lucy, it was the most natural thing in the world to kiss him. His lips were gentle until I grew more passionate, and then he kissed me most ardently, with his whole mouth and his tongue. You may call it scandalous, but it was nothing of the sort. It was magnificent. Exactly what I wanted. Exactly what I needed. We kissed for so long, until I could repeat all his tricks and could barely stand for breathlessness.

Georg talked, then. He told me he wishes to court me and asked could he meet my family in order to tell them his intentions.

I believe I squeaked like a mouse. It was not pretty. But

he understood my excitement and hugged me tight and kissed me again.

I protested that surely his family would object. He promised me they would not. He has also written to his friend the duchess to inform her he cannot possibly marry her. (His letters were not in secret code, he said.)

"My family and friends wish me to be happy, above all," he said. "They may be disappointed initially, but they will understand the moment they see how much I adore you."

He held me then, for a long moment, before whispering, "And even if the whole world objected, I would never let you go. I would move mountains to make you my own."

This is when I should have swooned. Or melted. Or fallen to my knees weeping. But I am me, so I did not. Instead, I looked up into his dark eyes and inquired, "Will you ravish me now?"

He laughed at this, but not meanly. He allowed me to feel something that proved he very much desired to ravish me, which made me flush hot all over. But Georg is a good man and does not want us forced to marry with scandal looming over our heads.

"I will kiss you at every opportunity," he promised. "And once we are engaged, we will have more freedom to be alone."

I stroked his beard. (It is very soft, just as I had hoped.) "Could you not be at least a trifle villainous?" I asked.

He started to turn toward the door, then turned back. "Very well, my seductress. I will be a trifle villainous."

I will not share the details of what transpired in writing, but rest assured that my dashing baron can be very wicked indeed when asked nicely. He has most excellently clever hands and an even cleverer tongue.

It occurs to me that I now understand why Catherine and Henry are always sneaking away to their room.

Please excuse me. I am yawning and I feel vastly better for having committed this tale to paper. I am confident now that I did not dream our passionate meeting.

Your blissfully happy sister,

Maria

P.S.

It is fully morning now. The roads are clear and we are to depart soon. It will not be long, then, before these letters are in your hands.

Baron Neufeld will be traveling with us. I do wish we could share a carriage, but now that we are venturing back into Polite Society, we cannot. Despite what I feared at the beginning of this adventure, I have not perished of ennui nor lost my sanity. In truth, it was a blessing to be here, away from all things "proper" for a time. I hope to partake of such adventures regularly. They are invigorating.

Looking out the window at the Twisted Tree, I realize it is not scary after all. It looks as though it should be, if you only glance at it. But it's something different, and if you take the time to study it, you will discover how beautiful it is. The curves of its branches shelter animals. The acorns it drops grow new trees. It is old and has seen much, and I think if we listen to what it tells us, we will be the wiser for it.

Perhaps someday I will return to the inn and greet the tree like the friend it is.

-M

Day 113

My beloved sister,

Thank you again for standing up with me at my wedding. I felt such joy having all those I love most with me on that happy day.

My husband and I have arrived at the Twisted Tree Inn. Husband! I love getting to write that now. That day I first entered this building seems forever ago and also yesterday. Life is so funny. But Georg and I will be forever grateful for the snowstorm that brought us together.

Married life is absolutely wonderful. The carriage ride passed in the blink of an eye with my beloved for company. We are not entirely like the heroes and heroines of my novels. We disagree at times, and we know there is more to experience beyond our happy ending. But in other ways, we are much like my favorite characters. We will make mistakes, yet we will persevere. We will live our adventure together, and I cannot imagine a more perfect partner beside me as I travel through my own story.

I do promise to keep you updated about any interesting goings on during our wedding trip. I warn you, however, that my letters will be shorter than you may be accustomed to.

I must go now. My husband and I have ever so many things to do. Wicked things. After all, he is my seductive villain.

Yours ever,
Baroness Maria Neufeld

Milton Keynes UK
Ingram Content Group UK Ltd.
UKHW040940141024
449705UK00005B/204

Her Fair Lady

~

CATHERINE STEIN

Copyright © 2024 Catherine Stein, LLC.

All rights reserved. No part of this book may be reproduced in any form without the written permission of the publisher, except as permitted by U.S. copyright law.

This is a work of fiction. Names, characters, places, and incidents are products of the author's imagination or are used fictitiously. Any resemblance to actual events or persons, living or dead, is entirely coincidental.

ISBN: 978-1-949862-51-5

Book cover and interior design by E. McAuley: www.emcauley.com

Her Fair Lady

Helena Wright has a single goal: retrieve her mother's heirloom pearls from the Earl of Fenwick. When her brother decides to crash the earl's house party disguised as a Bavarian lord, Helena has no choice but to play along. But the ruse throws her into the path of the beautiful and intriguing Amabel, Duchess of Mirweald. Amabel's suspicions are quickly roused, drawing the two women into a game of lies and flirtation. Soon they're spending more time together, peeling away more layers, and growing more intimate. As more truths are revealed, Helena and Amabel will need to confront their own buried desires in order to unearth the secret of true love.

Her Fair Lady is an homage to Shakespearean comedy. As such, it contains implausible situations, anachronistic turns of phrase, ribald puns, over-the-top supporting characters, and plenty of blundering. **Content warning for a side character with social anxiety.**

Dramatis Personae

～

Helena Wright - the sensible one, twin sister to Sebastian

Sebastian Wright - the reckless one, twin brother to Helena

Amabel, Duchess of Mirweald - a peeress with a penchant for meddling

Oliver, Earl of Fenwick - probably a thief, definitely a problem

Baron Georg Neufeld - unfortunately absent

The Sapphic Ladies' Club

    Georgia/George Beauclair - founder and president

    Maryanne - quietly radical

    Maryellen - lover of colorful language and illustrations

Sir Albert Fellowes - Maryanne's cousin, an over-enthusiastic director

Mr. Whitcomb - a doting husband with a flair for drama

Mrs. Whitcomb - a doting wife with excellent aim

Lord Tunsbury - a scribbler of dubious skill

Casper Hawthorne - armed and flirtatious

Mother and Stepfather - relatively relevant

~ day one ~

Murdering one's twin was a time-honored tradition. If Romulus could kill Remus for his own selfish gain and be deemed a hero, surely the world would forgive Helena Wright for strangling her brother.

Helena stomped up the servants' staircase, cursing Sebastian to perdition. Melting snow dripped from the hefty saddlebags slung over her shoulders, leaving a wet trail through the Earl of Fenwick's palatial mansion.

They'd had a plan. A sensible enough plan that she'd ridden through an ever-worsening storm in order to enact it.

Helena paused at the top of the stairs and leaned against the wall, squeezing her eyes closed. How hard would it have been to say, "I beg your pardon. We took a wrong turn on our way to the inn. Might we shelter overnight in your stables?" At the rate the snow was falling, they would be stuck here at least another day or two. Plenty of time to sneak into the house and retrieve Mother's stolen pearls.

"His lordship's chamber's at the end of the 'all," said the pretty, plump housemaid assigned to show Helena the way. "Oh! Do you speak English?"

Helena straightened up and tried not to snarl. This wasn't the girl's fault. "Yes. I was born in London, in fact."

"Oh!" the girl squeaked again. "So was I. But the air's 'ealthier here, they say, and five hours ain't too far to visit a

1

few times a year. 'Is lordship says family time is a blessing if you got a good 'un."

"I agree. Although sometimes even good family can try your patience."

Sometimes, your beloved twin adopts a ghastly Germanic accent and tells everyone he is a Bavarian lord and that you are his bloody valet!

There was no earthly way this would end in anything but disaster.

Helena adjusted the saddlebags and resumed her confident stride. She would simply have to complete her mission before everything blew up like Mt. Vesuvius.

The bedchamber looked fit for a king, with a spacious sitting area, a closet the size of a normal person's bedroom, and a massive bed that she was absolutely not letting Sebastian have all to himself. She dumped the saddlebags in the closet, atop the cot meant for the valet's use.

"Have I the honor of greeting Baron Georg Neufeld?" Helena mimicked the voice of the stablehand who had greeted Seb upon their arrival. "No. You bloody well haven't! You have the misfortune of greeting the most reckless, addlepated..."

She abandoned her ranting and shucked her wet cloak and jacket. She really ought to have expected this. And it was difficult to stay angry in a warm, dry room with a magnificent bed. This part of Seb's plan deserved high marks.

Helena hung her wet things, then emptied her saddlebags. Sebastian could deal with his own damn clothing, she decided, smoothing the wrinkles from her costumes. As punishments go, it wasn't much of one. Seb was as likely to wear her clothes as his own. They traded outfits back and forth so often neither of them was sure who'd purchased most of the things. Having an almost-identical twin did have its perks.

After completing her unpacking, Helena slipped out the door for a preliminary exploration. Mother's pearls—her precious, irreplaceable wedding pearls that had been a gift

HER FAIR LADY

from the twins' father—were somewhere in this house. The facts identified the Earl of Fenwick as the thief. She could worry about the particular excuse Seb had used to get inside at another time. What mattered was finding the pearls.

None of the guest rooms had doors that locked, since housemaids would be going in and out throughout the day. Lamp in hand, Helena poked her head into a few rooms. They all resembled her own. If it became necessary, she could search thoroughly, but she doubted Fenwick would hide stolen goods in the guest wing. Not when he had a palace full of better places at his disposal.

She moved quietly down the hall, alert for the sounds of nearby activity. A faint jumble of voices filtered up from the party below, but no doors creaked and no footsteps approached. Past the central staircase—a good deal nicer than the steep, cramped steps she'd taken before—was a corridor identical to the one she had just traversed. The family bedchambers would be there, most likely, along with rooms for the most notable guests. Helena walked to the first door and pushed it open.

The sitting room inside was as large as the entirety of Sebastian's chambers, and adorned with similar sumptuous fabrics and elegant furnishings. Partially completed embroidery rested on a settee, and several novels lay atop the various tables. Helena headed across the room to the connecting door. It led to an expansive bedchamber filled with an assortment of feminine personal effects.

She peeked into the dressing room and froze. Dresses out of a fairy tale shimmered in the light of her lamp. Helena stepped closer, reaching out a tentative hand. The fabrics were exquisite, soft to the touch and radiant with color. Beaded and embroidered details highlighted artfully draped skirts.

A stab of envy brought back her earlier anger, giving it a new target. The Earl of Fenwick dressed his countess like this and would still steal pearls from a mere barrister's wife! Did he

4 CATHERINE STEIN

not already have enough, the blackguard? Or was he financing his purchases out of the pockets of others?

Helena's fingers clenched. The lamplight wavered as her hands shook.

Breathe. Focus on the goal.

Now wasn't the time to vent her anger at Fenwick. Today had been long and tiring. A nice bed awaited her. Best to get some rest before determining next steps.

Helena slipped out of the room as quietly as she had entered. A second after the door clicked into place, the beam of her lamplight fell on the hem of a lavishly embroidered dress. She jumped, then slowly tipped the lamp upward to reveal a feminine shape gliding down the hall.

The woman approached at a measured pace, her figure becoming more distinct with each step. The lamp and the sporadically lit wall sconces gave off too little light to make out details, but what Helena could see left her frozen.

The woman was tall and regal as any queen. She moved with understated purpose, every motion deliberate, but never forced or exaggerated. This had to be Lady Fenwick. From tip to toe she exuded confidence. A born aristocrat for certain, even if her astounding dress weren't taken into account.

The woman stopped a few feet away from Helena, peering curiously down at her through a pair of spectacles. She was breathtaking, her sharp aristocratic nose and cheekbones softened by a round face and plump lips. The fashionable empire waist of her gown put her large, gorgeous breasts on full display.

Helena's cheeks warmed. This was hardly an appropriate situation for ogling a lady, but this woman was her every fantasy come to life.

"Baron Neufeld?" the woman asked. "You certainly wasted no time scampering up here. How did you manage to slip past me?"

God, even her voice was beautiful, like the glide of silk over skin.

Helena adopted the slight Germanic lilt her brother had affected as the baron. Better to be mistaken for Seb's alias than caught snooping. "I humbly beg your pardon. I am turned about."

"I can see that." The woman let out a short laugh. "Because unless your letters severely misconstrued your intention *not* to propose to me, you have no reason to be standing outside my chambers. Fenwick's room is across the hall."

Propose to her? She couldn't be Fenwick's wife, then. Who was she?

Helena gave the woman a polite nod and stepped aside. "Thank you for your assistance, my lady."

"Your Grace," the woman corrected. "In case you don't remember from your previous time in our country, the correct honorific for a duchess is Her Grace." She extended a hand. "But let us not stand on formality. We are old friends via our correspondence, are we not? You may simply call me Duchess."

Helena grasped the duchess' proffered hand. Prickles of awareness raced up her arm, despite the soft kid leather preventing skin-to-skin contact.

"I am honored, Duchess." Helena lifted the woman's gloved hand to her lips and kissed her knuckles. "And you must call me Neufeld."

The words came out huskier than she'd intended, and she abruptly released the duchess' hand and took a step backward.

"Let me not keep you from your rest any longer." Helena bowed. "Gute Nacht, Duchess."

"And a good night to you, Baron." The duchess swished by, her skirts brushing Helena's legs as she passed. "I hope come morning we will have more opportunity to get to know one another. I have a sense you are a man of many surprises." She opened her door and disappeared into the room.

Helena blew out a long breath. Her fingers still tingled

from the duchess' touch and her stomach flip-flopped from the near disaster. Tomorrow she would take more care.

As she crept back to her room, the memory of the duchess' mellifluous voice echoed in Helena's mind.

I have a sense you are a man of many surprises.

"You have no idea," Helena whispered to the dark. And she prayed it would remain that way.

Chapter 2

⌒ day two ⌒

AMABEL YOUNG, DUCHESS OF MIRWEALD—in her own right, thank you very much—was not a woman to be trifled with. Since inheriting the duchy at seventeen, she had refused to be quiet, unobtrusive, or conventional. Plenty of her fellow peers hated her, but every cut and snide remark was a reminder of the power they couldn't take from her. Power she didn't hesitate to wield.

Consequently, if Baron Neufeld was responsible for the glum look on the face of her dearest friend, he would soon be ruing every letter he'd ever sent her.

Amabel took a seat at the breakfast table next to the Earl of Fenwick. Oliver—as she'd known him since they were tiny children—stared disconsolately down at his plate, poking at his toast without eating it.

"You don't look like a man brightened by a night of energetic bedsport." As always, she kept her tone cool and her posture composed. After so many years, the role of duchess fit her better than even the finest of her gowns.

Oliver jolted at her words, mangling his toast. "I... what?"

Amabel dipped a knife into a dish of her favorite currant jam and applied a neat layer to her own toast. "I handed you the perfect opportunity for a night of debauchery. How on earth did you manage to bungle it?"

She'd all but thrown Neufeld at Oliver last night, and

7

when she'd encountered the baron in the hall she'd assumed he intended to spend the night in Oliver's room. Either the tryst had gone badly, or it hadn't happened at all.

"I can't believe you think I would hop into bed with the baron," Oliver whispered. "He's here to propose to *you*."

"Oh, pish." Amabel dunked her jam-coated toast into her tea. "Neufeld has no interest in me. He stated as much in his correspondence. His family believes we would be a good match, and he initially wrote to me to determine whether we would suit. He has since concluded—with my encouragement—that we do not."

She took a bite of her toast, reveling in the mixture of flavors and textures—crisp and mushy, sweet and bitter. A microcosm of the world's infinite varieties in a simple breakfast.

Oliver, who kept his food carefully separated, did not share in her pleasure. "And if he's a lying blackguard?" he persisted. "I don't want him to be. I liked him. But you know I have a poor history with charming men."

He did, the unfortunate man. Unlike Amabel, who kept all her lovers at a metaphorical arm's length, Oliver often threw his entire heart into an affair. A year had passed since Lord Rothmere had left him heartbroken and disgraced. The more time passed, the more Amabel fretted. All she wanted was happiness for her friend. She'd planned this house party for the express purpose of helping him. And here he was, forlorn, after but a single day.

"All charming men are liars, darling. It's simply a matter of whether their lies are meant to spread happiness or rob people of it."

Neufeld was a spreading happiness charmer, if she'd read his letters correctly. And given the way he'd gaped at Oliver last night, his lies were likely often for his own protection.

She dunked her toast again, a smug smile stealing across her lips. Here, there was no need to fear. Fenwick House was a safe space for the creatives, the radicals, and the queers. Her

HER FAIR LADY

friends were the voices that populated her magazine and aided in its publication. Recruiting other misfits to speak out against the world's wrongs was among her favorite pastimes.

A cluster of hungry guests flooded into the breakfast room. Whatever had transpired last night had not affected Neufeld the way it had Oliver, for he cheerfully settled into the seat across from the earl and began to chat about tea.

Amabel studied Neufeld as the conversation progressed. He was pretty, with wide dark eyes and short black hair that curled up at the ends. A bit of a rake, and one who seemed only to have eyes for other gentlemen. Clearly, the spark of interest she'd thought she'd sensed when he kissed her hand the previous evening had been her imagination.

Thank goodness for that.

The last thing Amabel wanted was a suitor. She took no interest in men, for one. Besides, she happily enjoyed casual relations with the members of the Sapphic Ladies' Club. Even if she had a woman for a suitor, what use was an affair of the heart? Romance could be left to Oliver. Either she would find him a suitably masculine woman to marry, or she would find him a man, marry him herself, and take them both off the market.

"And you, my dear Lord Fenwick, will be playing the heroic prince, as befits your rank both as a peer and our host," declared Sir Albert Fellowes, cousin to Amabel's sometimes-lover, Maryanne.

All the color drained from Oliver's face.

Oh, dear.

Amabel chewed her toast slowly, contemplating an appropriate response. Sir Albert's plan to put on a play for the ladies could provide a nice diversion for the snowbound party. But if it worsened Oliver's anxiety, it would have to be stopped. She *would* see Oliver whole and happy again, whatever it took.

Oliver excused himself abruptly and ran from the room.

10   CATHERINE STEIN

Before Amabel could put an end to the theatrical nonsense, Neufeld hopped up from his seat, leaving half his food uneaten.

"Excuse me. I should follow Fenwick. Get the house tour he promised."

Sir Albert beamed as the baron dashed away. "Wonderful, wonderful! Those two have such natural magnetism! They will shine as my star-crossed lovers!"

Amabel picked up her teacup, swiftly altering her plan. She would keep watch over Oliver and Neufeld and see how things played out. A fling would do Fenwick a world of good. And if that meant providing time alone with the baron, that was exactly what she would give him.

⁓

How like an aristocrat to have a copy of Debrett's Peerage splayed out on a podium in his library for all to marvel at.

Helena shoved the over-large maid's cap out of her eyes so she could read the text. The pompous tome did have some use to her, when coupled with the gossip the household staff had cheerfully offered up over breakfast. Helena had learned some basic facts about Fenwick: he wasn't married and he'd inherited the title from his grandfather three years prior. She'd also discovered the full identity of the woman from her midnight wanderings. Amabel Esther Sophia Young was Duchess of Mirweald in her own right, and had been for fourteen of her thirty-one years. The entry detailing the history of her duchy spanned more than a full page. Which explained her imperious demeanor. She could probably fell armies with a single condescending look.

"Title bestowed in 1223." Helena shook her head, causing her cap to slide down once again. "They must spawn excellent royal sycophants, seeing how no king has murdered them all and reclaimed the property for the crown."

Though the duchess seemed in no hurry to spawn the next generation. She had no children and had never been

HER FAIR LADY   11

married. At twenty-five, Helena had endured more than enough commentary on her unwed state. A peeress expected to continue the line must suffer endless badgering. Yet she remained a spinster and laughed at the idea of a Bavarian nobleman proposing. Helena quite liked her.

Helena stepped away from the Debrett's and tried again to wrangle her cap into place. The uniform she'd borrowed from the laundry fit well, but the cap was meant to cover the long hair most women wore. It drooped and sagged over Helena's short waves.

The door creaked open and Helena jumped. She clamped a hand down atop the cap to keep it from flying off as she whirled around.

"If you're looking for the Gothic novels, you'll need to go up to the next floor." The duchess made a brisk gesture at the ceiling.

Helena jerked her head down and stared at the floor, praying the duchess hadn't looked closely at her. The cap fell into her eyes, and this time she didn't push it back up.

She curtsied. "Beg pardon, Your Grace."

"My dear girl, never apologize for improving your mind. Men wish us to be empty-headed baby-vessels. We must therefore take it upon ourselves to learn and think. Moreover, we must encourage other women to do the same. I would never deny you access to books, and I can assure you that Fenwick feels the same. Please read as much as you like. Now, are you truly interested in…" The duchess peered at the shelf behind Helena. "*Taxonomy of English Grasses*, or would you prefer something more… adventuresome?"

A hint of a smile accompanied the duchess' final word, lending it a hint of mischief. Helena's stomach flipped in a mixture of excitement and panic. It would not do to discover that Her Grace had a naughty side or a playful one. Friendships and flirtations were out of the question.

You are the self-appointed Sensible Twin. Don't ever forget.

Sebastian would no doubt get himself into plenty of trouble, and Helena would have to be the one to get him out of it. A pretty peeress was a complication best avoided altogether.

"Would you like directions to the small library upstairs?" the duchess inquired.

Helena grabbed *Taxonomy of English Grasses* off the shelf. "No, thank you, Your Grace. Taxonomy sounds most improving." She curtsied again before scampering off. Enough reconnaissance of the enemy. It was time to find the pearls and get the hell out.

Chapter 3

ᴏ⌁

HELENA BUTTONED UP the waistcoat her brother had been using to playact as Baron Neufeld and considered her reflection in the looking glass.

Behind her, Seb flung himself dramatically onto the bed. "Damnation. I almost kissed him."

"Fenwick?" Helena nearly squeaked the name. They hadn't even been here twenty-four hours and already things were going topsy-turvy.

"He's sweet," Seb said dreamily. "He has adorable freckles and is very passionate when he's not afraid of the whole world watching. I don't know why he would steal anything, let alone an innocent woman's jewels."

Helena stuck to a recitation of the facts, her best tactic for maintaining a rational state of mind. "He was seen by the doorman tucking an unusual gray and pink pearl necklace into his pocket as he left the charity dinner. Multiple people have confirmed that he left the event conspicuously early and alone. It was the first time he'd been in public in over a year. People would notice him."

The thief's identity wasn't up for debate, and it didn't matter how nice he seemed or how much her romantically addle-headed brother wanted to bed him. Mother's necklace was somewhere in this house, and Helena meant to find it.

Fortunately, one glance out the window told her that the

13

snow continued to fall in earnest. No one would be leaving Fenwick House for at least a few days.

And now it was Helena's turn to take the stage.

She left Seb to play maid or valet—or to simply wallow in the bedroom—and headed down to the party. The role of Baron Neufeld came easily: a bit of swagger, a dash of flirtation, and a whole heap of self-confidence. Men could get away with almost anything, simply by acting as if they were entitled to it. This aspect of their so-called civilization enraged Helena, but that didn't mean she was above taking advantage of it. Especially in pursuit of justice.

She found a portion of the party relaxing in a large room with emerald green wallpaper and enviously cozy furniture. A tall woman decked in blue sat embroidering on one of the couches, while the man beside her chattered away about some kind of amateur theatrical.

"You'll love it, my dear," the man gushed. "I can't give away too much, because it's to be a surprise for the ladies, but Sir Albert assures me that the performance will have romance and drama to thrill your feminine heart."

The woman set her embroidery in her lap and smiled fondly at the man. "The same way you thrilled my feminine heart with a bouquet full of bees when we were courting?"

He turned red. "My dear Mrs. Whitcomb, can you never let me forget?" He looked around the room at the others gathered there. "I didn't know it was full of bees. They blended in with the yellow petals!"

A laugh to Helena's left made her turn. A handsome woman in a gentleman's suit came striding toward her. "If you lack for entertainment, Baron, spend time with the Whitcombs. They have the best stories of their life together. Not sure any of the tales are true, though."

"How diverting," Helena replied. "Thank you for the advice, ah…"

"Beauclair." The woman extended a hand. "George, today.

Her Fair Lady

The suit." She indicated her garments. "If you see me in a full suit, I'm George. A skirt, I'm Georgia. Otherwise, anything goes. And don't worry about lord/lady, mister/miss, he/she. I answer to most anything that's not an insult."

"Ah. Sehr gut," Helena replied, exhausting her entire knowledge of German. She shook hands with George. "A pleasure to meet you."

"Likewise. To be honest, I'd expected you'd be a prat 'til I saw you flirting with Fenwick this morning, and then I said, 'Eh, he's one of us, ain't he.' Welcome to the house of queers, Baron Neufeld of Bavaria."

The house of queers? Helena had her suspicions about the duchess, and Fenwick seemed to be of Seb's persuasion, but she would never have expected this. To speak openly of such matters, as if they were at a secret club in town? Or backstage at the theater?

Sebastian's behavior made a bit more sense now. He was right that this party didn't fit with their original image of Fenwick as a haughty thief. Still, scoundrels came in all varieties. And aristos were more often than not the worst of the lot.

"I am pleased to find broad-minded people," Helena said at last.

George chuckled. "Like-minded, at any rate. Not all too bright, though. Take Tunsbury, scribbling away at the desk over there. Writes the worst poetry. Don't let him read to you."

"George, darling." The duchess' satin voice slithered beneath Helena's garments, raising gooseflesh on her arms. "Don't tell me you're attempting to scare Neufeld away already. He only arrived yesterday. Besides, I'm sure he's a man of enough character to handle Tunsbury."

"Long as I don't have to handle him. Been there, done that. Decent tup, but, gad! The poetry!" George gave a cheeky grin and scampered off.

"Interesting chap," Helena mused.

"Yes," the duchess drawled. "The lovely Lady George. Founder of the Sapphic Ladies' Club, not that you would be interested in that, my dear baron."

Helena wanted to respond that, actually, she was quite interested, but she forced a chuckle. "Your club may not be for me, but I am always interested in interesting people."

The duchess tapped Helena's arm with her fan. "I'm sure you are. Now, tell me, Baron, how did you enjoy Fenwick's tour of the house?"

"It was most pleasant," Helena scanned the room to avoid looking the duchess in the eye. Damnation. She ought to have pressed Sebastian for more information. She didn't even know if Seb had seen the house, or if the tour had merely been a pretense for flirtation and almost-kissing. "It is a grand house, and excellently maintained."

"Indeed." The duchess fanned herself, causing a slight breeze to touch Helena's cheek. "My own home is not half so picturesque, I'm afraid. My predecessors were somewhat lax, and repairs have been ongoing for years. Fortunately, I have a dear friend and neighbor in Fenwick. We are rather like family." She paused, and her voice dropped ever so slightly. "Family who look after one another."

"He is fortunate to have so stalwart a lady at his side," Helena replied. "No doubt you are privy to all his secrets, clever as you seem." She glanced at the duchess, whose hazel eyes narrowed behind her spectacles.

"You flatter me, Baron."

"I speak only the truth."

"Is that so? It is a rare man indeed who can make such a boast." The duchess waved her fan lazily. "Or a liar. Which are you?"

"See? Clever!"

The duchess' full lips tilted upward in a calculating smile. "As are you, sir." She lifted her fan to hide her mouth. "As are

you." Hazel eyes tracked up and down, sending prickles of unease racing along Helena's skin.

Silly, she scolded herself. She'd doubled her brother dozens of times. Maybe hundreds. They'd played characters, switched places, been men and women and both and neither. No one ever saw through the ruse. They'd even fooled their mother on occasion. She had no reason to fear the duchess' penetrating gaze.

Helena took a step backwards. "And now it is I who must plead myself unworthy of your gracious words." She bowed. "It has been a pleasure, Your Grace. I will not take more of your time, but I look forward to future conversations."

The duchess snapped her fan closed. "Likewise." She nodded curtly and strode toward the Whitcombs. "Angelica, dear, do take a turn about the room with me. It will give the gentlemen a chance to get better acquainted."

Helena relaxed into her role as she greeted Lord Fenwick's friends. And if her gaze strayed to Amabel, Duchess of Mirweald a time or two—or three—it was only to assure herself that she was beyond suspicion.

Chapter 4

⟶ day three ⟵

*A*MABEL EXCUSED HERSELF after luncheon, giving no reason for abandoning the party. No one asked, naturally. She was a duchess, and therefore had no need to explain herself. No feigned headaches or urgent correspondence necessary.

Also, in this particular case, half the guests were intoxicated and all the guests were too busy gossiping about Fenwick and Neufeld to pay Amabel any attention. Even her fellow Club members were caught up in the drama.

She swept up the stairs toward her rooms, barely heeding her surroundings while her mind whirled. A bit of quiet to collect her thoughts would do her a world of good. Amabel didn't do well when confined, and even a large house like this one couldn't provide the same escape as a rambling walk. Outside every window, the snow continued to fall, like a taunt from the heavens.

You're stuck here, little girl. Stuck inside while the boys all play.

Or in this particular case, stuck inside with the boys, including one highly suspicious Bavarian lord.

Amabel had no clear evidence that Neufeld wasn't who he said he was, only her sense that something was odd. Their banter last night had bordered on flirtatious, yet this morning, his full attention had appeared fixed on Oliver.

"It doesn't have to mean anything," she muttered. "He likes Oliver best. And when Oliver's not around, he flirts with the closest person."

18

Her Fair Lady   19

It was common enough rake behavior, and the baron had seemed shrewd enough in their correspondence to be an effective charmer. Amabel's mind, however, wouldn't listen to reason. It continued to buzz, demanding her attention.

She turned toward the guest rooms, rather than her own suite in the family wing. A quick peek into Neufeld's room would tell her plenty. If the man was a danger to Oliver, she'd discover it and toss him out into the cold.

The *snick* of a door opening down the corridor caught her attention. *Neufeld's room.* Someone had beaten her to the punch.

The chambermaid who emerged wore a plain black uniform slightly too large for her slender frame. Strands of blond hair stuck out from a white cap that tilted down over her eyes. She jumped when she spotted Amabel, then executed a hasty curtsy.

"Your Grace," she murmured.

Amabel continued down the hall toward the maid, her strides smooth but purposeful. "The girl from the library," she guessed. "Reading the taxonomy book."

"Yes, ma'am." The young woman neither trembled nor looked away. Cheeky, for a servant caught leaving a room she had no business in.

"And how have you enjoyed your study of English grasses?" If the girl wanted to play games, Amabel would give her a taste of how it felt to take on a duchess.

"It's quite interesting, Your Grace. The *Phleum pratense*, for example, is a good food source for livestock. Unfortunately, it is also a common irritant for humans, and responsible for rather a lot of sneezing and itching eyes during its summer flowering season. Tall, cylindrical flowers, if you're seeking to avoid it.

"On the other hand, the pendulous sedge—that's *Carex pendula*—is a lovely grass. It has long, thin flower spikes that droop elegantly from tall stalks. Quite common in England and Wales in wet areas and clay soils. And in the event you find

yourself lost in an ancient swamp, the seeds are edible and the leaves can be woven into rope and matting." The girl had the audacity to curtsy again. "Your Grace."

A lifetime of practice kept Amabel's surprise hidden beneath her untouchable duchess demeanor. This young woman was more than cheeky. She was positively brazen. And Amabel adored brazen women. Nothing made a woman more attractive, in her opinion, than defiance of social norms.

How unfortunate that this particular rebel was an employee of one of her guests. And, apparently, some type of snoop or thief.

Amabel stopped a few paces from the other woman. Even shaded by the cap, something about her facial features seemed familiar. And not because of their brief encounter in the library.

"Who is your employer?"

"Baron Neufeld, Your Grace," the woman replied without hesitation.

She was quick-witted, Amabel had to admit. More attractive with every action. A pity.

"That would explain what you were doing in the baron's chambers." Amabel clasped her hands behind her back. "Except for the fact that Baron Neufeld arrived in a snowstorm that has not yet abated, and his only companion was his valet."

The maid tipped her chin up insolently, and a jolt of recognition hit Amabel. This girl had Neufeld's face. The same nose, the same cheekbones, the same puckish smile.

"I am his valet," she insisted. "I dress as I will, and I do my job, regardless of my sex. You are a woman in a position usually reserved for a man. I'm sure you understand."

"I do. That is not all you are, however."

The valet's expression hardened. "What are you implying?"

"You are a relative of Neufeld's," Amabel replied breezily. "You bear him a strong resemblance."

It all made sense. A half-sister, most likely, given a position close to her brother to keep her safe and provide her a certain

HER FAIR LADY 21

amount of freedom. She could afford to be mildly impudent, with a Lord as a brother. She was probably well-educated too, and liberal in her attitudes. Connected to the aristocracy, but not of them.

Amabel smiled. Yes, she understood this woman. "But have no fear," she added. "Your secrets are safe with me."

"You are perceptive, Your Grace. Please excuse me, I wish to check in on our horses before I resume my other duties." She curtsied again and started down the hall, sweeping past Amabel as though she were a piece of furniture rather than a peeress.

"Before you go," Amabel called.

The valet glanced over her shoulder. "Yes?"

"What is your name? In case we meet again, I'd like to know what to call you."

"Helena." She turned back abruptly and strode away, her movements as confident as any aristocrat.

"Helena." A fitting name for a fiery lady. A name for goddesses and saints and queens. The sort of name Amabel would enjoy gasping in the throes of pleasure, were the barriers of rank and hospitality not an obstacle.

It was not to be, in this instance. She couldn't seduce every spirited woman she met. This one, though, stung a bit more than most. They bantered so naturally. They would challenge one another, in and out of bed, she had no doubt.

"Well." Amabel turned back toward her own room. She'd made some new discoveries. She could delve further into the mystery of the Baron and his valet-sister later. First, she was going to talk to her friends and see if one of the ladies wanted a bedmate for the evening. She was obviously too lusty for her own good.

A healthy romp would banish thoughts of sassy Helena and her pretty smile.

Chapter 5

⟶ day four ⟳

AN UNINTELLIGIBLE MUMBLE came from the general area of the bed.

"What was that?" Helena asked.

"The baron is indisposed," Seb repeated. "I told everyone so last night. You can't waltz down there all spry and cheerful."

"I don't waltz anywhere." Helena shrugged out of her waistcoat and tossed it aside.

"You do," Sebastian insisted. "Especially when you play dress-up. It's a family trait. You can't escape it."

Helena ducked into the dressing room to survey their modest wardrobe. Her pilfered maid's uniform hung there, along with both pairs of traveling clothes, an extra suit, a few shirts and waistcoats, and their red party dress.

She rubbed the silk between her fingers, imagining the duchess' face if she saw Helena dressed as a Lady. Helena could do the Wright family waltz into the room, dress swirling, wearing Mother's recovered pearls. She would give the entire household a scathing rebuke and make the smug aristocrats cower. All while the duchess gaped at her in surprise and admiration.

Helena jerked her hand away.

Her mind was spinning nonsense. Toffs didn't submit to accusations by a commoner. And no gorgeous duchess was going to pay her the least attention. The last thing she needed

22

was to start believing the kind of romantic fantasies her brother did.

She reached for the last item in the wardrobe, a yellow dressing gown covered in garish yellow-brown embroidered vines. It had belonged to her stepfather until her mother had insisted on buying him a replacement. Sebastian had nabbed it immediately for their "costume collection."

Helena cinched the robe tight and ran her fingers through her hair. The too-large garment covered everything but her stocking feet and a rumpled bit of shirt. Perfect for an ailing lord stumbling out of bed for a snack. She applied a touch of gritty, dark makeup to her jaw to mimic a days' growth of beard—a trick she'd learned from her mother's theater associates, several of whom readily switched between male and female presentations both on and off stage.

"I'm popping down to the party," she announced. "You can wallow in bed all you want, but I'm getting some food and tea and taking a look around. I've had no luck finding the necklace up here, but someone in this house must know where it is."

Seb only grunted as she walked out the door.

A short time later, she stepped into the dining room to an earnest, "Still ailing, dear fellow?" from Sir Albert.

"Headache," Helena mumbled. "Tea and rest will cure me."

"Indeed, indeed." The baronet clapped her on the shoulder hard enough to make her stagger. "Drink up, lad, drink up. We'll need you hale and hearty to play our blushing damsel, eh?" He thumped her again.

"Mmph."

"Just so. Take some time to read over your lines as you recover. We'll be rehearsing tomorrow. Now, you must excuse me. I've a fencing lesson with Hawthorne. Cheeky boy, that one, but good with a sword, eh?" Sir Albert nudged her with his elbow and departed.

Helena blew out a relieved breath. Nothing short of the

24   CATHERINE STEIN

devil himself would keep her here long enough for either Seb
or herself to perform in that man's absurd theatrical.

Get the necklace. Get out.

She filled her belly with tea and toast, then returned to
her room, taking a different route to get a look into a few more
rooms. Let the games begin.

᠆

By late afternoon, Helena had developed a satisfactory mental
map of the house and had spoken briefly with most of the
guests. Each quick trip for food or tea provided a few more
possible hiding places for the stolen jewels. Minimal progress,
but better than nothing.

Most of the party had settled in the Green Salon for tea
and sandwiches. Helena poked her head in long enough to
grab a bite to eat, but didn't talk to anyone or linger more than
a moment. This was her opportunity. Fenwick would be busy
eating with his friends, leaving his personal study unoccupied.

And a private study was by far the most likely place to hide
stolen valuables.

Helena fingered the lockpicks in her dressing gown pocket.
A few minutes was all she needed.

The study door was locked, as expected, and Helena
twisted the doorknob a few times before kneeling to inspect
the lock itself. Both the door and the lock were sturdy, but
old. Even an amateur could have the door open with a bit of
practice. Helena had been picking locks since she was seven,
thanks to the enterprising woman who had minded the twins
during Mother's performances. Sebastian had gleefully learned
to cheat at cards, while Helena had developed the ability to
open every door in the theater.

She slotted a pick into the keyhole and probed the lock,
her fingers learning the bumps and dips as the tool moved. A
straightforward job. She applied a bit of pressure, then added
a second pick and a third. Tingles of anticipation blossomed

inside her with each shift of a tumbler, and when the lock clicked open, her triumph burst out in a happy little dance. It was silly, that carefree twirl, a remnant of her childhood. Not suited to the sensible twin.

Helena opened the door and stuffed the lockpicks back into her pocket. This ridiculous charade was getting to her, apparently. Honestly, masquerading as an ailing Bavarian lord and tromping through the house in her stepfather's appalling dressing gown? Mother had acted in farces less absurd.

The click of a hard-soled shoe on the floor made Helena jump. She spun away from the door and broke into a confident stride—just a man out for a stroll.

"Baron?" a polished voice inquired.

The duchess. Fuck.

Helena turned around slowly. "Ah. Duchess. Hello." She'd been doing her best to avoid the other woman today. Amabel Young was far too intriguing, with her sharp mind, commanding presence, and lush figure. She made Helena want to flirt like a shameless courtesan.

Which she might have done, had they been in London. And if the duchess wasn't the loyal friend of the enemy.

"Is this the way to the stairs?" Helena made an awkward gesture in the direction she'd been walking. "I still get lost in this house and my head is fuzzy today."

"It must be, for you to be loitering outside Fenwick's study," the duchess replied dryly. She moved purposefully down the hall toward Helena.

Helena backed away, holding up both hands. "Please do not come too near, Your Grace. My ailment may be only a headache, but I would hate to risk your health, should it prove to be something catching."

The duchess stopped and crossed her arms. Her brows knit together above her spectacles. Damn, but she looked good in the unladylike posture.

"For your sake, Baron, I hope it is a headache and nothing

26   CATHERINE STEIN

more… regrettable." Her gaze flicked to the study door, which
stood noticeably ajar.

"Many thanks for your concern." Helena bowed. "I'm
certain I will recover soon enough. But I must to bed now, to
recover my wits. Was I going the right way?"

The duchess's smile was tight, and her posture didn't
change. "You were. Continue to the end of the hall and turn
left. That will lead you to the stairs. And in the future, if
you are not feeling yourself, kindly ring for tea rather than
attempting to fetch it." Her smile grew, exposing a hint of
teeth. "How like a man."

Helena bowed again, while a litany of swears sounded in
her mind. Stupid, stupid, she was so damnably stupid! Foolishly
overconfident. She'd been caught near an unlocked door by the
shrewdest person in the house and she had no one to blame
but herself. If everything went pear-shaped, she couldn't even
flee because of the snow. Nothing left to do but brazen it out.

"Good day, Duchess." She turned away and headed directly
for her room, without a backward glance.

⌒

The scheming little minx. Admiration and irritation warred in
Amabel's mind as she watched the hideous yellow dressing
gown disappear around the corner. She did love an ambitious
woman. Even one who would go snooping through an earl's
private rooms.

Unless said ambitious snoop had nefarious intent toward
Oliver. No one trifled with Amabel's friends under her watch.
Not anymore. Not ever.

She walked to the study door and closed it. She'd have to
remind Fenwick to make certain it was kept locked.

"What could she want?" Amabel tapped one slipper as
she thought.

The maid/valet/baron's sister—if it had been her, Amabel
couldn't say for absolute certain—had Neufeld's protection.

Her Fair Lady

And likely his esteem and affection, since she appeared free to behave as she pleased.

Did she aspire to more? Money to run off on her own? A titled husband? Either could provide a motive for breaking into Oliver's study.

But maybe the girl was simply curious, and she'd taken advantage of the baron's illness to wander the halls and peek into open rooms.

"Maybe you're altogether too interested in the chit," Amabel grumbled.

She checked the study door again, to ensure it wouldn't swing open, and went to find Fenwick. She would protect him. Whatever it took.

I'm going to unravel you, Helena Neufeld, or whoever you are. I'm going to strip you bare, one way or another.

Chapter 6

⁓ day five ⁓

Amabel eyed Baron Neufeld as he sauntered toward the opposite end of the breakfast table. His suit was tidy, with a waistcoat of pale blue and a neckcloth the color of claret.

And who are you this morning? The real baron or his saucy sister?

She knew which she was hoping for.

"Neufeld! Here you are at last." Mr. Whitcomb raised a hand in greeting. "Thought you might miss breakfast entirely."

"Late night?" Casper Hawthorne smirked. "Please, have a seat and tell us what could possibly have kept you up."

Amabel raised an eyebrow at the fencing instructor. Honestly, the man was an inveterate tease. How Fenwick put up with him was a mystery. Though, perhaps it was good for Oliver to have someone to push him a bit. And Amabel knew Casper would never hesitate to defend their friend against anyone.

Neufeld riposted as smoothly as one of Hawthorne's fencing moves, cocking a hip and grinning down at the seated guests.

"I have better ways to occupy my lips than with idle gossip."

"Oh, ho!" Tunsbury cried. "His tongue is as sharp as your sword, Hawthorne. Perhaps he should give you lessons."

The baron took a seat beside Tunsbury. "I don't believe the swordmaster has much care for the cunning arts of a linguist."

HER FAIR LADY   29

Amabel didn't laugh with the rest of the party, but she tilted her head in a brief nod of approval. This "baron" was the sister. She was certain of it. And the cheeky lass was playing the crowd masterfully.

"Better for the ladies if he keeps his sword away from us," Maryellen piped up. An artist with a talent for drawing buxom beauties in flagrante, she rarely passed up the opportunity for ribald wordplay. "I hear he's known for finishing duels with a single thrust."

"Mmm. I'm a fan of a long, slow death, myself." Neufeld gave Maryellen a flirtatious eyebrow raise.

I see you Helena. What game are you playing? And can I play along?

When the latest burst of laughter from the crowd began to fade, Amabel stared down Neufeld's sister and said, "Tell us, Baron, is your experience here similar to what you might find at house parties in Bavaria?"

"Ah, no. Nein. In Bavaria, we have *castle* parties." Helena overemphasized the accent that had mostly slipped away since her arrival.

Amabel hadn't thought much of the change before. Neufeld had spent many years studying in England as a youth. She could hardly be surprised if he readapted easily to speaking English. Yet in their previous exchanges, Helena had spoken like a well-bred Londoner, neither foreigner nor housemaid. Either she, too, had spent time on British soil, or she adapted chameleon-like to her surroundings.

"And are your castle parties as diverting as this one?" Amabel asked.

Helena met her gaze. Even at this distance the duchess caught the twinkle in those dark eyes. "I couldn't say, Your Grace. Our parties involve a great deal more beer. If done properly, we remember little the next morning."

"How very Dionysian," Maryellen said. "But, then, all good house parties are."

30   CATHERINE STEIN

Sir Albert raised his teacup. "To the god of alcohol and theater! Clear your plates, chaps! Rehearsals begin now!"

"You'll have to catch me later, Sir Albert," Helena said smoothly. "I have not yet eaten a bite."

Oliver pushed his chair away from the table. "And I have correspondence to attend to. Good morning, all. I shall see you at luncheon."

The other Neufeld would have found some excuse to follow Fenwick from the room, but Helena remained in her seat and poured herself some tea. Amabel waited for the rest of the men to leave, then moved down the table to sit across from Helena.

She gestured at the other ladies. "And here we are. The wine god and his maenads."

Georgia smoothed out a non-existent wrinkle in her dress. "Oh, are we engaging in ritual debauchery? I wouldn't say no to entertaining our visiting Lord, but I fear that would make Fenwick jealous. We may have to engage in conversation instead. Maryellen, tell us what you're drawing for Amabel's next publication."

"Publication?" Helena lifted a brow and glanced at Amabel.

"A magazine for queer and liberal readers," Maryellen explained. "It encourages social reforms, advocates for the rights of the oppressed, and publishes art often deemed 'immoral.' For instance, an etching of two ladies kissing, or a poem about a person like Georgia, who is both man and woman."

Helena's face lit up like a child given a bag full of sweets. She was a striking woman, especially now, when her wide eyes and bright smile emphasized her delicate nose and the elf-like point of her chin. Her features were, perhaps, too angular to be considered traditionally beautiful, but Amabel had never been one to cleave to Society's standards. Beauty was an uncanny, shifting thing.

And this was the land of the Old Gods. Even a rational mind like Amabel's could be open to the possibility of the otherworldly. Maybe fae blood ran in the veins of the intriguing

Miss Neufeld. It would explain how she could swap places so smoothly with her brother. A touch of magic, invisible to only the most perceptive.

"What say you, Duchess?" Georgia swirled her tea as if it were brandy. "Should the next issue feature 'Mrs. Whitcomb's Embroidery Patterns for the Improvement of Young Ladies'?"

Amabel adjusted her spectacles to hide the fact that she'd missed part of the conversation. "I think that would delight our readers."

Maryanne leaned toward Neufeld. Ever soft-spoken, she struggled at times to be heard in group conversations. Here, among friends, all other noise ceased so as not to cover up her words.

"What you don't know, dear Baron, is that Mrs. Whitcomb's patterns all spell out rude words. It's rather a joke in our circles."

Helena grinned. "I know a few young ladies who would love that."

"Most young ladies love it, I find," Mrs. Whitcomb said proudly.

Helena laughed. "You clearly know the right sort of people."

"As do you, I wager." Amabel allowed a slight smile to crack her duchess facade. "It seems you fit in here exceptionally well. I would not have guessed it, based on your correspondence alone."

Helena's brows narrowed, though her smile didn't falter. "People are full of surprises, I always find."

"Indeed they are." Amabel rose from her seat. "Thank you for the conversation ladies." She gave Helena a pointed look. "And gentleman. I'm going to check the state of the weather and possibility of some outdoor entertainment for our party. I have been cooped up too long indoors." She nodded and swept from the room.

Helena's morning had been perfect. She'd fully searched two more downstairs rooms. She'd had an enjoyable—no, *marvelous*— conversation over breakfast with the ladies of the party.

It was therefore inevitable that her afternoon had fallen completely apart.

Her twin stood facing her in the center of their bedroom, his expression pleading. They were eye-to-eye, nose-to-nose, nearly identical to the casual observer, save for different colored cravats. Two versions of Baron Neufeld, wandering the same house at the same time. If she hadn't gone back to the room to use the Necessary... If she'd been at lunch...

What a mess.

As much as she wanted to blame Sebastian, Helena knew she was equally at fault. She'd hardly spoken to him over the last couple of days, too distracted with her games. She'd been playing, not working, having far too much fun donning disguises and bantering with the duchess.

And where had the snooping and flirtations got her?

Helena huffed.

Nowhere, that's where. She hadn't found the necklace, anything more with the duchess was an impossibility, and her soft-hearted brother had apparently gone and fallen for the thieving Earl of Fenwick. Fallen hard enough that he'd confessed his real identity, the sap.

Honestly, how can I love someone so much and find them so aggravating at the same time?

Composure settled over Seb's face. "Maybe we *should* tell him everything."

"Don't you dare."

No way in hell was she letting her beloved, *foolish* brother accuse an earl of a crime in a house full of his friends and allies. That was a good way to get dropped in a convenient ditch and never seen again.

HER FAIR LADY 33

She held up a hand to prevent Seb from interrupting. "You can be his friend. You can be his bedmate. But do not ruin this. I didn't come all this way, ride through shitty weather, and endure meddlesome duchesses, only to fail. You go have your fun; keep Fenwick busy. I'll find the pearls, and then we can leave."

A sensible strategy. She hadn't lost her head that much. She'd only been thrown a bit off course by an unexpectedly curious adversary. Time to correct and move on.

Sebastian appeared to consider the plan, then said, softly, "What if I don't want to leave?"

Helena's heart twinged. In a world where men weren't allowed to be dainty and gentle, Seb was both. Of course he'd taken one look at Fenwick's group of oddball friends and lost his heart.

She understood the temptation. A publication for queer readers. A Sapphic Ladies' Club. People who shared her ideals and sense of humor. God, how she wanted these things. But this was not and never would be the place. Fenwick House was a snow-covered fantasy palace. A fairy tale. A siren to her sailor, and Helena was keeping her ears fully plugged.

She put a hand comfortingly on her brother's shoulder. "You'll get over him, Sebastian. You always do. A month from now, another pretty face will come along and you'll move on." She gave him a pat. "Let's sit down and make a list of all the places we haven't yet searched."

Seb turned away and sprawled on the bed. "The billiard room, because it's always occupied. The kitchens. Fenwick's personal study. The butler's pantry."

"I've only glanced in the rooms in the family wing," Helena replied. "Try to search Fenwick's suite while you're romancing him. I'll do the others. Kitchens and pantry are unlikely hiding places, so we'll save those for last. The study we'll have to search at night, because the duchess is already suspicious and might

be expecting another break-in attempt. Ugh. I hate picking locks by candlelight."

Helena doubted Seb was listening anymore, but she was mostly talking to herself anyway. *Search the rooms, find the pearls, no flirting, no flirting, no flirting.*

Helena Wright was the Rational Twin. Helena Wright could resist the magic of this house.

She glanced out the window at the cold, gray landscape. The snow lay in deep drifts, but no more fell from the skies. In time, every storm ended.

Every fantasy did too.

Chapter 7

⟜ day six ⟜

*O*UTDOORS AT LAST!

Amabel breathed deeply as she led the household away from Fenwick House. Sunlight streamed from the cloudless blue sky, glinting off the heaps of snow and turning the frosty trees into shining jewels. The brightness made her squint, but she didn't care. They were out in the fresh air, free to stretch limbs too long unused.

The air smelled of winter: cold and snow and the tang of evergreen trees. With each pull into her lungs, Amabel lightened. Nature restored her, refueled her, and when she later retreated inside, it would be with a sense of peace and purpose.

Today, though, was for play.

Amabel turned and held up a hand, and the procession came obediently to a halt. Guests and servants alike peered at her from beneath cloaks and behind scarves. She let them wait expectantly for a few silent moments, then flung her arms wide and fell backward into the snow with a cry of, "Tally-ho!"

The crowd cheered. Amabel waved her arms and legs to create the first snow angel of the season.

And they were off. This was hardly the first time Amabel and her friends had gathered for such an event. Whenever the snow lay deep enough, at least a few of them tried to assemble to play like children. But years had passed since they'd had a snow this deep and this perfect for frolicking.

36   CATHERINE STEIN

The duchess rose to her feet and shook the snow from her coat. The angel wasn't perfect, but it was satisfactory for the first attempt of the winter. She started on a meandering stroll around the garden, enjoying the sting of the wind on her cheeks and the burn in her thighs as she tromped through deep drifts.

The others needed no further encouragement to take full advantage of the weather. Half-a-dozen snowmen appeared in minutes, while more elaborate creations formed slowly around them. The Whitcombs repeatedly tumbled one another into snowbanks, then "apologized" with kisses. Casper gathered sticks for an impromptu fencing lesson. All was indeed merry and bright.

More time than usual passed before a familiar *thud* and subsequent shriek announced the opening salvo of a snowball fight. Amabel ducked behind the nearest bush.

A nearby group of housemaids, led by a woman in a knitted blue cap and scarf, hurled snowballs at a snow pyramid that had to be Oliver's doing.

"We're under attack! Take cover!" the earl cried out. He grabbed Baron Neufeld's arm, and both men disappeared behind the pyramid, narrowly avoiding a snowball launched by the housemaid in the blue cap.

"You there, with me!" Amabel commanded. The group of maids remained half-hidden behind a fallen snowman. A couple of footmen rushed to the duchess' side. "Defensive fortifications, now. I'll make the ammunition."

A clump of snow hit the bush, breaking apart and showering her with powder. She retaliated with a high, arcing throw that landed inches shy of Oliver's pyramid.

I always was a better commander than soldier.

"Aim for the pyramid and call your friends," she told the footmen. "This will be a long fight!"

Amabel rolled ball after ball as she assessed the situation. Lord Tunsbury had joined Oliver and the baron as one faction.

HER FAIR LADY

Casper and several admirers made up another, though they were too busy flirting to pose much of a threat. The Whitcombs would be her biggest challenge. Mrs. Whitcomb's gentle elegance hid a keen eye and a powerful arm. She rarely mentioned her boyhood in a London gang, but she didn't hesitate to use the skills she'd developed during the time. Without reinforcements, Amabel and her associates would fall quickly.

The duchess sprang from her semi-protective spot and raced to the nearby cluster of housemaids. She seized the cloak of the woman with the blue scarf and hat.

"You started this war, so I'm claiming you for my team." Amabel pulled the woman around to face her and froze.

Most of the woman's face was covered by hat and scarf, but those golden-brown eyes and the slim point of her nose were unmistakable.

"Helena," Amabel gasped.

A look of absolute terror passed over Helena's features before she schooled it into an expression of polite calm. "I would be honored to join your team, Your Grace." She gestured to the other maids to follow. "To the bush! Bring all the snowballs you can carry!"

The group scurried to obey, joining Amabel's men behind the shrubbery. Helena whipped off her cloak and flung it over the bush before ducking down behind.

"There, now they can't see us. You two, help the men build up our eastern defenses. And you—Martha, was it? You keep a lookout behind us. How's your aim, Your Grace?"

Amabel lifted a single eyebrow. "Someone thinks she's the general in this battle, I see."

Helena didn't falter. "I'll do the throwing, then. Along with the big fellow, once the fortifications are a few inches taller. You can throw, I presume?" she asked the footman.

"Yes, ma'am," he replied.

Amabel shifted close to Helena. "You've never been in

38   CATHERINE STEIN

service a day in your life, have you?" she asked quietly. "You give orders like a professional, but you clearly don't know how to take them."

Helena's eyes narrowed. She rose up, threw three snowballs in rapid succession, then crouched down again. "It's a game, Your Grace, and one I'm good at. Would you instead have me pretend to be something I'm not?"

Amabel had to swallow a laugh. The absolute nerve of this woman! "You do play fearlessly. I can respect that."

"No other way to play. I play to win, whatever the odds. Even if I fail, I know I've tried my hardest."

Helena checked on the fort builders, then launched another attack on Oliver's pyramid. This time she was too slow taking cover, and a snowball struck a glancing blow to her shoulder. She flicked the snow off her clothing.

"Put your cloak back on," Amabel chided. "You'll catch your death."

"Nah. The action keeps me plenty warm." Her smile was hidden behind her scarf, but her cheeks lifted and her nose twitched in the most adorable way. Begging to be kissed, the little witch.

Bugger. Amabel needed a distraction.

She rolled a snowball and heaved it at Casper, who stood— bravely and foolishly—in front of his group, directing them where to attack. She hit him squarely in the back, and he crumpled dramatically to the ground.

"Our king hath fallen!" cried Sir Albert.

A groomsman snatched up Casper's stick sword and raised it above his head. "Vengeance for the king!"

The whole group stormed Amabel's fort, and her orderly strategy collapsed into chaos. Snow flew everywhere. Limbs flailed and bodies tumbled to the ground amid shrieks of mingled outrage and laughter.

Amabel ran for the nearest tree. Before she could even catch her breath, someone crashed into her from behind. If

she'd been any less balanced, or the person any larger, she would have fallen on her face. She spun, raising her hands to defend herself.

"Sorry." Helena fiddled with the clasp of her cloak. "Was running and dressing at the same time."

Amabel had a fleeting vision of pushing Helena flat on her back in the snow. She crossed her arms and turned up her nose instead.

"Why did you follow me?"

Helena's cap had gone askew, revealing expressive dark eyebrows that lifted in amusement. "You conscripted me, Princess. I wouldn't want to be thought a deserter."

Amabel gaped, then snapped her mouth closed. "Princess?"

"Duchess didn't seem lofty enough."

Only a lifetime of restraint stopped Amabel from fulfilling her fantasy of shoving Helena into a snowbank. "You have quite the mouth for a valet. Do you speak like this to the baron?"

"No, I'm much ruder to him." Helena curtsied. "Your Highness."

Amabel adjusted her spectacles to hide the smile she couldn't stop. Dammit, she liked this sassy spitfire. Even her friends sometimes slipped into deference to her title. But Helena wasn't cowed or impressed. If anything, she appeared disdainful. Bloody refreshing, that.

"I've formulated a plan. I'll use your body as a shield and your sharp tongue to slay our enemies." She gestured for Helena to proceed. "Lead on."

"Oh, I couldn't possibly put myself ahead of your royal—"

A snowball slammed into the tree above their heads, and they both whirled around. Georgia, Maryanne, and Maryellen crouched in the snow ten or fifteen yards away, holding fistfuls of snow and shields of evergreen boughs.

Amabel didn't think. She leapt toward Helena, flinging an arm out to push the smaller woman behind her. Her hand caught only air, as Helena plowed into her, shoulder-to-

shoulder. They both staggered. Amabel's left foot hit an icy patch. She flailed and her arm snagged on Helena's cloak. The next thing she knew, they lay in a tangled heap in the snow, blinking at one another.

"What?" Amabel gasped. "What did you do that for?"

"*You* knocked *me* down." Helena tried to disentangle herself from her scarf. In the background, the other ladies hooted with laughter.

"I did not. I was trying to protect you from the snowball attack."

"Wasn't I supposed to protect you, Princess?" She yanked the scarf away, exposing her smart and delectably kissable mouth. Her eyes twinkled like the sunlight off the snow.

Amabel scowled. "And yet here I am lying in the snow, at the mercy of our enemies. I ought to sack you."

A tiny cloud formed when Helena exhaled. "It wouldn't be the first time."

The shiver racing through Amabel's body had nothing to do with the snow seeping through her clothing, and everything to do with the tempting treat spread out beside her, rosy cheeked and defiant. Beautiful. Devious. And mere inches from her mouth.

"Go ahead, Highness," Helena whispered. "I dare you."

Amabel leaned in until their noses bumped. "I'm done playing games." She climbed to her feet, shook the snow from her outerwear, and strode toward the house.

day seven

HELENA SHUFFLED PAST the Painted Salon in her maid costume, head ducked, pretending she couldn't hear the laughter and happy chatter happening inside. Playtime was over.

"You! Neufeld's maid!"

Helena went still as a statue at the sound of the duchess' voice.

"Join us," Amabel called.

Blasted duchess. Blasted duchess with her haughty manners and her charming spectacles and her body just begging to be caressed.

Helena walked into the room as deferentially as she could manage, which probably wasn't very. A week into this charade and she was fed up with roles and lies. Especially after the way she'd succumbed to the temptation to be fully herself during the snowball fight.

Go ahead, Highness. I dare you.

Shite and bugger. She'd been a right prat to a duchess. And enjoyed the hell out of it. Perhaps this was her reckoning at last.

"Yes, Your Grace?" Helena curtsied to the Sapphic Ladies' Club members. George sat sprawled in an armchair, her long legs stretched out before her. Maryanne and Maryellen snuggled together on a couch, paging through a sketchbook.

"Ladies, this is Helena, Baron Neufeld's personal assistant." the duchess introduced her. "She showed wit, skill, and tenacity

41

42   CATHERINE STEIN

in our snowball war yesterday. I think she would make a fine addition to our club, at least for the duration of our party."

Helena's eyes widened, but she managed not to gape stupidly. Another invitation. What was the duchess up to now? So much for "done playing games."

"One can never have too many ladies, in my humble opinion," George said, her mouth twitching in a delighted smirk.

"Are you a relative of the baron, Helena?" Maryanne asked. "You look rather like him."

Helena inclined her head. Seemed the cosmetics she had applied to deemphasize her resemblance to her brother had failed. "A distant connection, milady."

"Oh, Maryanne is fine. We all use given names here."

George gestured to the single remaining seat in their circle—an empty place on a couch beside Amabel. "Sit. Tell us all about yourself. Or don't. We were discussing which of Maryellen's drawings should accompany my poem in the next issue of Amabel's magazine."

Helena sat. She only caught the duchess' eye for an instant, but the sly gleam there was enough to set her heart racing. She focused on the conversation. "I didn't know you were a poet."

George crossed her legs at the ankles. "Oh, I'm not. I scribbled a verse last night to shut up Tunsbury and his awful odes to pudding."

"It's very good," Maryellen chimed in. "It sounds like it's about food, but each fruit is actually an allusion to a woman's 'fine attributes.' Very classical. Which is why I think it needs to be paired with the frolicking goddesses sketch."

Maryanne gazed forlornly at the sketchbook. Her lips moved, but Helena couldn't make out the words.

"What was that, dear?" the duchess asked.

"Oh." Maryanne looked up. "I was merely lamenting that choosing the goddesses means I won't have my own copy of the parasol woman after all."

HER FAIR LADY   43

Maryellen took the other woman's hand. "You can have the original. I'll frame her for you."

Maryanne turned pink. "Oh, I would love that!"

"Show Helena the book so she can give her opinion," Amabel suggested. She glanced Helena's way. "You're comfortable with erotic drawings, I trust?"

"Certainly."

Maryellen rose and handed the book over. It was open to a sketch of two women half-clothed in Grecian-inspired robes. One was draped across a stone altar, while the other knelt between her dangling legs, orally pleasuring her.

"Frolicking indeed. I like the expression on her face. She's certainly enjoying herself."

Helena turned a page and found the parasol woman. She stood tall and proud, shielding her face behind the parasol while putting her whole voluptuous body on display.

A flash of arousal hit Helena hard. This woman wasn't Amabel, but she conveyed a sense of power and confidence, and her body shape was similar, if idealized. The drawing was beautiful, but the image it conjured in Helena's mind was far grander: the Duchess of Mirweald, naked to the world, but still aloof and untouchable. Unless one could manage to slip behind that parasol with her.

Helena flipped through a few more sketches, not registering much beyond the fact that they were all of pretty women. Her bothersome mind remained stuck on the woman sitting next to her and impossible fantasies.

Pull yourself together, Helena Wright!

"I'm sure any of these would be well-received," she babbled, "but the Grecian ladies do make sense if they're accompanying an ode. Perhaps some of the other drawings could be matched to future poems. Make it a feature, with an alluring nom de plume. A sort of modern Sappho. Art and poems from 'The Lady of Lesbos.'"

"Yes!" George pointed a finger at Helena. "I like you. You've

got a good head on your shoulders. You should contribute to the next issue."

"Oh, I couldn't—"

"Nonsense." Amabel patted Helena's thigh, as if they were long-time friends. Flaming desire raced right through the layers of skirts to pool in Helena's belly. "I'm sure you have some special skill or idea. A creative talent?" Her eyebrows arched above her spectacles.

Helena wanted to wipe the devious smile right off the duchess' face. Either by snarling at her or by kissing her.

Yes, Your Grace, I'm a well-practiced liar and skilled improviser. Is that what you're implying? Shall I perform for your magazine?

Truthfully, other than the family penchant for acting, Helena didn't have much practice with creative endeavors. She didn't paint or write, didn't embroider. Didn't sing or play an instrument. Organizational tasks suited her better. Putting things in order and making sense of them soothed her and gave her a sense of accomplishment.

"I'm excellent at making lists," she replied. "Perhaps I could... give theater recommendations."

"Ah." Amabel shifted to make better eye contact with Helena. "You have a familiarity with the theater, then? Perhaps Sir Albert ought to have recruited you."

Everyone laughed, but Helena narrowed her eyes at the duchess, for only an instant. *Stop trying to provoke me, Duchess. It's none of your business who I really am or why I'm here.*

Helena set the sketchbook aside and smoothed down her skirts. "I must return to my duties, I'm afraid. Ladies, Your Grace." She rose, then curtsied, holding Amabel's gaze as she did so. Her Royal Highness smiled. Haughty minx. "Thank you for the introduction to your club." She whirled around and strode from the room, head held high.

Once well out of earshot, she muttered, "What if I recruit some populist reformers for your publication, Princess? Some anti-aristocracy crusaders."

Her Fair Lady
45

A grin spread across Helena's face. She knew several people who fit that description. One of them could submit a piece entitled, "Why Nobility Shouldn't Exist."

An image formed abruptly in her mind of Amabel nodding in approval and applauding her. Damn. She just might do, at that.

Helena squeezed her eyes closed. Ugh. Why, why could she not stop liking this woman? They were adversaries. Opposing forces. Thief and investigator.

Helena resumed the walk to her chambers. Sebastian had spent last night in Fenwick's room. If he did so again tonight, she'd take the opportunity for a thorough search of the earl's study.

Soon. She'd be gone soon. And then she'd never have to think about the fantasy-parasol-woman-slash-duchess, with her sly smiles and seditious magazines and lesbian friends. Never again.

Chapter 9

⌒ day eight ⌒

*T*HE RAIN HAD BEGUN shortly after midnight, and now it came down in earnest. Helena sent up a prayer of thanks. The patter on the roof and windows would help cover any creaking floorboards as she went about her business, and the downpour would eat away at the piles of snow. Maybe her luck was changing.

Soon enough she'd have Mother's pearls in hand. She'd grab Sebastian—from the earl's bed, if need be—and they'd gallop away and never look back.

No, no, no.

Helena clenched her jaw and marched resolutely toward Fenwick's study. No fantasizing. Fantasizing about leaving was as bad as fantasizing about staying.

Rational and realistic. Rational and realistic.

She made short work of the lock and eased the door open, ears pricked for the sound of footsteps. Only the *tap, tap* of rain on the windows disrupted the silence.

Helena stepped into the room and closed the door carefully behind her. She pulled a hand towel from her pocket and dropped it at the foot of the door. Using the toe of one boot, she nudged it up against the crack. Only then did she fully open her lantern.

The room was nothing special. A nice desk, a few

HER FAIR LADY

bookcases, a globe that looked decades out of date. A potted plant stood by the window.

She started with the desk. Fenwick kept things tidy, and all his papers and writing implements had been tucked away into drawers. Helena found receipts for household accounts, records for the estate, and two drafts of what looked like book reviews focusing on queer subtext. She'd read nearly a full page before she realized what she was doing.

She slipped the papers back into place with a wistful sigh. Maybe Amabel—no, better to think of her as the duchess— would publish them in her magazine. Surely Helena could find a copy in London.

She straightened up and rolled her shoulders. The desk was a bust. Nothing but what was supposed to be there and no secret compartments.

The same held true for the bookcases and the paintings on the walls. Nothing out of the ordinary. No hidden safe. She checked beneath the rug and in the potted plant. Ran her hands along the baseboards and the undersides of chairs.

"Ugh."

Helena sat heavily on the floor and stared up at the ceiling. She'd found the one aristocrat who was doing what he was supposed to do. This was an honest room. A place for a man who was doing right by his household and his tenants. The exact opposite of the lair of a jewel thief.

What a waste of time and effort.

Helena struggled to her feet, locked up the room behind her, and trudged back toward the stairs. God, she was tired. More than a week and nothing to show for it but a lack of sleep and a frustrating semi-flirtation with a peeress.

Nothing made sense, dammit! She was beginning to believe Seb's claims that Fenwick was innocent. He seemed nice. Kind. Shy, yes, but honorable, and with excellent taste in friends. He'd certainly earned Amabel's regard.

Amabel. God, there was another mess of confusion and

contradiction. She'd haunted Helena's dreams the last few nights, appearing with and without clothes, peeking cheekily from behind parasols, luring Helena with her mellifluous voice.

The sound of a footstep at the top of the stairs made Helena freeze. She snapped her lantern fully closed and stepped back into the shadows. Her gaze traveled up the staircase to where a halo of lamplight limned the face of the Duchess of Mirweald.

"Good morning, Helena," she called out.

Helena thumped her head against the wall behind her. "This is getting ridiculous."

Confound it!

Amabel made her way down the stairs toward Helena the Defiant, working through new strategies in her mind. What in God's name was the woman up to? She didn't seem to be a thief. A quick peek into her room had revealed nothing more than an assortment of clothing. No weapons, no contraband.

But she was up to *something*.

"Trouble sleeping?" Amabel asked sweetly.

"No more than you, it seems." Helena opened her lantern, obliterating the shadows she'd tried to hide in. She wore the same ugly yellow dressing gown she'd worn when playacting as ailing Baron Neufeld.

"Who are you really, Helena? Because you're not the baron, and I don't think your brother is, either."

"I really don't see as it's any of your business, Princess. I'll be popping back to my room now, if you'll excuse me."

There she went, getting her defenses up and spitting barbed words like a cornered cobra. Amabel would never get any information from her this way. They'd almost been friendly during the snowball fight. And then again with the Sapphic Ladies' Club. There had to be a way to talk to her without snipping at one another.

Amabel gestured toward the stairs. She'd try being nice

and see how that worked. "By all means. I'd hate to keep you from your rest."

Helena sniffed. "Sarcasm, Your Highness? A bit vulgar, don't you think?"

Amabel took a step toward the other woman. "I was entirely sincere."

"Oh, really?" Helena tilted her chin up. "So you don't suspect me of nefarious deeds? You're merely questioning my identity for a bit of sport?"

"Perhaps I'm only trying to get to know you." Amabel adjusted her spectacles. "You're an interesting woman."

"I'm not an ingenue from a Gothic novel, Your Grace. Duchesses don't befriend housemaids."

Gothic novels, eh? Amabel had read her share of those. Helena appeared determined to paint her as a villain. Perhaps it was time Amabel gave her what she wanted.

Amabel took another step closer, letting her hips sway. "You're no housemaid. You'd have been tossed out on your ear for insubordination on your first day of work. You're a troublemaker. An instigator of chaos."

Helena gasped in outrage. "I am the sensible twin!"

Twin. Well, that was an interesting bit of information to file away for further contemplation.

"Are you now?" Amabel let her gaze drop to Helena's lips. They were lovely lips: rosy, even in the dim light and enticingly bow-shaped. The small divot at the center of her top lip looked particularly fetching. Highly kissable. "I suppose that does explain how easily your brother has upended the life of my dear friend." She leaned closer, until their noses nearly touched. "If he hurts Oliver with whatever scheme you two are—"

"He would never," Helena snarled. "You know nothing."

Amabel let her voice drop deeper. "I know that I protect the people I love. And if that means protecting them from you, I'll do it. No matter how clever and pretty and charming you are."

50   CATHERINE STEIN

Helena inhaled sharply. She rose up on her toes and stared directly into Amabel's eyes. "You're not always right just because you're a duchess. Now shut up and kiss me."

For the first time in many, many years, Amabel did as she was told.

Lord, what a relief! Thoughts of possibilities and decisions flew from Amabel's mind, flung aside by the press of Helena's pliant lips. Her body swayed instinctively closer to the other woman, for once not constrained by "shoulds" or "musts." She'd given herself freedom to act, to do as she wished and damn the consequences.

The kiss began slow and exploratory, lips brushing gently as they learned the shape of one another. Helena parted hers first, and Amabel answered with a flick of her tongue into the gap. Helena tasted of tea and tooth powder, conjuring up fantasies of nighttime rituals in Amabel's mind: Helena stripping away her daytime costume. Slipping beneath soft sheets. Perhaps pleasuring herself or wrapping her limbs around a lover.

Helena's tongue touched Amabel's, and the kiss deepened. It was still soft, still experimental, but hunger lurked beneath. They licked and teased and nibbled, each tiny movement promising so much more. New places to taste, soft skin to touch, whole bodies to map with mouths and hands. Already Amabel's insides churned with desire, a hot little spark snapping and dancing deep within, begging for the fuel that would rouse it to a roaring flame.

Flame!

Amabel jerked backward. She was still holding a burning lamp. Even enclosed as it was, it could start a fire if she dropped it or crushed it between them.

"Pardon me." The lamp flickered as she gestured with it. "Fire hazard."

Helena stared, pupils blown wide. Her words came breathlessly. "Right. Sorry."

Her Fair Lady
51

Amabel shook her head. "Listen to us. Why are we apologizing for kissing? It was lovely." *It wasn't enough.*

"Not apologizing for the kissing. Just for..." Helena glanced down at her lantern. "The circumstances."

"Wrong time and place. But I would be amenable to a further opportunity for us to get to know one another."

Helena rolled her eyes. "You wanna fuck, Princess? I'm up for that. Or down. However you like it."

"As you say." This was familiar territory. "Casual, fun relations. No expectation other than mutual pleasure. Yes?"

"Of course. That's what house parties are for, aye?"

"Indeed. Tomorrow then. Well, today, technically. In the evening. Come to my room and we'll indulge ourselves."

Helena pressed a finger to her bottom lip. "No more interrogations?"

"Never in the bedroom."

"Okay. I accept. Tomorrow, then. Goodnight, Amabel." She nodded and jogged up the stairs.

Amabel watched until Helena disappeared from sight. Her lips tingled from the kiss, and cold had begun to seep through her dressing gown. Evening couldn't arrive soon enough.

Chapter 10

A THUMP FOLLOWED BY LAUGHTER sounded from beyond the Earl of Fenwick's bedroom door. Helena didn't pause or turn. She didn't want to know what her brother was getting up to in there. He was having fun, that's what mattered.

And now, after more than a week of frustration, she was going to have a little fun herself. She tapped on Amabel's door.

The duchess answered immediately and ushered her in with a smile and a wave of her hand. She wore a simple blue robe—though clearly of fine silk; she was a duchess, after all—over a white nightgown. The soft lamplight highlighted the red in the long tendrils of auburn hair hanging loose around her shoulders. Helena flexed her hands. She'd love to twine those curls around her fingers, or spread them across a satin pillow. Gorgeous, gorgeous Amabel was Helena's for the night. Unreal.

"I'm so happy you could join me," Amabel said, her velvety voice sending shivers down Helena's spine. "It's such a pleasure to see you." She gave Helena a deliberate once-over.

Helena fought the urge to squirm. She was no feminine beauty fit for a gallery wall. Not with her short-cropped hair, barely-there bosom, and a plain men's nightshirt that wasn't even white anymore. Probably she looked like a lost waif fresh off the streets of London. But this lost waif would bloody well look a duchess square in the eye.

52

"How do you manage to look so feisty in bare feet and an old nightshirt?" Amabel mused. "It's extremely seductive. You could teach the heroine in the novel I'm reading a thing or two."

Helena followed Amabel's gaze to a nearby chair, where a Minerva Press novel lay face down, pages splayed open to mark her spot.

Helena winced. "I don't know if I can be with someone who cracks book spines," she said, only half in jest. "Do you dog-ear the pages too?"

"Not in Oliver's books. But in my own, yes. Are we entirely incompatible, then?"

"'Fraid so. Though I may be able to overlook this obvious failing of yours for tonight only. It's just a silly Gothic novel, after all."

Amabel pulled a handkerchief from her pocket and began to clean her spectacles. "Silly books have merit too, my dear. Art touches people in many different ways."

"Mmm. True. You're awfully clever for a duchess." Helena cocked a hip.

"And you're clever for a charlatan with questionable taste in literature."

Helena walked over and picked up the book. She leafed through it, taking care not to lose Amabel's place. "These sorts of stories do have intriguing parts to them. It's only that I can't stand the naive, swooning heroines."

The duchess waved a hand dismissively. "Oh, the heroes and heroines are merely part of the world, like the old ruins and the secret dungeons. They're props. You have to look to the other characters. That's where the beauty lies. The healer woman who saves the day, or the sly old monk who might also be a spy. They have all the wit and wisdom in these stories. I can recommend you a few books with particular favorites of mine."

54   CATHERINE STEIN

"I could perhaps be persuaded to try one or two." Helena replaced the book on the chair, exactly as it had been.

"I'm also frequently drawn to the villains." Amabel closed the distance between them. "The wily, seductive ones especially. They're quite terrible, at times. But I've found that when the world tells you you're a sinful aberration it becomes quite easy to sympathize with monsters." Her gaze drifted languidly to Helena's lips, then down to the open V at the top of her nightshirt. "Can you really blame them for wanting to watch the world burn?"

"No." Helena reached for the tie of Amabel's dressing gown. One gentle tug and the knot unraveled. "I'd be right there with them, roasting my celebratory feast on the flames."

"I knew you were a wicked one." Amabel gave her shoulders a small shake, and the dressing gown slithered to the floor. The dark peaks of her nipples showed through the fine linen of her nightgown. "Let's be bad girls together, shall we?"

"Yes, let's." Helena leaned in for a soft, lazy kiss. A gentle prelude to open the show. "Shall we sit? Or do you prefer to go directly to the bed?"

Amabel slipped her fingers through Helena's already-tousled hair. "The choice is yours, my dear."

Had she just been given free rein to boss around a duchess? Yes, please.

"Then on the settee with you, Princess. For Act One I want to unwrap you like a gift."

Amabel took a seat on the nearby chaise, her every movement slow and elegant. She lay back and swung her legs up in a graceful arc, leaving her spread out across the couch like an odalisque.

Helena took a moment to ogle her soon-to-be lover. "Jean-Auguste-Dominique Ingres wishes he had you for a model."

"Ah. *La Grande Odalisque*." Amabel fluttered her eyelashes. "You are familiar with the art scene, my clever little chambermaid? Have you ever been to Paris?"

HER FAIR LADY

"Sadly, no. But I read up on gallery showings and the latest news. The arts are humanity's greatest treasure."

Amabel beckoned Helena closer. "Then let us make beautiful music together. And perhaps someday I shall take you to the Continent for further indulgence."

Helena's heartbeat stuttered. What a vision. Amabel with a parasol resting on her shoulder, strolling through an art exhibition. Or sitting regally in a theater box at the opera.

A hot flush spread over Helena's skin. She had to remember that the duchess was only flirting. Her words were part of the game. Wandering museums and visiting cafes with an elegant lady on her arm was not part of Helena's future.

She climbed onto the chaise, straddling Amabel's legs. This was one fantasy she *could* have, and she wasn't wasting another second. She reached for the top button of Amabel's nightgown and slipped it neatly through the hole. She caressed the small patch of skin she had exposed, then moved on to the second button. And the third.

"Lovely." Helena dragged a finger along the exposed edge of Amabel's left breast. A few more buttons, and she was able to open the nightgown enough to survey the full expanse of that magnificent bosom. "In a fair world, these would be on display all the time."

Amabel's musical laugh echoed off the walls. "In a fair world they'd be light enough not to require stays to support them!"

"Ah, yes. I forget that not everyone is as fortunate in that regard as I am." Helena cupped Amabel's breasts, squeezing gently. The warm, pliant flesh overflowed her palms. "But I do love a generous handful." She squeezed a little harder, drawing a sigh from Amabel. "It can't be helped. I'm just a girl with a weakness for soft, plump titties."

Amabel chuckled again, but the noise turned into a moan as Helena lowered her head to take one dusky nipple into her mouth. She sucked greedily, flicking and teasing and circling

the taut peak with her tongue, while her hands continued fondling both breasts.

"You taste so sweet," she murmured, moving to the opposite nipple. "Rich. Like a decadent cake."

Gentle fingers combed through Helena's hair. "Utter rubbish, my dear, but thank you. Mmm. That feels wonderful."

Not rubbish at all. Amabel tasted incredible beneath Helena's tongue. She could feast all day and not feel as though she'd missed a single meal. A whiff of something sweet and fragrant clung to Amabel's skin, filling Helena's nostrils with each inhale.

"So good, Princess," she said, before trailing kisses down into the valley between Amabel's breasts, savoring each new mouthful. "This *is* sinful, I think, because I'm greedy for you." She nuzzled the underside of one breast and received a languid sigh.

"Is greed a—mmm—sin though? To excess, perhaps. But wanting..." She broke off and arched up into Helena's touch. "Ah. Yes. Desire. *Need.* Those are—ooh—essential to life."

Helena sat up in order to push Amabel's nightgown up past her thighs and belly. "Are you always so philosophical during sex, Highness?" She slid down the couch and lifted one of Amabel's legs over her shoulder, spreading her wide. "Or am I special?"

"Every lover is special. But you particularly make me want to tease you."

Helena grinned. What a beautiful answer. She pressed a kiss to the inside of the duchess' thigh, just above her knee. "Then I shall tease you in return."

She kissed slowly up Amabel's thigh, lingering on any spot that made the duchess twitch. Amabel was already glistening with arousal, but Helena had all night. There would be no rushing this. By the time she felt the brush of tight auburn curls against her cheek, Amabel was panting. Helena pulled away and began her ministrations all over on the opposite leg.

HER FAIR LADY

"Vixen," Amabal hissed.

"The pot calls the pan burnt-arse," Helena retorted, then nibbled a love bite on the fleshiest part of the other woman's thigh. "But you are a delicacy nonetheless." She wriggled in an attempt to soothe the persistent throb of her own arousal. Relief could come later, after she'd tasted every morsel.

"Helena, *please!*"

The whine in Amabel's voice sent a surge of triumph through Helena. "Oh, yes, Princess. Beg for me."

Another wiggle to settle herself, and she finally set her tongue to Amabel's folds. She licked her up and down, gauging her reaction to every swipe before dipping the slightest bit inside her.

Amabel's hips lifted off the chaise. "Yes, please."

Helena continued to take her time. She alternated circling Amabel's clit and slowly fucking her entrance, until the duchess was writhing beneath her.

"More, dammit!"

Helena would have laughed if her tongue weren't currently buried inside her lover. So demanding. So needy.

She turned her attention to Amabel's clitoris, sucking and tonguing with increasing pressure. She eased one finger inside Amabel, then a second when the duchess gave another plaintive whine.

Surrender, Princess. Let it all go.

Helena held the other woman down as her thrashing grew wilder, threatening to topple them off the couch. Any words were garbled now, mixed with gasps and moans. Amabel's hands found Helena's hair again, clamping down hard enough to send tiny spikes of pain into Helena's skull.

Come on, duchess. Almost there.

Helena redoubled her efforts, and Amabel came with a cry. Her whole body spasmed beneath Helena's grasp, and she mewled and panted though wave after wave. At last, she pushed Helena away and sank into the cushions.

"You're so beautiful," Helena said.

The duchess was never anything but beautiful, of course, but now she was positively glowing. Pink arousal stained her fair skin. Tendrils of hair twisted and hung in all directions. Her pupils were blown wide, her lips parted, and her chest rose and fell in deep, exhausted breaths.

"Bloody gorgeous. Disheveled and debauched looks good on you."

Amabel laughed. "Give me a moment and then I'll make you look the same way."

"A moment and no more. I've been waiting since last night."

She'd been waiting since the night she'd arrived. Something about the duchess set her blood on fire. And, yes, she was a lusty woman. But usually not to this extent.

Helena tried not to dwell on that as she untangled herself from Amabel and rose to her feet. She walked into the bedroom to the washstand and cleaned her face and hands. As she finished up, a hand settled on her back.

"Into the bed with you," the duchess commanded. "And dispose of that nightshirt on the way. You won't be needing it."

Helena turned around and pulled the nightshirt off, but remained where she was. "Do you think you're in charge now?"

"Not yet." Amabel walked to the nightstand and opened a drawer. "But I will be. Would you like a toy to play with?" She withdrew a polished dildo and held it out to Helena. "I can use it on you, or you can continue to be stubborn and defiant and use it on yourself while I watch."

Helena's mouth went dry. "That. Yeah. Give it here."

"Ah, ah." Amabel held the toy out of reach. "On the bed first."

This time Helena obeyed. She settled herself into the cozy bedding, propping her head up with a fluffy pillow and spreading her limbs wide. "Acceptable?"

HER FAIR LADY

"Lovely." Amabel sat on the bed beside Helena and handed her the dildo. "May I touch you while you pleasure yourself?"

Helena pressed the toy between her legs, getting it nice and slick before rubbing it over her clit. "Have at it."

Amabel bent to kiss Helena with deep, intoxicating kisses. She didn't tease so much as luxuriate, mapping out Helena's lips with her own before moving on to explore other areas. Her mouth and fingers were feather-light on Helena's skin. Helena hadn't considered herself particularly ticklish, but under Amabel's questing hands she bucked and writhed. Bloody hell, she was sensitive in places she'd never have guessed. The hollow of her elbow. The length of her collarbone. A flick of the duchess' tongue into her navel made her cry out and nearly jolt off the bed.

All the while, she kept up a steady rhythm with the dildo. She teased and stroked herself near to the peak before finally thrusting the phallus inside her. She dropped her free hand to her clit, applying soft pressure as she worked her way back toward climax.

"I love how you even tease yourself," Amabel murmured. "You truly delight me, Helena. In so many ways."

The breathy words stoked Helena's desire just as much as Amabel's velvet touch gliding over her nipples, and she had to slow her pace again to keep from coming too soon.

Not yet. Not quite yet.

This had to last. It was almost certainly her one and only time to enjoy sex with Amabel.

Unfortunately, Helena's body didn't agree with her brain. Her hips jerked to take the dildo deeper and press her clit against her fingers. Oh, fuck, it was all so good. And the way Amabel smiled down at her—there was nothing haughty in that smile. No condescension or smug satisfaction. Amabel's eyes were soft, her head tilted to one side. She looked... smitten.

Helena's control snapped. Her eyes closed as her movement became frantic. She had never imagined this. She was no mere

object of desire. Amabel *liked* her. Enough to be a bit vulnerable with her. And damn if that wasn't the sexiest thing ever.

A few more thrusts and Helena was coming apart under her own hands, trembling through the orgasm. She sighed and went limp. When she opened her eyes, it was to that same adoring gaze.

"You are a treasure, my dear," Amabel said. She pressed a kiss to Helena's lips, then her brow.

Helena had to close her eyes again. Too much. Too much.

"You can stay here as long as you like. Or return to your room. Your preference."

"Sleepy," Helena replied. She wasn't, really. Simply spent. And not yet willing to let this dream fade.

⌒

Helena stared up at the canopy of Amabel's luxurious bed and listened to the slow in-and-out of her breathing. The duchess had been asleep nearly an hour according to the clock on the mantel. Helena had tried to doze, but her restless mind continued to churn. The weather had obliterated most of the snow, and in another day or two she'd have no more excuse to stay. She ought to be up and about, doing her utmost to find Mother's necklace before it was too late.

Amabel knew she was a fraud. Fenwick knew Sebastian's real identity. It was only a matter of time before the whole story came to light and they were thrown out for good. And here she was, wasting time in bed with a woman who'd never be more than a party fling.

Which was fine. Party flings were fine. Tonight had been spectacular, yes, but that didn't mean it needed to be repeated.

Helena slipped out of the bed, careful not to wake Amabel, and donned her nightgown. She glanced into the mirror above the dressing table to see how disheveled she looked.

Yeah, you look well-bedded, Helena Wright. Pity it's only this once.

Her Fair Lady

The sparkle of a gemstone caught her eye. Two jeweled hair pins lay on the table beside a large wooden jewelry box.

Helena sucked in a sharp breath. Amabel had made it clear how loyal she was to Fenwick. What better place to stash stolen pearls than a duchess' personal possessions? No one would dare accuse her of theft. And she surely had so many pieces with her at all times that the addition of one more would be easy to overlook.

Amabel remained sound asleep on the bed, giving no indication of waking anytime soon. All Helena had to do was open the box and take a look. Maybe peek into a drawer or two. She could be done and gone in under a minute.

Helena watched Amabel sleep as the seconds ticked by. A woman at peace. No title, no duties. Just witty, compassionate, tenacious Amabel. Helena bit her lip, took a deep breath, and turned toward the door.

Once she reached her room, she threw herself on the bed and buried her face in a pillow.

"Shit, shit, shit, shit."

Chapter 11

⟶ day nine ⟶

AMABEL DIDN'T DANCE through the beams of sunlight angling through the windows of the Painted Salon, but if she'd been alone she might have done. Her heart hadn't felt this light in ages. Not since before Oliver's seclusion, at the least. But today, all was right with the world for once.

Last night had been beyond her wildest hopes. Helena was every bit as fun in bed as she was out of it. Amabel admired her more with each new layer she unwrapped. And now she could look forward to revealing a few more layers over the coming days.

Then there was Oliver. He'd been absolutely radiant with joy the past few days. He and Neufeld—Amabel really needed to learn the man's real name—appeared utterly besotted with one another. Oliver was constantly smiling, often laughing. Amabel thought her heart might burst from happiness to see him so at ease.

Georgia skipped across the room to nudge Amabel with her elbow. She'd dressed in a delightful mix of masculine and feminine styles, pairing an elegant bodice with breeches and hunting boots.

"Fenwick's head over heels, eh? Haven't seen him so happy in ages. Guess we'll be keeping the baron, then. Does that mean we get to keep Helena too? You two gamahuched yet?"

"A lady doesn't kiss and tell."

Georgia sighed. "You always say that. Can't you give a girl a few details?"

"I am a duchess, dear. I must be proper and discreet."

"Eugk. Glad I'm the fifth daughter of a marquess. He married off my sisters and now I can run around like a hoyden."

"Would that we could all be so fortunate."

"Well." Georgia nudged Amabel again. "Maybe you'll find your own Baron Neufeld one of these days."

Amabel nodded, her gaze shifting to Oliver and Neufeld, who were gleefully trouncing another pair at whist.

Perhaps it was time to put everything out in the open. If Oliver's affair was to continue—and she wanted it to continue as long as it made him happy—then Neufeld needed to confess. Not just to Oliver, who seemed to know more than he was willing to admit, but to everyone.

"Excuse me," Amabel said to Georgia. "I have business to attend to."

"Business between a certain lady's thighs?"

Amabel didn't dignify that with an answer. She turned away with chin up and glided out of the room.

She headed directly for the stairs. Yes, indeed. It was time to solve her mystery once and for all. She'd have a sensible chat with Helena, learn what the twins were really up to, and then pick a time to divulge all.

Much to her chagrin, it took Amabel the better part of an hour to track Helena down. She'd been nearly ready to give up and return to the party when she'd finally located the other woman poking about in the library, once again dressed in her maid's costume.

"I returned the taxonomy book," Helena said when Amabel entered the room. Her current location was nowhere near the taxonomy books, but a glance told Amabel that the statement was technically true.

"And now you're searching for something equally scintillating?"

"Something like that." She ran one finger along the book spines as she moved from one shelf to the next.

Amabel took a seat in one of the plush reading chairs, crossed her legs at the ankles, and spread her skirts out. "Don't you think it's time you told me the truth?"

Helena turned slowly and crossed her arms over her chest. "How much more truth do you want, Duchess? You know my name and you've surmised that neither I nor my brother is actually Baron Neufeld of Bavaria."

"'Surmised' is the key word, Helena, dear. Most of what I know I have discovered on my own. You reveal so very little. Everything you wear is a disguise. You haven't even divulged your true surname."

"Wright. My name is Helena Wright. I assumed you knew, since my brother revealed his identity to Lord Fenwick days ago."

"I'm glad to know he didn't try to seduce my friend under false pretenses. But, no, I didn't know. Oliver has been tightlipped. I suspect he likes keeping his lover's secret. He's a bit of a foolish romantic, I'm afraid."

"So is Sebastian."

"Helena and Sebastian Wright." Amabel motioned for Helena to take a seat. She hesitated, but eventually complied, her arms still stubbornly crossed. "Who are you, I wonder. You haven't stolen anything to my knowledge, yet you entered this house under an assumed name. Why?"

"Weary travelers caught in a snowstorm. Didn't want to freeze to death."

Amabel hummed, but let the half-truth go unchallenged. "Tell me something about the real you, Helena Wright, and in return I will tell you something about myself."

Helena thought for a moment, then finally relaxed her posture. "You wondered about the theater. My mother is an actress. We grew up in a world of costumes and performances. It was a good space. Free and queer and joyful. Not much

Her Fair Lady 65

money, lots of hard work, but an endless variety of people and knowledge. Seb and I didn't opt for a life on the stage, but it will always be a part of us."

"Yes, I see that in you." *You come from a place where art and fantasies are powerful. Where one can visit other worlds. Maybe even get a glimpse what this world* could *be.*

"What about you, Duchess? How did you come to be a publisher of illegal materials?"

An easy question. Amabel smiled. "Oliver and I grew up together. We are, as you know, both queer. The previous earl—Oliver's grandfather—lived in a dedicated partnership with both his countess and his mistress. The three of them had like-minded friends. So we never had to wonder about the fact that we were different than most of our peers. I grew up knowing the way things ought to be. And while I am duchess in my own right, as a woman I do not get a vote in the House of Lords. So I use my money and connections to influence the world in my own way. Hopefully someday everyone will enjoy the same freedoms I possess."

"Well, I approve." Helena's grin made her eyes sparkle. "Keep up the good work."

"Thank you. Look at us, having a conversation without any bickering!"

"Oh, that won't do." Helena leaned forward in her seat. "You're still a princess, even if you're a smart and rebellious one."

Amabel copied Helena's movements, putting them within arms' length of one another. "And you're still a menace, even if you're a cute one. Just think what we could do together."

Helena's eyes flicked toward the doorway. "Like what we did last night? I've been thinking about it all day."

Amabel twitched, as close as she ever came to flinching after years of posture training. She'd not been thinking about last night—in this case—but about the two of them running her magazine together. Helena had the right sort of mind for

66   CATHERINE STEIN

it, as well as connections in the London art world. They'd be able to extend their reach, gather more ideas, take input from a broader range of people. And it would be plain old *fun* to work with her.

But that was nonsense. Helena would depart when the party was over. If her brother stuck around for Oliver's sake, she might see Amabel on rare occasions. But they weren't friends, were barely lovers, and certainly not partners in any sense.

Amabel allowed her smile to become seductive and rose from her seat, extending a hand to Helena. "Shall we retire for the afternoon? That maid costume isn't you at all. I think you need breeches for practicality or a ballgown to dazzle your admirers. But nothing at all will suit you for the next few hours."

Helena's warm fingers closed around Amabel's. "Well, then. Let us make haste!"

Chapter 12

⌒ day ten ⌒

HELENA ADJUSTED HER CRAVAT until it puffed just so
from the top of her waistcoat. No maid's uniform today. She'd
returned the drab thing to the laundry. Whoever it belonged
to could have it back. Helena wouldn't be going out in disguise
today. She'd be going as herself.

Since leaving Amabel's bed yesterday, Helena had spent
a great deal of time mulling over their conversation. Maybe it
was time to divulge some of the truth. Fenwick knew already,
and he would support Sebastian. Once the situation had been
explained to the rest of the party, Helena and Seb could pull
the earl aside for a frank discussion. If he really was the good
man Seb seemed to think he was, he would explain his role in
the necklace theft and return it to its rightful owner.

"Am I fantasizing again? Or indulging my brother's
whims?" Seb had been suggesting they confess everything
for days. Maybe he'd been right all along. Or maybe Helena's
judgment was clouded by her infatuation with a certain peeress.

Blast.

She tugged at her cuffs. Sebastian had taken the good
cufflinks again, the rotter. This pair never seemed to stay put.
She slipped them off and dropped them atop the dressing table.
There was a third pair in their saddlebags, she thought.

Helena strode into the closet and pulled a bag from beneath
the unused valet's cot. She stuck one hand down into the bag

67

68   CATHERINE STEIN

and rummaged around, feeling for anything hard among the various stockings and gloves. Her fingers brushed something smooth and round. When she shifted her hand, she felt another round object chained to the first. And another and another.

She flinched.

"What?" Helena closed her fist around the item and yanked it from the bag. The moment she saw the rope of pink and gray pearls, she dropped it like it had burned her hand. "What the absolute fuck?"

Mother's necklace winked up at her from the carpet. It was here. In her room. In her bag. For how long?

Helena scrambled to her feet and backed out of the closet. This wasn't happening. It couldn't be happening. Seb wouldn't lie to her like that. He wouldn't let her continue a pointless search just to keep her occupied. He wouldn't make her stay here after the job was done. He wouldn't waste her time like that, wouldn't insult her like that, wouldn't leave her fumbling around long enough to possibly start developing feelings for a bloody duchess!

Or maybe he would. Maybe he was having so much fun fucking the damned Earl of Fenwick that he didn't care. Maybe this had all been a game to him. Like how her banter with Amabel was all a game. And Helena was nothing but a pathetic pawn.

She stomped back into the closet and snatched up the necklace. "I'm changing the rules," she snarled. "You do not get to do this to me. Any of you."

It was time for them all to come clean. And she'd fight dirty to make it happen.

⌀

Well, well, well. Amabel flattened the letter from the real Baron Neufeld on the breakfast table, where everyone around it could read it if they wanted to. Here was her opportunity, delivered to her with the morning post.

HER FAIR LADY   69

"It seems the baron intends to marry." Amabel directed her words at Oliver, who sat across the table beside Mr. Wright.

The floor is yours, gentlemen.

Lord Tunsbury waved a spoonful of marmalade. "Marry whom? Fenwick? Because I know a vicar who might assist with that."

"That's dated yesterday." Casper Hawthorne, who sat to Amabel's left, leaned so far over his cuff nearly dipped into her tea. He began to read aloud, anger rising in his voice with every word. "'On the morrow we will at last be departing the inn…'"

Amabel reached for the letter, but it was too late. Casper's face had gone red with rage, while Mr. Wright had turned the color of pea soup.

"I suppose this is my cue to explain," Wright sighed. "Not my preference, but needs must."

"You think this is a joke?" Casper snarled. "Who the fuck are you?"

Oliver jumped to his lover's defense. "Whoa. Casper, relax. It's a simple misunderstanding."

Casper brandished his butter knife at Wright. "Explain yourself."

Oh, for the love of God. Why did men always have to be so emotional about things? She really should have taken that into account when she'd decided to expose the truth. The letter had seemed like a blessing from above only moments ago. She shifted her chair back a few inches so she could easily rise if things got any more out of hand.

Wright, fortunately, had come prepared. "My name is Sebastian Wright. I'm not Baron Neufeld, and I don't know a thing about the man except that the boy in the stables assumed I was him when I arrived. I used that to get into the house, and I honestly can't say I regret the lie. It got me out of the snow and I met all of you. I had no compelling reason to tell the truth to strangers, and by the time I discovered how well I fit

70   CATHERINE STEIN

in here, well… This moment was bound to happen. And I told Oliver days ago, if that makes any difference to the rest of you."

Either his theater background had made him an excellent liar, or he was telling the truth. Given how happy he'd appeared during his time here, Amabel suspected the latter.

Casper, unfortunately, did not. "It bloody well does not," he roared. "Who are you? A thief? A spy? A confidence trickster? A blackmailer?"

"God, no, stop!" Wright held up both hands, babbling his apologies.

Amabel stopped listening to him. The door to the breakfast room had flown open, and Helena Wright came charging through, her pretty face twisted with rage and an ugly rope of pearls clenched in her hand. She headed straight for her brother, not even looking in Amabel's direction. She shook the pearls at Wright.

"Goddamn you, Sebastian Wright, how long have you had these? How could you keep this from me?"

Every single person at the table gaped at Helena.

"I swear to Almighty God I haven't been drinking this morning," Whitcomb said. "Why the devil are there two of you, Neufeld? Or whoever you are."

Two of you? Amabel had to shake herself to make sense of Whitcomb's question. She'd entirely forgotten the average person couldn't tell the twins apart at a glance.

They *were* very much alike, she couldn't deny that. But now that she knew Helena, all the subtle differences seemed glaringly obvious. The slight difference in their voice, for instance, even when Helena spoke in a low register. Or the way they both walked. Helena was too purposeful for the flirty hip sway her brother affected. Her face was different as well, a little bit softer, with eyes that pierced more than shimmered.

Helena stomped her way across the room, still ranting at her brother. Amabel couldn't make heads or tails of the argument. The pearls certainly didn't belong to her or to Oliver.

Her Fair Lady   71

No one else in the room had jumped up crying, "Thief!" Yet Helena was acting as if her brother had committed a hanging offense.

"We were partners," she shouted. "We were in this together. I came here for a *purpose*, not so you could play Fuck-the-Toff for a week!"

The word "purpose" knocked the wind from Amabel's lungs. There it was. The proof that the Wrights were up to no good. It was what she'd been searching for since that first night, and now… Hell and damnation. What a fool she'd been to let her attraction to Helena push it to the back of her mind.

Sebastian openly glared at his sister. "I am *not* playing. And what do you care, anyhow? You'd handle it and I only had to 'keep Fenwick busy,' wasn't that what you said?"

Oliver turned white as a ghost. Casper raised the butter knife and lunged.

"Stop it!" Amabel caught Casper by the collar and yanked him back down into his seat. "All of you, stop this at once!"

Not a single person obeyed her. Perhaps they couldn't hear over the sudden clamor, as the entire party began to talk at once. A chair crashed to the floor. Tunsbury staggered away from the table and fled, clutching his belly as if he were about to cast up his accounts.

"Quiet!"

Casper swore right over her. Helena hurled insults at Sebastian. Across the table, Oliver trembled, hands clutching the tablecloth.

No, no, no. This couldn't be happening. After all this time, after her meticulous plans for this party and the past few blissful days, to be falling apart now?

Sebastian pressed close to Oliver, murmuring something soothing, but getting no response.

"Stop," Oliver moaned. He pressed his forehead to the table and clapped his hands over his ears. "Stop. Please, stop."

Casper growled and Amabel shook him. "Get away. This is not about you."

The swordmaster wrenched himself from her grasp and sprang to his feet, snarling something unintelligible. He slammed the butter knife back down on the table, catching the edge of a teacup and sending it flying. The tinkling crash of breaking porcelain hardly registered through the cacophony. Casper stormed off to a corner of the room.

Amabel curled her hands into fists and tried to summon up all her strength. One—small—problem fixed. Now for the next.

"So they were twins all this time?" Whitcomb clung to his wife's arm. "I still don't understand."

"Helena," Amabel demanded. "What is the meaning of this?"

Helena glanced in her direction. "It's nothing to do with you." She reached for her brother. "Come on, Sebastian. We're leaving."

"Don't touch me," he shot back. He caressed Oliver's hair. "Sweetheart, please. How can I help?"

"Leave him be," Amabel ordered. "You've done quite enough already." She looked from one Wright sibling to the other. "Both of you. And I demand a full expla—"

"You're Helena the maid?" Maryellen interrupted. "The valet? But also the baron?"

"Oh, are you a spy?" George popped up from her seat so fast she overturned her chair. "Please tell me you're a spy. Who wants to place a bet? Spy, yes or no. And if yes, a spy *for whom*?"

"Oh, dear, oh dear."

Mrs. Whitcomb hauled her flustered husband from his seat, bumping the table in the process and sending another teacup crashing to the floor. Amabel wanted to scream.

You are a duchess, you are a duchess, you do not throw a tantrum like everyone else in this godforsaken room!

HER FAIR LADY

"Excuse me." Sir Albert waved frantically. "Excuse me. About the theatrical?"

Amabel rose from her seat and squared her shoulders. She picked up a candlestick from the center of the table and thumped it one, two, three times like a judge calling for order with his gavel. A few heads finally turned her direction.

"Out! All of you, get out this instant! Except you, Wright... and Wright."

Amabel's eyes met Helena's. For a moment the world seemed to stop. And then the anger faded from Helena's expression. One corner of her mouth turned up in a sad half-smile as she shook her head. She turned and walked away, chin defiantly in the air.

Helena's departure seemed to spur something in the rest of the party. They all scrambled from their seats, chattering amongst themselves.

Amabel gazed down at Oliver, who continued to hide his head and whimper.

"You should go too, Mr. Wright. I'll assist Lord Fenwick."

Wright nodded. A tear rolled down his cheek. He dashed it away with the back of his hand and ran from the room.

"Oliver." Amabel took her seat once more and reached across the table to pat her friend's arm.

He took his time straightening up before uncovering his ears and opening his eyes.

"I handled that badly," Amabel apologized. "I ought to have brought all of this up with you long ago."

Oliver blinked at her. "You knew?"

"Not all of it. I knew they were masquerading as Neufeld, among other disguises. I didn't know the why of it."

I should have pressed Helena. I should have insisted on the full truth instead of letting her tempt me into bed.

"And you said nothing."

She considered several options before speaking.

I was trying to protect you.

I wanted to let you enjoy your fling.

I was distracted by the vexing Miss Wright.

I was so close to solving the mystery myself.

"I had no idea you'd actually fallen in love with him," she said, extending a conciliatory hand.

"Excuse me." Oliver stood and turned away.

Amabel let him go.

Chapter 13

⟶ day eleven ⟵

*B*ONG!

Helena lay on her bed, staring up into the darkness as the clock in the hall tolled the hour. One a.m. seemed an appropriate time to contemplate one's life choices.

Just me and the ghosts of my mistakes.

She counted off the days she'd been here on her fingers, cataloging one poor decision after another. She'd be ceding her title of Sensible Twin to Sebastian, that was certain. Assuming she ever saw him again. She'd gone to the stables multiple times throughout the day to check if he'd ridden away, but both horses remained in their stalls, happily munching on treats from the groomsmen.

The door creaked and Helena bolted upright, fumbling for the lamp and matches on the bedside table. She hastily struck a match and it flared to life, revealing her brother in the doorway.

"Thank God." She lit the lamp and blew out the match. "I was worried about you. I almost thought you'd left, except the horses are still in the stables. Where have you been?" When he didn't answer, she hopped off the bed and strode toward him. "Seb, I'm so sorry. I should never have confronted you like that. My mind's been in such a muddle all week, and when I found the pearls in our bags, I snapped. I reacted impulsively and out of anger, and that was wrong of me. W-we were a team.

76   CATHERINE STEIN

A-always together. And now I feel like I've driven a wedge between us, and... and..."

"Hey." Seb embraced her. "I still love you, Hellion."

Hellion. Lord, it had been ages since she'd heard that nickname. She really had been a hellion, once. The girl who picked locks and wore trousers and sometimes went to school in her brother's place just to prove she could get away with it. When had she lost that girl?

She managed a weak laugh. "You haven't called me that in years."

"Well, you had to go and turn all sensible on a chap. Nice to know you still have your wild moments."

Plenty of them, judging by the past week and a half. Sleeping with a duchess! Good Lord. Maybe she'd been repressing her impulsive side too long, and this was the result.

As the twins undressed for bed, Helena dragged an explanation about the pearls out of her brother. They'd been in a box of props for the bloody theatrical, of all places. And Fenwick couldn't remember how they'd come into his possession. Helena didn't have the heart to suggest the earl might still be lying.

Especially after Seb began to cry.

Her poor, sweet, darling, romantic brother. Helena hugged him tight as they both burrowed beneath the covers. This was all her fault. He deserved so much better. And if Fenwick cared for Sebastian even half as much as Seb cared for him, he deserved better too.

She could only pray that Fenwick and Amabel wouldn't throw her out before she had a chance to atone.

～

Casper was probably exaggerating his desire to murder Mr. Wright and dump his body in a bog.

Probably.

Amabel wasn't entirely certain she cared one way or the

HER FAIR LADY 77

other. She'd yet to decide whether Wright was a villain or not. This morning her concern was solely for Oliver. Which is why she found herself standing in his study, sipping a cup of tea, while Casper leaned menacingly in the doorway behind her.

"Get out," Oliver commanded. "I'll have no more talk of murder or dueling. It's not funny and I'm bloody well sick of it! Come back when you can stop acting like a bullying older brother who hits anyone who looks at his siblings funny."

Casper gasped. "I beg your pardon!"

"He's right, Hawthorne. There's no need for histrionics." Amabel waved a hand to shoo Casper away. "The proper solution is to send Mr. Wright packing with a warning to stay away lest we take more drastic measures in the future." She turned her focus to Oliver. "Speaking of which, why haven't you sent him away?"

"I don't know, Amabel," Oliver replied in the most sarcastic tone she'd ever heard from him. "Why didn't you tell me you'd noticed suspicious goings on?"

Was he actually *chiding* her? Amabel's spine went so rigid she could have removed her corset and still not slumped. "I was attempting to unravel the mystery and resolve the matter in a way that would cause the least disruption. I perhaps was hasty in allowing Hawthorne first glimpse at the letter from the real Baron Neufeld. But I could not have known Miss Wright would choose that moment to expose herself to the world."

Amabel's mind immediately filled with images of how enthusiastically Helena had exposed herself in the bedroom for their mutual pleasure. *Oh, bugger. Poor choice of words.*

Blast Helena Wright anyway. Blast her and her wit and charm and stalwart sense of her own self-worth.

"Resolve the matter." Oliver spit the words back at Amabel, shaking her from her maudlin thoughts. "Take care of things behind my back like I'm a poor little child who can't make a decision for himself."

78   CATHERINE STEIN

"I did not say that." She wasn't mothering him. She was simply... helping. Freeing him from certain responsibilities.

"Nor did I," Casper added. "It's only that after your exile—"

Oliver pounded his fist on the desk, and Amabel jumped, sloshing her tea. "I'm incompetent? Weak? Afraid of everyone and everything?" He sprang to his feet. "Maybe I am. Maybe I'm pathetic and helpless and need looking after. But did you ever once think to *ask?* No. You all simply barge in and start doing things for me. Yes, I needed help. I even wanted help. But not one of you ever bothered to ask what I wanted."

Amabel had no words. She stared open-mouthed at her oldest friend.

"I'm done here," Oliver said firmly. "Don't follow me. I've had more than enough of your meddling. I won't be your charity project any longer." He stormed out.

"Sh-should we go after him?" Casper asked. His usual swagger had been fully supplanted by a look of utter bewilderment.

Amabel shook her head. Oliver was right. She hadn't asked. She'd never asked. Every day she woke up and set about doing whatever she thought was right without even thinking to consult anyone else. Which maybe was fine in certain cases, like her duties to her estate. But when it was Oliver's life she was controlling...

"Well, fuck," she blurted.

⁓

They met in the library again, as if it were their special place. As if "they" actually existed. Which it didn't, obviously. Certainly not anymore. Helena's purpose here was fulfilled, and she'd be leaving with Mother's pearls and—maybe—her brother as soon as she'd undone some of the damage she'd caused.

"We need to fix—"

"We made a mess—"

Helena gestured at Amabel. "Sorry, you go first."

HER FAIR LADY

"I'm a duchess, of course I go first." Amabel's tone was sharp. Not her usual wry banter, either. This was more caustic. And directed inward, if Helena was reading her correctly. "We made a mess of things, didn't we?"

"Yes. We did." She couldn't keep the edge out of her own voice, either. She ought to have left things well enough alone. Left Sebastian to his own devices. He was an adult. He could take care of himself. But most of all, she ought never to have gone to bed with Amabel. No, check that. She should never have *flirted* with the duchess in the first place. Not once.

Amabel sighed heavily. "I ought to have sat you down to discuss the matter the moment I suspected you of deception. Gotten the facts directly instead of hunting for clues like some sort of Bow Street Runner."

Helena shook her head at the aristocratic non-apology. "I wouldn't have told you a thing. I thought Fenwick was a thief when we arrived."

Auburn eyebrows arched in disbelief. "Oliver has never stolen anything in his life!"

"That does seem to be the consensus, yes. But he did leave a charity gala with my mother's necklace, and we came here to retrieve it. Whatever happened, I'm not going to make a fuss over it. I have what I came for and I'll be on my way as soon as I can. I never intended to disrupt your party. I never meant to hurt anyone. And I certainly never meant to break anyone's heart, especially Sebastian's. I owe him and Fenwick a full apology before I leave."

"As do I. My triumphant reveal of the truth ended in complete disaster. I haven't precisely been thinking straight these last few days." Amabel's gaze met Helena's.

Helena quickly looked away. "No, neither have I. What can we do, though? I'd like to give them some time alone. If their feelings are genuine—which my brother's certainly are—a few moments together with no fear of outside interference might be all they need."

80 CATHERINE STEIN

"Oliver's feelings are absolutely genuine," Amabel said firmly. "That man doesn't have a dishonest bone in his body."

"Right. Then we'll arrange for them to be in the same place at the same time and keep the rest of the party distracted while they talk." Helena snapped her fingers. "They'll be together tomorrow evening, for the theatrical. Seb won't leave Fenwick on his own then, even if they haven't made up."

"Oh, good heavens." Amabel rubbed her temple. "I'd forgotten all about that damned thing. Oliver never wanted anything to do with it. I think he only went along with it to be near your brother. If only we could give him an excuse not to—"

Her gaze snapped to Helena's face at the same moment an idea sparked in Helena's brain. They smiled at one another.

"We need a copy of the script."

Amabel nodded. "Not a problem. Follow me."

Chapter 14

⌐ day twelve ⌐

AMABEL ADJUSTED HER DRESSING GOWN into an elegant drape as she strode toward the little nook the gentlemen were using as a dressing room for their theatrical performance. True, she was about to barge in on potentially half-dressed men while in a state of dishabille, but she would do it in a manner befitting a duchess.

"I found it on the floor, all right? The clasp was broken. It could have belonged to anyone."

That was Tunsbury's voice. Amabel held up a hand to halt Helena.

"I'd run up some debts of honor—you know how it is—and suddenly there was a solution, lying right in front of me."

Helena looked pleadingly heavenward. "Of course it was him. Who else would do something so inane? Probably stuffed the pearls in Fenwick's pocket because he feared someone would try to claim them."

"Shush." Amabel waved a hand at Helena. "I think that's exactly what he's saying," she whispered.

"It seemed harmless. How was I to know a pair of charming twins would storm your house, take on a secret identity, make everyone fall in love, and break your heart?" Tunsbury sounded near tears.

Amabel rolled her eyes—something she usually only allowed herself to do in private. "Oh, for heaven's sake. Come along, Helena."

81

She stepped into the doorway. "Tunsbury, stop blubbering. The ladies are waiting for the play to begin and I believe you're in the first scene. Into the next room with you all. I need a moment alone with Fenwick. Mr. Wright, you may remain as well. Quickly, gentlemen, I haven't all day."

She clapped her hands twice, but the men merely gaped at her. Tunsbury recovered first, and bowed, probably thinking it concealed his flaming cheeks.

"As you wish, Your Grace." He hurried into the Green Salon, where the rest of the ladies awaited what was sure to be both a tragedy and a farce.

It took a few moments—and a promise from Casper not to duel anyone—to get the rest of the room cleared, but with a bit of shooing, Amabel finally got herself alone with Oliver and the Wright siblings.

It also took that long for Oliver to notice her state of undress.

"What are you wearing?" he blurted. "Or *not* wearing?"

Amabel didn't have time for lengthy explanations. The play was about to start, and the audience was getting restless. "Get out of those clothes."

Oliver stumbled."I beg your pardon!" He covered his eyes when Amabel tossed the robe aside.

"Calm yourself, Fenwick. I'm not here to seduce you. You of all people know I have no interest in men. But I have wronged you and I owe you a good turn. Now hand over your costume. I'm taking your place."

Sebastian Wright stepped in front of her, hands on his hips. "Is that an order? Because I didn't hear a 'please.'"

Amabel actually winced. Clearly it would take some time to break her bad habits. "You have my apologies, Oliver. I have been trying to control your life, and that has hurt you and hurt our friends. Now here I am, doing it again. Allow me to offer you a choice. Miss Wright and I are willing and able to take

HER FAIR LADY

your places in the theatrical. We've read the script. If you don't want to perform for the ladies, we will. What is your decision?"

"I accept your apology and your offer. Sebastian can speak for himself." Oliver threw a lopsided papier-mache crown at Amabel. She fumbled with it, then placed it on her head as regally as possible.

Sebastian, meanwhile, kicked a messy blond wig to Helena. "Be my guest."

The men disrobed with impressive alacrity, and within minutes, Amabel did up the last remaining buttons on the Prince's wrinkled and distastefully ostentatious green and gold doublet. She nearly rejected the flimsy prop sword Oliver handed over.

"I couldn't swat a fly with this thing!" she protested, as she relented and belted it to rest at her hip.

Sebastian fastened the last of Helena's buttons, adjusted her wig as best he could, then kissed her cheek. "Have fun, Hellion. And thank you."

"Here he comes now," Mr. Whitcomb's voice boomed from the next room. "Our great and noble prince, himself!"

Amabel ran for the stage, Helena right behind. This was it. No more time to talk. And she'd have to admire Helena in the dress during the performance. It would help her get into character.

"Greetings, my brave and loyal knights!" Amabel stepped through the curtains (repurposed bedlinens) as she spoke. "You find me now a changéd man, as I have known beauty unlike any in the world."

Out in the audience, Mrs. Whitcomb gasped at the sight of Amabel on stage and covered her mouth to hide her giggling. Georgia laughed out loud. Maryellen and Maryanne exchanged a look.

Amabel held out both hands in a gesture of supplication and continued on with Oliver's lines. "Beauty rare and fleeting, like the tender rose, whose petals fall when summer's days are

o'er." The line had originally said spring, but Amabel wasn't about to go on stage and spout incorrect botanical facts. Also, summer fit the meter better.

Despite his near hysteria only minutes before, Tunsbury didn't miss a beat. He carried on with his part as if a duchess hadn't stepped without warning into the lead role of an all-male production.

"Is my lord taken ill that he raveth so?" He stage-whispered to Whitcomb.

"Aye. Afflicted sore with love, methinks."

"Love." Amabel pressed the back of her hand to her forehead. "Love. Too small a word for what I feel. This sickness claws its way from beneath my breast and threatens my poor heart to rend in two."

Helena peeked around the curtain. "Oh! What? The Prince draws near, and with his knights. How will I hide this passion that cannot be? For I am no royal, worthy of his regard!"

"Ho!" Tunsburry shaded his eyes with a hand and craned his neck. "Is that the Lady Alice beyond yonder shrubbery?"

Helena gasped and threw open her parasol.

"Alice!" Amabel cried. "It is she my heart desires and no other! But where has she gone? Come good sirs, I must find her that she may know the depths of my regard."

Helena squealed and tried to duck behind the curtain as the others chased her offstage, but the open parasol snagged on one of the bedsheets, and it came tumbling down on top of her. The audience roared with laughter. Off to stage right, Sir Albert wrung his hands and flushed scarlet.

"He needn't worry," Amabel murmured to a giggling Helena as the men untangled her and set about rehanging the curtain. "The mishaps are the best part of any amateur theatrical."

Out on stage, Casper introduced himself as the villain of the piece. As he shouted his lines, he also showed off his

fencing moves—to great applause. From Amabel's vantage point, he looked like a life-sized shadow puppet.

"I do hope he won't be stabbing me with a real sword."

Helena lifted up on tiptoe and whispered, "Not into all the thrusting, Princess?" She pulled off her blond wig and threw it into a corner. "I couldn't see through all the hair in my eyes and couldn't get the parasol closed. Lady Alice is adopting a new hairstyle."

Mr. Whitcomb turned from his work on the curtain. "What the deuce are you ladies doing here? Where are Fenwick and Wright?"

Tunsbury snorted. "Where do you think? Ooh, there's our cue. Ta!"

The two "knights" returned to the stage, summoned by the villain for his dastardly scheme. Amabel and Helena found themselves alone backstage, standing with their shoulders touching.

"You were excellent," Helena said. "I would never have guessed this was your first stage role."

"My dear, being a duchess is much like being an actress, except the performance never ends."

"You don't need to act with me."

"Thank you."

Ah, if only life were that simple. Find a person who let you be fully yourself and spend as much time with them as you could. But Helena had no further purpose here. She'd said she was leaving. The time to explore that possibility was at an end.

"Are you ready for our climactic love scene?" Amabel asked. Best to keep to the task at hand.

"I remember all the lines. Even the bad ones."

"Oh, were there good ones?"

Their eyes met, and they both dissolved into a fit of uncontrollable laughter. By the time they had to retake the stage, they were both red-faced and wheezing.

86   CATHERINE STEIN

"At least we look like we've come from a passionate embrace," Helena gasped.

Amabel had to cough several times before delivering her lines, prompting Tunsbury to improvise with, "Still ailing, Your Highness? Such are the trials of love." He was a lousy poet, but he had a knack for acting.

The play went on in this manner for a number of scenes. Lady Alice and the Prince had no more than a few lines each, as Sir Albert had adapted his writing based on Oliver's reluctance to participate. Amabel spent most of the time admiring Helena. She looked lovely in the red gown, which had clearly been tailored to flatter her slim figure. A rosy pink still highlighted her cheekbones, and she wore a smile of genuine pleasure. Trading places with Oliver and Sebastian had been a brilliant idea.

A brilliant idea that had Helena shining like a star. This was how she'd been the day of the snowball fight: still sharp-tongued and fiery, but also playful and relaxed. This was how she deserved to be every day.

A round of applause to end a scene marked their moment. The love scene was at hand. Sir Albert pushed a potted plant onto the stage. Amabel and Helena entered to stand on opposite sides of the "hedge."

Amabel parted the leaves of the plant to gaze longingly at Helena. "My dear Lady Alice." *My dear Miss Wright.*

Helena curtsied, lowered her gaze, and looked up through her lashes. "Your Highness."

Amabel's skin burned. Good Lord, what had she gotten herself into? A little fake flirtation and she was gaping like a besotted fool. For a few horrible seconds, she forgot every line she'd so meticulously memorized yesterday.

"I-I beg your forgiveness," she stammered. "Er...for my intrusion. But I must speak, though I fear my words come too late."

"I will deny you nothing, sir. Surely you must know this.

My loyalty to you knows no bounds." Helena smiled shyly and twirled her parasol.

Dammit, why was she so good at this?

Alice, not Helena. Alice, not Helena.

Amabel clasped her hands to her chest. "Darling Alice, always will I treasure your goodness and fealty, though they are but fleeting shadows when I cannot have your heart."

"My heart?" Helena blushed. She actually made herself blush, right on cue. Her eyes sparkled like fresh-fallen snow. Amabel wanted to mash their lips together and kiss her senseless.

Somehow she managed to keep reciting her lines.

"Your heart, my love. I know it is not mine to claim, but I yearn for it. My own has been yours since the moment I laid eyes upon you."

Amabel reached into her doublet for the folded script that was meant to portray a love poem. She lost a button in the process, but this time the audience didn't laugh. A surreptitious glance told her they were all paying rapt attention. Her stomach lurched.

"Your Highness," Helena gasped, accepting the letter and unfolding it. She pretended to read, blinking rapidly to simulate tears. "Oh! Oh, my love! Can it be true?"

"Aye. 'Tis true. You are as dear to me as all the earth, the moon, the stars, and all the universe."

At this point in the script, Alice invited the Prince to climb over the hedge to see her. Which meant Amabel was supposed to climb up onto the potted plant and leap down with "a triumphant cry." There were, however, certain things that a duchess did not do, even if she had taken up the role of actress.

She walked around the plant.

The audience laughed and one person clapped.

Helena, still blushing and playing shy, had her parasol open again, held in front of her to form a barrier between them. Amabel took a step toward her, extending a hand.

"My lady, Take my hand, as you have taken my heart."

Helena played the timid heroine to perfection, slowly shifting the parasol out of the way as Amabel moved closer. Her hand trembled when their fingers finally brushed.

"Dearest," Amabel breathed, going completely off script. "Unrivaled beauty. I am yours."

Helena's smile turned coy. "Then, Highness, I must also be thine own." She raised her parasol to hide her face from the audience.

Amabel pulled her into an embrace and kissed her.

Chapter 15

*S*OMETHING ABOUT THIS KISS was different. It was sweet and soft, but also possessive. Amabel's hand cupped Helena's cheek, holding her in place with a firm, but not constricting grip.

I want you to stay right here, Helena imagined the duchess saying. *Stay here, in my grasp. Be mine.*

Helena wanted to linger in the moment. It was worth savoring, this kiss. Each press of lips and slide of tongues begged to be analyzed. This was a kiss every snake-oil salesman would weep for, if it could be bottled and sold. Pure and glorious.

Until Casper Hawthorne came leaping over the plant, nearly knocking both Helena and Amabel off their feet.

The parasol clattered to the floor, and they stumbled apart. Casper brandished a stick.

"Haha! The kingdom is mine!" He poked Amabel in the back.

Amabel staggered, drawing the pitiable papier-mache sword from her belt. "No," she croaked. "This kingdom will never be yours, foul knave!" She stabbed Casper in the gut as best she could (the sword bent nearly in half), then collapsed.

"Alas, I die!" Casper fell flat on his back. The force of his crash rattled the stage and made one of the curtains fall again.

Helena dropped to her knees beside Amabel, biting her lip to keep from laughing.

89

90   CATHERINE STEIN

"Alice, my love," Amabel gasped. "My time draws near. But I will see you once more beyond this life." She clasped Helena's hand, kissed it, and then slumped over. It was an elegant death, worthy of a duchess.

Helena had only a single line left to deliver, but she'd had enough of meek Lady Alice. She flung herself atop the body of her lover, wailing and beating her fists on the floor. She cursed the gods, especially Eros, and screamed so loud it hurt her throat. At last, she lifted her head, looked directly at the audience and cried, "Thus my heart breaks and I live no more."

As she crumpled back atop Amabel, the audience burst into hearty cheers.

"Bravo! Brava! A triumph!"

Amabel began to snicker. Then she snorted. And suddenly she and Helena were once again carried away by half-hysterical laughter.

They laughed as they untangled themselves and helped one another to their feet. They laughed as they took their bows to a standing ovation. They were still laughing as the audience stormed the stage to congratulate the actors.

"Oh, Lord." Helena leaned on Amabel for support and dashed away tears of mirth. "That was utterly absurd."

"It was brilliant!" Georgia enveloped them both in a fierce hug. "You were so funny and romantic and silly! I loved every moment!"

"I'm glad someone did." Amabel bent down to retrieve the papier-mache crown she'd lost during her death scene and placed it back on her head. "I would hate to have done all this for nothing."

Helena bumped Amabel's shoulder, the way she might have done with Sebastian. "You did it for *fun*. Doesn't matter what anyone else thought of it." She frowned. "You did have fun, yes?"

"I did. Quite a lot of fun, as a matter of fact." Her gaze

caught briefly on Helena's lips. Seemed Her Royal Highness was also thinking about their interrupted kiss.

"So did I," Helena admitted. "I wouldn't want the stress of a professional stage career, but I do love a chance to perform once in a while."

"All the ladies should perform the next play," Georgia suggested. "Also, the story needs proper kissing. No more of that parasol nonsense. And it should be much queerer."

"Excuse me." Tunsbury slung an arm around Mr. Whitcomb's shoulders. "We knights are wildly in love. Couldn't you tell?"

"You'll have to duel my wife for my hand, darling," Whitcomb drawled.

Tunsbury leapt away. "Eh. Fuck that!" He caught Helena looking at him and flushed. "Miss Wright. Sorry about… well, everything. I was a fool. Let me make it up to you. Need any cash? Hit a run of good luck the day before the party, so I'm flush right now."

Helena held up a hand and shook her head. "Keep your money and stop gambling. Maybe try your hand at acting if you're bored. You were excellent tonight."

He looked down at his feet. "Oh. Thank you. Perhaps we can put on another show together some day."

"I'd like that."

"Oh, yes," Maryellen jumped in. "And your brother can participate too, even if Fenwick doesn't want to. Imagine all the fun tricks we could pull with both of you in the show!"

Helena winked. Grinning, she turned to Amabel.

The duchess didn't return the smile. In fact, she looked nearly as dour as she had after the disastrous reveal of Helena and Seb's true purpose here.

"Let's not get carried away making plans." Amabel's smooth voice had slipped back into its aloof peeress tone. "I'm sure the Wright twins have their own matters to attend to. We cannot simply keep them here for our entertainment."

Helena tried to maintain her smile. "Yes, we do need to be getting home."

Her insides twisted in knots. *Ask me to come back. Ask me to prolong our affair. Tell me you want me. Tell me we can try to be more than a fling.*

"But you'll be back, won't you?" Maryanne asked from just over Helena's shoulder. "Fenwick and your brother won't be parted for long. They're simply mad about each other. So I'm sure we'll see you again soon enough."

Helena left the question unanswered. "I ought to change out of this gown. Excuse me, everyone."

She left the stage and ducked back into the nook, where her dressing gown still lay on the floor. She slung it over her arm and left by the opposite door. Just past the threshold, she paused and looked back over her shoulder.

Some silly little romantic part of her expected Amabel to be there, following her. The nook remained empty, and that little part fizzled away.

Helena didn't look back again. She had bags to pack.

Chapter 16

~ day fourteen ~

*L*ADIES." AMABEL CLAPPED her hands to draw the attention of the chattering club members.

The other four women sat together on the largest couch in the Painted Salon—George perched on the arm, while Maryellen and Maryanne flanked Mrs. Whitcomb. Their heads all bent over Mrs. Whitcomb's embroidery hoop, which said "Bugger All This" in flowing script. She was currently finishing a dainty floral knot to dot the i.

Amabel pushed a high-backed chair directly in front of the couch and sat. "Ladies," she repeated. "This is our last time together before the party ends, so we must attend to business."

George pointed at the embroidery hoop. "Bugger business. This is a social club, not a courtroom. And I'm the president, not you."

Maryellen draped an arm across the back of the couch. "Honesty, Amabel, what has gotten into you? You've been so stern these last few days. I thought everyone was happy and everything was settled after the theatrical."

Mrs. Whitcomb paused her embroidery and looked up. "Is it not obvious, dear? The duchess is missing her charming companion. I know all the signs. After my darling Mr. Whitcomb and I began courting we inevitably had to part for a time. I was certain—foolish youth that I was—he would never return to me and that everything I'd thought lay between

93

94   CATHERINE STEIN

us was entirely my imagination. I was, as you might expect, in a foul temper, and was quite rude to everyone around me. But, of course, the true cause of my upset lay in my own fears and unspoken feelings."

"Ooh. Zing!" George wiggled her hips and stared pointedly at Amabel. "Arrow of truth right to the heart."

"Nonsense. I am simply moving on from the frivolity of the party and considering more serious matters."

Helena had left. That was a simple fact and Amabel wasn't fretting or doubting anything. They hadn't been courting. They'd both agreed the liaison was casual. Amabel missed the banter and their physical connection, but surely that was allowed.

"But, Amabel, love, you *shouldn't* move on from frivolity," Maryanne said gently. "It was so lovely to see you having fun. You were so much more relaxed, so much happier. It had been so long since any of us had seen you truly happy."

The other women all nodded.

"Wha—" Amabel shook her head. "No, I—"

"Even when you were grumbling and sneaking around the house—yes, we did notice, don't interrupt." Maryellen held up a hand. "You were just happier. Like you'd discovered something endlessly fascinating. And then that something turned out to be a pretty woman."

"No. No." Amabel couldn't seem to stop her head waggling back and forth. "I've been happy. Plenty of times. I was curious. Trying to help Oliver."

"Helping, helping, helping." George pointed an accusatory finger. "And not letting anyone help you. We're not going to stand for it any longer. You miss Helena. Admit it."

"You know what Helena would say." Wicked amusement gleamed in Maryellen's eyes. "Admit it, *Princess*."

The pet name did her in. Amabel buried her face in her hands, smearing her spectacles with fingerprints and long-unshed tears. "I miss her. I do. She made me happy."

HER FAIR LADY   95

"Right." George slapped her thigh. "So go get her."

Amabel peeked out between her fingers. "I don't think she feels the same way."

"You can't know unless you ask," Maryanne pointed out. "Tell her how you feel, find out how she feels. Or kiss her behind a parasol again. She seemed to like that."

Amabel lifted her head and straightened her shoulders. "Thank you, all of you. You are true friends."

George smirked. "Nah. We only want to get Helena back into the club. Completely selfish."

Amabel truly smiled, for the first time since Helena had departed. "Sometimes we all need to be a little selfish, I think."

~ day fifteen ~

It was good to be home. Helena smiled across the parlor at her mother and stepfather, who sat snuggled close together as the family took tea. The mended necklace hung around Mother's neck. She ran her fingers idly over the pearls, beneath the adoring gaze of her husband, who had never shown anything but the utmost appreciation for the great love in her past and the two children she'd brought into his life.

"Well, I can't say I approve of your methods," Helena's stepfather said. He attempted to frown like a proper barrister, but his smile was too wide to fully suppress. "But I must congratulate you both for restoring such a precious heirloom to your mother." He kissed his wife's cheek.

A truly fortunate woman, Helena realized. How many people could boast of having one such partner, let alone finding a second after many years of widowhood?

Helena fluffed her skirt to hide the fact that she was crossing and uncrossing her legs yet again, trying to ease the unrelenting restlessness in her bones.

You could have had that, whispered a voice from the deepest

recesses of her mind. *Amabel could have been that partner for you, if only you'd said something.*

"Now tell us what else happened on your adventure," Mother prompted.

Helena froze.

"And don't try to tell me nothing happened," Mother went on. "I know my children, and you're both fidgeting like you're fit to burst."

"I met someone!" Seb blurted. He turned pink. "Um, it's Lord Fenwick, actually. Oliver. He's the sweetest man I've ever met. His friends are absolutely lovely, and he wants to meet you and says I can bring the whole family to Fenwick House at any time, and… and I just love him so much." He hopped up from his seat to fetch himself more tea. "Sorry for babbling, I'm nervous. I know it's strange, me being with an aristocrat. Also, it happened pretty suddenly, so—" He shrugged.

"They're rather disgustingly smitten," Helena admitted. "And very well suited. Fenwick is a good man, and I know he'll make Seb happy."

Her brother beamed at her. "Love you, Hellion. Now what about your duchess?"

"Duchess?" Their mother's gaze snapped to Helena. "My goodness, you children are incorrigible!"

"No, no, it's not like that," Helena protested. "It's… We…" The noise of horse hooves and carriage wheels gave her an excuse to turn to look out the window.

"Whoa." Seb sauntered toward the window. "Fancy ride. Looks like somebody important's popping by for a visit."

Stepfather rose from his seat and offered Mother a hand up. "Has your earl come to pay a call already, Son?"

"No, no. He doesn't like to go out in public much, and I told him to stay home. And that's not the Fenwick crest." He craned his neck. "It's familiar, though. Some kind of tree?" A note of amusement crept into his voice. "Hmm. The Duchy of Mirweald, maybe?"

Helena couldn't see the crest from her seat, but she didn't need to. She'd seen the stylized tree and crossed feathers on Amabel's trunks and other possessions. Besides, the gilded trim and sleek black paint told her enough.

But what did this mean?

Her body had gone numb. She couldn't move her limbs. The whole world had gone foggy, as if she were standing outside reality looking in.

Vaguely, she heard the housemaid scurry into the parlor.

"H-her Grace, the Duchess of Mirweald."

Amabel swanned into the room, bedecked in peacock blue, with diamonds at her throat and feathers in her elaborate updo. Helena wanted to kiss her until that perfection was mussed. Or tease her until her regal expression became a wry smile. Her traitorous body remained still as stone.

"Your Grace, such an honor." Mother curtsied. "You and Helena must have so much to discuss. Come along, Sebastian, you can finish telling us all about Lord Fenwick in the next room." She linked arms with her husband and son and escorted them out. "Feel free to join us whenever you're ready, girls," she called as she disappeared from sight.

"Well." Amabel pulled a handkerchief from her pocket and wiped her spectacles. "It's a family trait, I see. I don't think I've been called a girl since…" She sniffed. "Perhaps not ever."

"Amabel." Helena's voice sounded distant to her own ears, but at least her body had started to obey. "What are you doing here?"

"I believe I have made a mistake." Before Helena could respond, she continued, "I suppose I've made any number of mistakes in the past fortnight, and God only knows how many in my lifetime, but I'm here to rectify one particular mistake, if you'll allow me."

"Of course. Would you like to sit down?"

"No, thank you. I find I am in need of movement." She clasped her hands behind her back and began to pace in front

of Helena. "I let you go without a word, when in truth, I had much to say. I understand that this may make no difference whatsoever in our circumstances, but I cannot allow my feelings to go unspoken."

"Amabel." Helena sprang from her seat, reaching for the other woman. Her heart galloped and her blood hummed as fear and hope tangled and sparked inside her.

Amabel stopped pacing and took Helena's hands. Stark longing radiated from her hazel eyes, and she tugged Helena closer.

"Helena, darling. I hardly knew what I had in you until I felt its absence. These last weeks have been a revelation. From the first, you made me laugh, you annoyed me, intrigued me, made me think and question everything. You challenged me, Helena, in a way few people ever do."

"You challenge me too, Princess. You keep me constantly off-balance, and I think I need that as much as I hate it."

Amabel's answering laugh was a glorious thing, light and joyful. "Oh, indeed. We might be very good for one another, in fact."

"Yes."

Amabel brought one of Helena's hands to her lips and kissed it. "Most of all, my dear Miss Wright, you made me think about what Amabel wants, not what the duchess wants. And what Amabel wants is to be happy, to be loved, to live true to herself. You bring fun into my life. You value me as I am. I would love to keep you in my life, my heart, and my bed, if you will have me."

Helena pressed close to Amabel, bringing their lips into kissing range without closing the gap entirely. "I want that. I do. But you are a duchess, and I'm no one. I don't want to live on your largess, or be nothing but your mistress. I want to be a part of your community. I want to contribute."

Amabel kissed her gently. "You already do, dear. The ladies are all begging me to bring you back, and they don't even know

you as I do. Come help me run the magazine. You said you were good with lists."

"I am. I like organizing and I do know plenty of theater people and— Oh!" Gears clicked into place and her mind began to whirl with possibility. "I can solicit advertisements. Lure your readers to shows and businesses. I can help with distribution to the right people. We can promote creative endeavors and safe spaces. If you use your aristocratic connections and I use mine, we can expand the reach, get information to those who need it, maybe even facilitate the creation of new clubs or offshoot publications on specific topics. We'll need to discuss discretion, of course, to keep everyone involved safe, but just imagine what we can do!"

Amabel threw her head back and laughed. "Helena, you are vastly more beautiful than your Trojan namesake ever was. We'll do it. We'll do everything you suggested and more. We're going to turn this whole damn world upside-down, you and I."

Happiness flowed from every inch of Helena's body, and she poured all of it into a deep, hungry kiss. "Yeah?" she asked, when she paused for air.

"Yes," Amabel promised. "Or we'll burn it all down and start from scratch."

Helena wound her arms around Amabel's neck and tangled her fingers into her hair. "Let's be reckless together. Starting right now."

And they were.

About the Author

AWARD-WINNING AUTHOR CATHERINE STEIN believes that everyone deserves love and that Happily Ever After has the power to help, to heal, and to comfort. She writes sassy, sexy romance set during the Victorian and Edwardian eras. Her stories are full of action, adventure, magic, and fantastic technologies.

Catherine lives in Michigan with her husband and three rambunctious kids. She loves steampunk and Oxford commas, and can often be found dressed in Renaissance festival clothing, drinking copious amounts of tea.

Visit Catherine online at
www.catsteinbooks.com
and join her VIP mailing list for a free short story.

Follow her on Instagram @catsteinbooks,
or like her page on Facebook @catsteinbooks.

Potions and Passions

The Earl on the Train - Book 0.5

How to Seduce a Spy - Book 1

Mishaps & Mistletoe -
A Holiday Novella -Book 1.5

Not a Mourning Person - Book 2

Once a Rake, Always a Rogue - Book 3

Love at Second Sight - Book 4

Sass and Steam

Love is in the Airship - Book 0.5

A Shot to the Heart - Book 0.75

Eden's Voice - Book 1

What Are You Doing New Year's Eve? –
A Holiday Novella - Book 1.5

Priceless - Book 2

Dead Dukes Tell No Tales - Book 3

Arcane Tales

The Scoundrel's New Con - Book 1

The Spinster's Swindle - Book 2

Mad Scientists Society

The Courtesan and Mr. Hyde - Book 1

The Electrical Affairs of Dr. Victor Franklin - Book 2

Lords of Dystopia

Earth Earls are Easy - Book 1

Other Books

Mating Habits - Book 1

Idle Nature - Book 2

Available at your favorite online retailer.
www.catsteinbooks.com

Thank you so much for reading.
If you enjoyed the book and are so inclined, I would love for
you to leave a review. Happy readers make an author's day!

I love hearing from readers,
so feel free to contact me on social media, or email:

catherine@catsteinbooks.com